||| || ||||||||| | || ||||||||||||||||| ||| 2014

✓ S0-AEW-321

Praise for Heather Ashby's Love in the Fleet Series

FORGIVE & FORGET

"Bold and steamy with a suspense taken from today's headlines and a love that breaks all rules."

— Cathy Maxwell,
New York Times Bestselling Author of *The Devil's Heart*

"Heather Ashby writes authentic Navy stories with heart and a good dose of humor."

— Geri Krotow,
Author of *Navy Orders*, Whidbey Island Series #2 and
U.S. Naval Academy Graduate

"Heather Ashby writes characters that are anything but standard issue. This exciting high seas adventure showcases a world of honor, duty, and selfless service. But most of all, it's a lovely example of how love conquers all."

—Terri Osburn,
Author of *Meant to Be* in the Anchor Island Series

"A thrilling novel...takes the reader into adventure on the high seas that involves suspense, danger, and intrigue, as well as forbidden love. This is a feel good read that rings true in every regard. It is especially exciting to know this is the first in a series. I'll be eager to read the rest!"

— Susan Brandenburg,
St. Augustine Record

"A fantastic debut! Heather Ashby kept me entertained all the way through with engaging characters and a story that had me right there living it."

— Kim Law,
Author of RITA-nominated, *Sugar Springs*

DISCARD

"Heather Ashby's characters are appealing and realistic, her depiction of life aboard an aircraft carrier is fascinating, and the suspense and romance crackles throughout. *Forgive & Forget* is a compelling, compulsively readable love story that's as hard to put down as it is to forget."

– Colette Auclair,
Author of *Thrown* (December 2013)

"Although her novel's characters are at sea, Ashby isn't. She has a sure grasp of romance and adventure in a war zone...An up-to-the-minute-tale for today's military and civilian adventure reader and a complete treat for readers of romance."

– Jeane Westin,
Military Veteran and
Author of *The Spymaster's Daughter* and *Love and Glory*

Forgive & Forget

The Love in the Fleet Series
by Heather Ashby

FORGIVE & FORGET

FORGET ME NOT
(*coming December 2013*)

Forgive & Forget

LOVE IN THE FLEET

Heather Ashby

Palmer Public Library
655 S. Valley Way
Palmer, AK 99645

HENERY PRESS

FORGIVE & FORGET
A Love in the Fleet Story

First Edition
Trade paperback edition | July 2013

Henery Press
www.henerypress.com

All rights reserved. No part of this book may be used or reproduced in any manner whatsoever, including Internet usage, without written permission from Henery Press, except in the case of brief quotations embodied in critical articles and reviews.

Copyright © 2013 by Heather Ashby
Cover art by Doug Thompson
Author photograph by Straley Photography

This is a work of fiction. Any references to historical events, real people, or real locales are used fictitiously. Other names, characters, places, and incidents are the product of the author's imagination, and any resemblance to actual events or locales or persons, living or dead, is entirely coincidental.

ISBN-13: 978-1-938383-44-1

Printed in the United States of America

For
The women of the United States Navy

and

For Pete, my anchor

ACKNOWLEDGMENTS

In thanksgiving for my Army son's safe return from both Afghanistan and Iraq, I donate half of my royalties to organizations that benefit wounded warriors and their families. Go to HeatherAshby.com for more information on how the sale of this book benefits our troops.

I write for men and women who have ever been associated with the Navy, and for readers who would like to vicariously join the Navy and see the world for the duration of this book. I try to strike a balance between military and civilian worlds so that all my readers can enjoy the story. Apologies for smoothing over some military terms for civilian readers and for altering billets and shipboard life where necessary. I take responsibility for all mistakes.

Special thanks to the people who made this novel possible: Lieutenant Junior Grade Louise Jordan McClean, USN 1942-1945 - Thanks, Mother, for sharing your love of the Navy and your love of books with me. And thanks for taking the watch. I'm grateful to Bates McClean and Eva Hansen Lamb—my great-grandmother who published her first book in 1894. Thanks for the writer gene, Father and Oma.

Thank you Anne Lamott, Pat Conroy, Natalie Goldberg, Kaye Gibbons, Anne Morrow Lindberg, and Harper Lee for inspiring me to write. Thank you Suzanne Brockmann, Catherine Mann, Lindsay McKenna, and Merline Lovelace for the inspiration to write military romance. Hugs to my Golden Heart Firebird Sisters, my fellow RomVets, First Coast Romance Writers, and all the Hens in the Hen House for your advice, encouragement, and support.

Thanks to Ellen for your friendship through the years and for challenging me to write a romance novel. Special thanks to Cathy, Jeane, Geri, Susan, Kim, Terri, and Colette for your awesome quotes and to my beta readers who read this book at every stage of its life: Diane, Michael, Mary, Donna, Morgan, Laura, Margo, Nancy, Gary, Linda, Gina, Colleen, and Lisa. I'm eternally grateful to the Navy personnel who shared their sea stories and helped authenticate the book. You know who you are. Thanks to PBS "Carrier" for helping me wrap my brain around going to sea on an aircraft carrier and hugs to Sandy, Melissa, Andrea, Loni, and "Trixie"—the best shipmates a girl could ever have.

Thank you, Molli Nickell at Get Published Now for all your guidance and cheerleading and to Michael Straley for capturing my passion for the Navy in your camera. Special thanks to Doug Thompson for breathing life into Hallie, Philip, and their world on *Forgive & Forget's* awesome cover. And to Nikki Lamont for breathing life into me and keeping me focused on writing my books the way they needed to be written. I could not have done this without Maria Connor at My Author Concierge for handling my technology needs and talking me down from the ledge by saying, "I'll take care of it." Extra special thanks to my awesome critique partners: Suzanne Galbo, Kelly Martin, and Catherine Rull - who is the best line editor in the world! I really appreciated those holiday and weekend edits, *from Australia yet*, so I could meet my deadlines, Cat.

I am so blessed to have the best editor ever, Kendel Flaum, who makes me stretch and grow as a writer—even when I don't want to—and who believes in my stories and in me. Extra hugs to my dearest friend, Jane Blanchard, for loving my books and for loving me all these years. And to Pete, my First—and only—Mate, who takes care of everything so I can write. Thanks for being the anchor, honey, so I can be the sails. Finally, I am grateful to God for bringing my son home safe and whole from war, allowing me to write the books of my heart to send out to the Fleet in thanksgiving. I am so blessed to have you as my agent, making all the right things happen in my literary journey—and in my life. Full speed ahead!

Chapter 1

Her mother had always boasted, "I have something better than a son—a daughter with balls." Hallie smiled and stretched in the confines of her bunk as she remembered that classic line. Well, maybe her mom hadn't used those exact words when Hallie was a little girl, but she'd grown up understanding that being ballsy was a good thing. Sometimes it was the only way for a girl to get what she wanted out of life.

Especially Chutzpah Barbie. This model came with both blue and white dress uniforms, complete with patent leather pumps, chic hats, and white gloves. For her everyday work uniform she sported a navy blue-and-gray camouflage outfit, bloused over steel-toed combat boots, and a pair of stainless steel dog tags to adorn her neck.

McCabe, Hallie L. 023-71-7048/USN/B-NEG/PROT. Blood transfusions and a Protestant chaplain were additional and hopefully never required.

Other accessories included navy blue coveralls, an orange life vest, and her very own battleship gray Kevlar combat helmet. A green canvas seabag in which to stow the extra outfits and accessories was also provided compliments of Uncle Sam.

And the set of balls? Standard equipment on Chutzpah Barbie.

Fortunately, everyone but the duty section was gone for the weekend, so Hallie slept in after her mid-watch. Having perfected the Navy shower, she used her two minutes of hot water wisely. She appreciated the shower while the ship was still on shore power, knowing hot water might become a precious commodity once they deployed.

Donning capris, a tank top, sandals, and sunglasses, Hallie walked to the quarterdeck, requested permission to go ashore, and snapped a crisp salute to the Stars and Stripes. As she strolled down the gangway of the USS *Robert C. Blanchard*, Petty Officer Hallie McCabe knew every pair of male eyes topside was watching her disembark. One lone wolf whistle confirmed it. She considered sending up a one-fingered salute, but reminded herself she was a professional.

Although she was excited about shipboard duty, she loved to escape to her cousin, Rebecca's. Rebecca and her husband lived in Jacksonville Beach, and Hallie liked spending nights there after her classes at the University. She also appreciated home-cooked meals, a real bed, and showering for as long as she pleased.

The upcoming picnic at Rebecca's apartment complex promised to be outstanding. The Towers were hosting a luau complete with a whole pig that had been roasting since dawn. After greeting Rebecca and her husband, Hallie grabbed a glass of red wine and sauntered down to the beach. Standing in the surf, digging her toes deep into the sand, Hallie let the waves wash over her ankles.

Miles away from industrial Naval Station Mayport and the noisy hustle and bustle of life on a Navy ship, Hallie sipped her wine and looked with longing at a cluster of sailboats. She inhaled the salty air and exhaled deeply. Utter and total relaxation. Her world seemed balanced when she stood at the edge of the land, staring at the horizon. Shipmates warned her once they deployed she'd see so much ocean, sky, and horizon she'd want to puke. But Hallie disagreed. She had clawed through too much red tape to get this billet on an aircraft carrier and she could not wait to deploy.

Nobody took the wind out of Hallie McCabe's sails.

Come to think of it, she missed sailing. Hadn't done it since her mom got sick.

"You a sailor?"

Hallie turned to find a tall man standing nearby. *Nice.* She would have called him handsome, were he not wearing BCGs—government issue glasses, nicknamed "Birth Control Glasses," because they made anyone wearing them so ugly no one would want to have sex with him, or her. Between the glasses and his haircut, he was definitely military. Had to be an officer if he lived at The Towers, but at least he wasn't a pilot with those glasses. Pilots wore aviator shades with cocky attitudes to match. Hallie didn't do pilots. Plain and simple.

"I can find my way around a boat."

He tucked his shoes under his arm and offered his hand. "Philip Johnston." He nodded toward the apartment building. "Do you live at The Towers? I don't think I've seen you around."

Something told her to keep her military status quiet. Couldn't she just be herself today? "I'm Hallie McCabe. I live with my cousin and her husband in three-oh-four. I'm a student at the University of North Florida. How about you?"

"Apartment four-oh-five. Right upstairs. Hey, let me know if you ever want to go out. Sailing, that is. I've got a sweet little fourteen-foot day sailer for the summer. Joined a boat club with a friend."

"Are you serious? Yes. Yes. And *Yes.*"

A corner of his mouth tipped up in a slow smile. "Well, tomorrow's Sunday and I happen to have an opening for a first mate. My buddy canceled at the last minute and I hear the weather's going to be awesome."

Before thinking, Hallie blurted out, "I'd love to. I haven't been sailing in years." A little voice in her head scolded her that she didn't know a thing about this man. But another voice whispered that ax murderers didn't usually carry a pair of Topsider boat shoes in their right hand and a Corona with lime in their left. Ax murderers probably skipped the lime. "You're not an ax murderer or anything, are you?" She flashed him a sweet smile, then sipped her wine.

Philip's face blossomed to a grin. "Not quite. I'm an engineer. Been too busy lately to murder anyone. I'm in the Navy. On the *Blanchard*."

Hallie choked on her wine, coughed, and sputtered. She raised a hand to indicate she was okay. And in the time it took her to clear her throat, she amended her policy about not dating anyone from her command. And double oops. He said engineer, which meant officer. Fraternization between officers and enlisted was forbidden, and although she'd dabbled in that territory before, she'd never dabbled with an officer from her own command. Hallie lived by the mantra: Never get your honey where you get your money.

She'd never had a problem with that mantra. Until today.

"The Navy. How interesting." She tried to ignore the ribbon of guilt curling in her gut. Hallie did not consider herself a rule breaker. She was more of a rule rationalizer. It wasn't like they were in the same chain of command or anything. She didn't work for the guy. The *Blanchard* was the largest class of ship in the Navy, with a crew that would swell to five thousand once they deployed. If she hadn't bumped into him on board yet, chances were she never would. Plus he was an engineer. Those guys practically lived down in the hole. What was wrong with enjoying a day out on his sailboat and then quietly disappearing?

"Not always. Right now I'm the Auxiliaries Officer."

Hallie's stomach sank. The AUXO was Trixie's new boss. Hallie's bunkmate, Trixie, was rude and crude, so Hallie rarely listened to her drivel, but perhaps she should have listened closer when Trixie had trashed her new boss: "On a geek scale from one to ten, he's a twenty-five."

But Trixie was wrong. This was no geek. This hottie with the broad shoulders, dark curly hair, and deep brown eyes with lashes any woman would kill for, could pass for a Greek god. Well, if he would just lose the glasses—they smacked of *Geek* god.

What did Trixie say his nickname was? Bill Gates?

"So what exactly do you do?"

"I'm kind of an air conditioning specialist and a glorified plumber."

No way did Bill Gates have Philip's sexy smile—and she doubted he had sexy toes either. What was wrong with her? Lusting after a man's toes? *Officer* toes that fit into expensive, custom-made boots that walked the same decks as her heavy government-issues.

"...And trust me, there's plenty of sewage on an aircraft carrier." He huffed out a half laugh like he couldn't believe he'd just said that.

Great. Hallie had been lusting after his toes and he'd been waxing and waning about sewage. "Well, I guess the only way is up."

His eyes crinkled with laughter. "Not if you're the sewage."

Hallie thought he was adorable. Unaffected and refreshing. He reminded her of Clark Kent and she felt flooded with warmth, imagining Philip throwing his glasses off and turning into Superman.

While they ate dinner and discussed sailing and Hallie's journalism classes, Philip kicked himself with both feet. He cursed himself for leaving his sunglasses on the sailboat, which—with his regular glasses being repaired—left him trying to pick up a major babe in his BCGs. No wonder his nickname was Bill Gates. And not because of the money either.

He couldn't believe how stupid he'd sounded after meeting the most beautiful woman he'd ever seen, with innocent blue eyes that searched his while he talked about sewage. "Way to go, dumb ass," was what his best buddy, Sky, would've said. "Just keep talking about sewage. That'll win her over."

After dinner Philip invited Hallie to walk on the beach. The sun sank in the west, but its fingers reached around and reflected the foam on the waves as they crawled onto the sand. The air was thick and scented with the sea—and the essence of Hallie McCabe.

As they walked barefoot through the surf, he mentioned his upcoming deployment to the Persian Gulf in July.

"How do you feel about that?" she asked.

"Excited. I'll be responsible for the plumbing network of essentially a small city. And I'm charged with keeping the A/C up and running. The temperature gets well over a hundred degrees in the Middle East and I hear it'll be a daily ordeal keeping all our electronic equipment cool." He chuckled. "And it's not like we could just open the windows, because one, the air is filled with blowing sand. And two, there are no windows on an aircraft carrier. But I like a challenge. Plus I've never been through the Suez Canal, so hopefully I'll have some time to get off the ship to explore."

"But what about the danger? We're still at war and you're headed into a hot zone."

"I worry about my friends who are pilots. I know guys in the boarding parties too. That's got to be scary, boarding fishing boats and merchant vessels, not knowing if there are pirates or weapons on board."

Hallie jumped in. "You know what I think is the scariest? This enemy knows the terrain. They watch and wait and strike whenever they choose. And they take advantage of rules designed to prevent casualties. Actually, they don't even care about casualties, even civilians. I say it's changed the face of warfare.

"Used to be combatants only took chances up to a certain point, but the bottom line was to stay alive while completing their mission. Now, the terrorists don't care if they die because it makes them martyrs. Just like the Kamikaze pilots in World War II."

Philip stopped walking. He stared at her, stunned this insight was coming from her pretty girl mouth.

"So the Middle East is a frightening place, but I guess an aircraft carrier would be safer than any other kind of vessel. I mean, carriers are huge," she said.

"Its size makes it a bigger target," Philip responded, finally catching up to her. Like there's a big, red bullseye painted in the center of the flight deck—or rather on the sides. That's what we worry about most, floating bombs disguised as fishing boats. We'll be traveling with five smaller ships as escorts. While they protect us from other ships or, say, a missile attack, it's the common fishing boats that tend to be the biggest threat. That's what happened with the USS *Cole*."

"Surely you have ways of knowing what's out there so you can protect yourselves." She gazed at him with trusting eyes, as if he had the answers to all the world's problems.

"Yeah, but the Rules of Engagement are tricky. Even if we know there's a threat, we often can't fire unless the bad guys fire first. And then it may be too late."

He thought the rules sucked, but he wasn't going to say that.

Hallie didn't miss a beat. "Wasn't that the problem in the *Cole* bombing? We knew what was happening at the last minute, but had to wait for permission to fire on the terrorists. By then it was too late and seventeen sailors died and...well, it was bad."

Philip's jaw dropped. Seventeen was not a number you pulled out of the air. And he was completely blown away she had a clue about Rules of Engagement. If he'd thought she was the woman of his dreams two hours ago, the idea was now locked onto his brain like a heat-seeking missile. "Even though I'm a major rule follower, I'd have trouble waiting for permission in a situation like that."

His mouth kept talking, but every other cell in his body focused on how to get this woman to marry him, bear his children, and grow old with him. There was way more to her than just being a babe, although the babe part would definitely not be a problem.

Mesmerized by her blue eyes sparkling with intelligence, he said, "You know, I think you'll go far as a reporter. I can feel your passion for it."

Hallie sucked in a breath and stepped closer, bringing her face a few inches from his and—as if on impulse—she reached up and removed his glasses. "Sorry, but I've wanted to do that all afternoon. You have beautiful eyes, Philip. You should think about contacts or glasses that show them off. You know, eyes are the window to the soul and all that?"

Energy crackled between them. Sky's voice screamed in his head: "That's your cue, shit-for-brains. Kiss her."

But no way was he going to. One kiss was not going to be enough. So there he stood on a beach at sunset with an incredible woman who had removed his glasses and although a major organ was doing his thinking for him, it wasn't his brain. Even though he had an open invitation to do something—anything—he didn't take the bait. What if he screwed it up and she canceled their sailing date? So he told Sky's voice in his head to shut up, played the gentleman card, and did not reach for her.

"What? You thought I wore BCGs all the time? Uh...we call them 'Birth Control Glasses' in the Navy, because if you wear—never mind." Great. Now he was talking about birth control.

Her face lit with amusement. "Nobody would want to..."

"...have sex with you," he finished for her.

Which was all he could think about. Jesus, she had eyes that could make a man forget to breathe.

"My regular ones are in the shop. I keep these for spares and I wear them when I'm down in the hole." He could practically hear Sky's voice bellowing at him now.

Philip scrambled to clarify but the damage was already done. He laughed it off. "That's the engineering spaces on a ship, where all the snipes work."

Her lips twitched in amusement as she replaced his glasses. "Snipes."

There went his window of opportunity. "Engineers and Machinist's Mates. Connoisseurs of boilers, engines, and turbines. Snipes." At least she laughed along with him now.

"So," she took his arm and headed up toward the seawall, which bailed him out. "What time tomorrow?"

"How about eight?"

"Sounds good. I'll bring lunch and meet you in the parking lot. Today was fun. I can't wait to go sailing tomorrow." And as they climbed the steps of the seawall, a sudden luminous smile lit her face as she added, "Shipmate."

* * *

"I can't believe when the chick removed your glasses and said you had beautiful eyes, you didn't say, 'The better to see you with, my dear,' and then fucking kiss her."

Philip laughed right along with Sky as they debriefed on the phone. "This one's different, Sky. I wasn't going to take a chance on messing things up."

"Okay, okay. But here are some pointers. Never discuss sewage with a chick again, all right? Don't even say the word. Even if it is your bread and butter. And dude, I don't care if you work down in the hole of a ship, do not use those words around a female unless she's one of your snipes. No wonder we named you Bill Gates." Sky muttered something unintelligible, then continued. "So I've been replaced, huh?"

"I prefer my first mate in a bikini, and no offense, but you don't have the man boobs to pull that look off."

"Good one, Bill. Listen, I'm proud of you, buddy. And rules are rules. 'Rule Number Two: If either man can replace the other with a hot babe in a bikini before lines are cast off, then the first man gets the sailboat and the loser is shit out of luck.' You won, hands down. And it's not like I haven't pulled that on you a time or three. So tell me about the chick."

"Hallie's not a chick, Sky."

"They're all chicks until proven otherwise."

Philip lay across his unmade bed with his arm thrown across his forehead and a stupid grin on his face. "She's tall, athletic body, long blond hair, and these blue eyes that look at you like you're her hero."

Sky sighed. "Aw, I love it when they do that. Jeez, I can't believe I'm living vicariously through Bill Gates and his BCGs on a Saturday night. What does she do?"

"She's a student."

"Oh, my God, you're not robbing the cradle are you? Has she reached the age of consent? Did you give her your real name?"

"She's twenty-four, smart ass. Goes to UNF and she's smart. Very smart. We talked about real stuff. Not like most of the women we meet. You know, the ones who blabber on with all their friggin' small talk? She even knows a lot about the Navy."

"Maybe she's prior service."

"Hallie? In the military? No way. She knows a lot because she's majoring in television broadcast. I mean, she knew details, like, about the *Cole* bombing. She understands the complexity of Rules of Engagement."

"Let me get this straight. You stood on the beach with a hot chick at sunset and instead of kissing her, you discussed Rules of Engagement? Shit, man, the only rules of engagement you should have been thinking about were the ones that might engage her in your bed. You could have had her screaming, 'You may fire when ready, Gridley!' What am I going to do with you, Bill? For an engineer you really are a dumb ass."

"No, I am the man with a sailboat and a smokin' hot first mate in a bikini. That's what I am. And you are the loser who is shit out of luck tomorrow."

"Two points for Bill Gates!" Sky called out to no one in particular. "Okay, looks like you won this round, buddy. You want to go out for a beer later this week—if you're not, like, *married* by then? We could meet halfway."

"If I don't have a date. Because, as Rule Number One states: 'An evening spent with a hot chick trumps a beer with a wingman every time.' See ya."

Philip thumbed off his phone and tossed it on the bed. He felt better about the fiasco on the beach after talking with Sky. Surely he'd done the right thing by not trying to kiss Hallie—at least tonight. "Better safe than sorry" had always been his mantra. Probably why he didn't get girls the way Sky did. But charming women was not Philip's strength—especially beautiful, self-assured women like Hallie. And there was more to her than just being hot. How many young American women could quote the bombing of the USS *Cole* chapter and verse?

He lay awake thinking about what his mom had told him for years, "Just be yourself, Philip. Be your sweet, wonderful self." She didn't get it that guys didn't want to be thought of as sweet or wonderful. They wanted to be *men*. But when he watched his buddies in action, he realized his mom might be right, because apparently he hadn't acquired the asshole gene.

"Don't worry, Philip," she'd say. "When it's time to settle down, the smart women will be looking for a man like you. The kind they can count on. And you'll know when she's The One. You'll just know."

He would spend the entire night lying on his back, hands clasped behind his head, staring at nothing, thinking about Hallie, and figuring out how to keep from fucking this up.

Chapter 2

Rashid clicked send and closed his laptop. He needed to eat before the restaurant closed. Forking up the pancit with one hand, he used the other to dip fried lumpia into the sweet sauce. He glanced around the Filipino Café as he ate his fried rice noodles and spring rolls, and watched the two other customers peruse the shelves of Filipino groceries for sale. The thing he missed the most about Rosie was the food. God, that woman could cook.

He'd been hanging out here in his free time since he'd lost her. The mall had Internet access and the food was to die for. A knowing smile curved his mouth. Never really thought about that saying before. The flavors brought back good memories of Rosie. He took out a photograph that had been taken right before they were married. His family hadn't approved of her because she was Filipino. He had told them to go to hell. They loved each other and that was all there was to it. Rashid reminded himself he was doing this for her. He tucked Rosie's photo back into his wallet and looked around his new favorite place, which was perfect for his needs.

Who would suspect a terrorist to hang out in a Filipino restaurant? Filipinos were notoriously good, decent, peaceful, God-fearing people. And security around here seemed to be nonexistent. Anchorage Mall was a ghost town these days. Ever since the upscale super-mall had been built across town, this one had become a dead zone. The few remaining stores all displayed similar signs: "Big Sale! 75% Off" and "Everything Must Go." Pretty soon they would be giving the shit away. What were they going to do with this hulking mess when every single store had shut its doors?

Not his problem.

While he ate, he watched people sporadically walk by—hopeful sales clerks and retirees getting their exercise. Earlier he'd seen a few young couples with strollers headed to the indoor playground. It was a good place to take kids on a hot June evening. At least the air conditioning in this dump worked. That was a plus.

He and Rosie had planned to have kids someday. Hell, they had had all kinds of plans for their future, plans that weren't going to happen. His thoughts were interrupted by a couple of teenaged slackers walking by with jeans hanging half off their asses, dragging on the floor, and underwear hanging out. No way would his kids have dressed like that. Where did these losers come from?

A slow smile spread across his face, knowing he was probably the only person here with a direct line to al-Qaeda. Scratch probably. There couldn't be a hundred people in this entire mall tonight. No competition. How about the city of Jacksonville? Or the state of Florida? He knew there were plenty of sleeper cells in the U.S. and plenty of individual moles like himself, but he was still one of the select few. And one with some really good information.

The mall had provided him with a contact for the ultimate revenge. It had been a merchant at one of the gold kiosks who connected him with his sadiqs—his new buddies—in the Middle East. Ibrahim was the only person who had offered him kindness and understanding after he lost Rosie. He had tried to convince Rashid of the healing power of Islam and initially it did sound promising. But when the merchant asked about his allegiance to the U.S. government and the Navy in particular, Rashid's eyes had lit up. That's when he knew the partnership could be beneficial to both parties.

At first al-Qaeda had been hesitant to trust him because he refused to wholeheartedly embrace "the one true faith." They questioned if he was some kind of double agent who might expose their terror cells in the United States, but once they discovered what he could provide, they had accepted him into their network with open arms.

Rashid was surprised at how little they understood U.S. Navy ships' movements and he was shocked by their complete ignorance of an aircraft carrier's vulnerabilities. Stupid Arabs. Didn't they know a nuclear carrier was essentially a fuel and ammo dump? That with the right kind of explosion as a trigger, the three-and-a-half million gallons of jet fuel plus the bombs, missiles, and bullets on board would make for quite a night of fireworks?

Al-Qaeda told him they would provide a fishing boat laden with explosives and just enough devout "fishermen" willing to die when their boat collided with the ship. Not that one boat could do much damage to something as large as an aircraft carrier. But between the jet fuel and the ordnance, all the tangos needed to do was provide a spark.

He was stunned that his sadiqs did not seem concerned about the deadly aftermath two nuclear reactors could cause. They were too overjoyed about the possibility of taking so many American military lives at one time. By the time the ship deployed, there would be five thousand souls on board. More than had died on 9/11.

And it was all in Rashid's hands.

He'd been up front with them. He wasn't going to do that Muslim shit. Well, not in so many words. He'd be respectful and let them think he cared about their cause. But deep down he didn't give a rat's ass about western influence infiltrating and corrupting the Middle East or a Palestinian homeland or even oil for that matter. Mostly he just wanted to fuck over the U.S. Navy. And if the bad guys got involved, his actions would be that much sweeter.

But he wasn't giving up beer—or pork for that matter. Rashid wolfed down the sinigang na baboy, drained his Budweiser, and paid his bill. Then he headed home to his quarters aboard the USS *Blanchard*.

Chapter 3

Sunday dawned bright and clear, promising to be another Florida scorcher. Fortunately, a steady breeze blew across the St. Johns River—a perfect day for sailing. Despite the light chop on the water, Philip said it was nothing he couldn't handle. And he didn't yet know what a good sailor Hallie was.

Yeah, he *really* didn't know that.

They ate breakfast at the marina and Hallie felt a tug at her heart as she watched Philip eat. Last night at dinner she'd observed he was a lefty.

Southpaw guys turned her on. The way they curled their wrists around to write. Or ate scrambled eggs. Or—

Do not go there. It's just sailing.

She made a mental note to think like a civilian. What was she thinking last night when she'd stood on her soapbox and spouted off about how the terrorists had changed the way of warfare? And, duh. Most civilian women did not know details of the USS *Cole* bombing.

Hallie knew she was in trouble the instant they arrived at the sailboat and Philip found his sunglasses. Earlier that morning when he'd shown up in his BCGs and a day-old beard, he'd taken on sort of a Buddy-Holly-wanted-for-rape-in-Texas look, but when he turned around wearing his sexy, wraparound shades with that stubble she nearly lost it. He was drop-dead gorgeous. How silly that a pair of glasses could make that much difference, but they did. Maybe he felt safer behind the dark glasses. No. It wasn't just the glasses. He exuded an air of confidence now that he was on his boat. His own turf, so to speak.

Goodbye, Clark Kent. Hello, Superman.

"I love it out here where I have control over my world," Philip said as they motored out of the marina. "You know, a sailboat is a lot like life. I can't control the wind or the water, but I can manipulate the sails and work with whatever the weather throws at me."

He laughed a genuine laugh. Perfect, white teeth flashing. The kind where she knew the laughter reached his eyes behind his sexy sunglasses. Wait. It wasn't the sunglasses that were sexy. It was him. Those incredible shoulders stretched out a faded blue T-shirt that hung over board shorts. Long, tan, muscular legs. Boat shoes. No socks. Sweet. A Ralph Lauren ad with the perfect sailor boy.

Hallie was in a crapload of trouble now. Had she bitten off more than she could chew with her little charade? This was a really nice man, the kind of guy she might hurt if she just disappeared. And did she want to disappear? Not so much anymore. Hallie hadn't felt this comfortable around a man in a long time. Maybe never. Except for Rebecca's dad. Like her Uncle Pete, Philip made her feel safe. And respected. He was quality. He was a gentleman.

An *officer* and a gentleman. From her ship.

Reality stabbed her in the solar plexus. No way could she see this guy again. Somehow she'd have to let him down easy. Her experience with men in the past had been that they would eventually stop thinking with their brains and show their true colors. Maybe if she gave Philip enough time, he'd—what did they call it in the commissioned ranks when an officer messed up? Fall on his sword? That would give her a valid excuse for not dating him again. Her heart fluttered in her chest when she realized she *wanted* to continue to see him.

"You must have grown up sailing," she said, untangling lines.

"Not really. My parents were originally from Oklahoma, so they were more into football. I started sailing in college with Sky, my roommate at the Naval Academy. He's a helicopter pilot over at the Air Station and since we're both here for the spring and half the summer, we joined this boat club."

Philip pulled out a battered, straw cowboy hat and cocked it on his head, giving the Ralph Lauren model a Marlboro-Man-goes-to-the-America's-Cup makeover.

"Nice hat, Cowboy."

"I come by it honestly. My dad always wore jeans and boots and a cowboy hat when he wasn't in uniform. His call sign was 'Spurs' if that tells you anything."

Her heart hitched.

Call sign.

"He was a Navy pilot. He's retired now, but they all have call signs—the name they go by when they're flying. Usually some funny story behind how they got them." He held up both palms in surrender. "I have no idea why his nickname was Spurs and I don't want to know. He sent me this hat for Christmas one year and it's been my lucky sailing hat ever since."

"So he flew airplanes?" Dumb question. As opposed to what?

"Yeah, P-3 Orions. Big four-engine propeller jobs used for anti-submarine warfare and reconnaissance. He and Sky love to get together and shoot the bull."

Whew. Not F-14 Tomcats. "How about we pony up and hit the trail?" She gave him a little giddy-up click and a wink as she helped him unfurl the sails.

Together they raised the mainsail and headed out into the St. Johns River. Philip nodded his approval and seemed impressed that Hallie knew how to manage the sails. The breeze kissed her face and ruffled her hair as they headed up the river and under the Buckman Bridge, passing the Naval Air Station, quiet on a Sunday morning.

"So is this what sailors do on their day off?" Hallie asked.

"This is so different from what I do all day long—or all night long on a bad day. Here, I am out in the fresh air and sunshine. It certainly doesn't smell like oil—or sewage." Philip's mouth curved into a crooked smile. He was so much more relaxed than last night, joking about sewage today.

"But you like your job, don't you?"

"I love taking things apart and fixing them. My dad tried to talk me into flying, but it didn't interest me. "

Extra points for you.

"Whenever he used to take me to the airfield to hang around his squadron, I was always more interested in how the aircraft worked than flying them. I'm just not a flyboy kind of guy."

Good. Hallie wouldn't be there otherwise.

"Water is my thing." He waved his arm indicating the sailboat and the sparkling water of the river. "Sailing, swimming, and ships. My mom was a competitive swimmer and she introduced me to it when I was little. I competed all the way through school, even at the Academy. I still swim whenever I can."

That explained his incredible shoulders. Hallie reached for the sunscreen, then whipped off her T-shirt, exposing her bikini top—and much more.

Attention. On. Deck.

Desire punched Philip squarely in the gut. Never had he seen a more perfect female body—and he had spent a lot of time around women in bathing suits. But none of them compared to this woman. Or this bathing suit. Usually when a woman was tall and slender, she had small breasts to match her build. Maybe Hallie had stepped into the wrong boob line when they were putting her together, because these babies were all but spilling out of her polka dot bikini top. And there was no question they were the real McCoy. He somehow knew Hallie McCabe was genuine through and through.

"I love to swim too. Well, just freestyle, you know." She continued to apply sunscreen to her shoulders and—oh, God—down into her cleavage. *Did cleavages sunburn?* "What's your best stroke, Philip?"

"Breast. I mean, butterfly. I mean, I'm good at breast, but better at butterfly." Glad he was tan, he felt heat clear to his scalp.

"Cool." She indicated the river. "Maybe you can show me a thing or two today."

He wasn't going to touch that one with a ten-foot pole.

When Hallie bent down to apply lotion to her legs, a lock of her hair slipped free and curled down over her right eyebrow. She mindlessly pulled it back behind her ear, but it fell again. He'd watched her tuck it numerous times last night. She seemed unaware of how often she did it, or how much it turned him on. Suddenly he understood why Muslim women covered their hair. This golden tendril was that seductive.

Hallie finger-combed it back, then piled her long, sun-kissed hair onto the top of her head and handed him the bottle of sunscreen. "Would you mind putting some of this on my back?"

His breath caught. Sky's voice tickled his ear: "Think of it as an engraved invitation." Philip hissed shut up to his brain as he took the proffered bottle. He rubbed sunscreen into the baby-soft skin of her perfect back—above and below two sets of skimpy strings that separated him from nirvana—and struggled to keep his groans to himself. How easy it would be to pull those strings and slide his hands around to caress her polka dots. Yeah, like he'd ever do that. He slid his thumbs down her backbone to the top of her shorts. Or he could just slip his fingers down inside. Wait, what the hell was wrong with him? Shoulders. Stick with her shoulders.

"Mmmm. That feels so good," Hallie mumbled. "I haven't had a good backrub in ages."

Philip leaned in closer, rubbing lotion into her neck. "You must be studying too hard. Your muscles are in knots."

He caught a whiff of something fruity in her hair, which combined with the coconut in the sunscreen served to thicken the blood in his veins. He'd probably never drink a pina colada again without thinking of this moment. Remembering himself, he backed off and capped the sunscreen. "That should keep you safe for a few hours."

At least from the sun.

He went back to fiddling with the sails, hoping she hadn't seen her effect on him.

Hallie reached for the bottle of sunscreen and looked at him expectantly. "Your turn."

"Oh, no, that's okay; I don't burn," gushed from his mouth too quickly. Not only was that true, but he wasn't ready for her hands on his body. Not yet.

She pointed to his shirt. "Peel. Everyone needs sunscreen. It's not even the damage now you have to worry about. Skin cancer may not show up for years. There are lots of people making foolish mistakes in their twenties that they'll pay for later."

He pulled off his shirt, bared his back to her, and hoped he didn't make a foolish mistake in his twenties, like exploding on contact. "I suppose you've reported on this."

"As a matter of fact, I have. And I got an A." She began to apply the lotion to his back, "Let's get this on you before you burn to a crisp and regret it later. Maybe years later."

He barely heard her talking now.

"Basal cell carcinoma...middle layer epidermis...melanoma..."

The cool, slick feel of her palms on his skin shot straight to his groin and he wondered just what he might regret today—the hell with years from now. The sunscreen wasn't protecting him from anything. As a matter of fact, it made things a whole lot worse. It was all he could do not to groan out loud as her thumbs worked their magic into each tender muscle.

Stopping at the base of his neck, she teased and probed. "Aha, you've been working too hard as well. It always shows up in the neck."

She dug into his shoulder muscles, pulling and slipping and pushing. Unintelligible grunts of pleasure slipped out of him. He didn't know which felt better, Hallie touching him or someone kneading away his tension. Philip forced himself to think about quadratic equations and the sewage intake valve on the ship.

Anything but her hands on his body.

"Thanks, Hallie. That's good." He twisted away from her. "I better concentrate on sailing before we capsize." Or I take you right here on the deck of this sailboat.

He redirected. "Hey, how about getting me a water bottle?"

Philip might get a moment's respite if she would turn away to the cooler, because he certainly needed cooling off.

Unfortunately, he looked back at the wrong moment and caught her reaching into the cooler. Her perfect ass leaning over in those shorts—could you even call those things shorts?

He closed his eyes to block out what his primal brain was trying to tell him was beneath them. No. Forget it. That made it even worse.

Philip went back to equations.

They sailed for several hours, mindful of storm clouds to the east. Mostly they chatted about their boating experiences. Often they remained comfortably quiet, enjoying the sunlight sparkling on the water and the slap of the waves on the hull. Philip shared tales of growing up in a Navy family and moving around the world. Hallie talked about growing up with her mom and her cousin's parents. What a strong woman her mom had been up until breast cancer took her four years ago.

"Sorry to hear that, Hallie. What about your dad?"

Hallie bit back bile, swallowed, and composed herself. "He was never really in my life. Thank God I had my aunt and uncle. I don't know what I would've done without them when Mom got sick. They took care of everything, including me."

Instinctively, she ducked her head and continued talking as Philip brought the boom around. "My Uncle Pete is awesome. He has always been a dad to both Rebecca and me. He taught us to sail and how to throw a baseball—like boys—and took us to Orioles games every summer. Mostly, I love him because I know I can count on him."

She glanced out at the horizon, lost in good memories of Uncle Pete—which helped take the sting out of thinking about her asshole father.

She reigned in her attention, stood, and reached for the sails. "Hey, let's drop anchor. You want to take a dip?"

"No, thanks. I am one."

"What do you mean?"

A wry smile tugged at Philip's lips as he pulled in the sails. "My buddies are always teasing me about being a dip. A nerd. A geek. They call me Bill Gates."

She knew it. "Nicknames can be hurtful. I should know. I had nicknames in high school that mortified me."

"I'm sorry to hear that. But ours is all in good fun. It's kind of like a pilot's call sign. You don't get to pick your Navy nickname, so you might as well be happy with the one you get."

Philip finished furling the sails, then sat across from her, and spread his long arms along the gunwale with his foot propped on his knee. He grinned, showcasing beautiful white teeth, his broad shoulders and chest now fully exposed to her.

"Poor Sky got the nickname 'Skylark' because he got so many demerits for skylarking at the Academy. That means not paying attention. Or getting caught daydreaming."

Hallie knew what skylarking meant and she was doing it right now as he rambled on about his buddies. Because she was taking in Philip's naked swimmer's torso for the first time and, besides his well-developed physique, Philip had a happy trail. She'd also heard it called a treasure trail, but either way she could only imagine the happy treasure at the end of the trail of hair from his navel down to his...Hallie could do the math. Tall man. Long arms, legs, fingers, toes, and—

Long officer's arms, legs, fingers, toes, and—

From her ship. That snapped her back to the present. "Hopefully you'll end up making as much money as Bill Gates."

"That used to be my reply, but I gave up on it years ago. I got the nickname at the Academy and it follows me wherever I go.

Truth be told, I guess I am kind of geeky. I'm not much of a party guy." His face brightened. "Although there is a party at my Captain's house on Saturday. It's more a social obligation than anything else. Would you like to go?"

Adrenaline shot straight to her gut.

A party at his Captain's house? Which meant her Captain's house. And gee, wouldn't it be fun to chat with her boss, Commander Scott, while they sipped cocktails and nibbled on appetizers? Not freaking likely.

"Sorry, Philip. I have a big paper due the following week. I really need to work on it all weekend."

"Does that mean you wouldn't be up for sailing again next Sunday?"

A smile lit Hallie's face. "Now that I think I could manage, especially if I work hard the rest of this week. Tell you what. Let's plan on sailing next Sunday and if you get home early from the party Saturday night give me a call. Surely I can take a study break—but only if it involves a glass of wine."

"Deal," he said.

Hallie stood and peeled off her shorts. "Come on, Cowboy. Let's see you swim."

The water was chilly for mid-June. Philip struck out with a strong freestyle stroke and left her in his wake. He swam back underwater until he popped up, surprising her. Her mouth eased into a smile she couldn't control as he playfully splashed her.

"Thanks for coming today, Hallie. I'm glad you're here."

"Me too." Suddenly the water didn't feel quite so cold.

She begged him to demonstrate his butterfly stroke and was it ever beautiful. Oh, how he could cut the water. Those powerful shoulders twisting and turning, his long, strong arms pounding the water between breaths. The upper half of his body rocketing out of the river, as he stroked away from her. For a second she imagined those long, strong arms stroking her. And as to the pounding? Her nipples hardened and it had nothing to do with the temperature of the water. Then reality reared its ugly head.

Step away from the officer—or would that be swim away?

The storm clouds continued to move in, so they headed home. About halfway back the heavens opened, drenching them. Philip tied his hat on Hallie's head, as if that was going to do any good, but she was touched by the gesture. She had trouble pulling in the mainsail because the wind kept blowing it out, so Philip took over and let the wind take them back under sheets of rain. He gave Hallie the tiller and seemed impressed with her sixth sense as they tacked their way through the storm.

Drenched to the bone, once they reached the marina, Hallie laughed as she ran under the eaves. Dripping wet, she removed his hat, shook it off, and handed it to him. "Here's your hat, Cowboy."

Philip gave her a look that licked her body.

He dropped the hat on the ground, slid his sunglasses into his wet hair, and pulled her gently to him. Angling his head, he kissed her slowly and tenderly. Rain poured down around them, splashing at their feet. Water trickled down their faces, making the kiss even more sensual.

He slid his fingers through her wet hair and gently tipped her head backward, cradling it in his hand. The first swipe of his tongue took her breath away. She returned the caresses. Slow. And deep. His mouth was firm, his lips soft. Urgency shot through her when be backed her against the wall. He pressed his soaking wet body to hers, but did not move further, even though the treasure at the end of his happy trail had apparently voted to take things to the next level.

Philip broke the kiss and rested his forehead on hers. "I'm sorry. But as somebody so eloquently put it, I've wanted to do that all afternoon."

"Me too," she whispered before reigniting the kiss. Philip complied willingly. Her hands dug into his hair pulling him closer. Glad her back was to the wall, Hallie felt as if her knees might buckle.

A low moan slipped past her lips. What was she doing? She had no business kissing this man. But then his tongue delved into her mouth, sweeping away all the rules. His stubble scoured her chin, but Hallie didn't care. Nothing in the world mattered except this kiss.

Lightning flashed and they jumped apart. The thunder that immediately followed shook the deck and vibrated the air around them. Philip grabbed her hand and pulled her around the corner into the building. A pulse throbbed in his neck as he fought to catch his breath. "Is it my imagination or did the earth just shake with that kiss?"

Hallie willed her heart to stop racing and answered with a good-natured smile. "Not bad for Bill Gates."

Chapter 4

"When Does Friendship Become a Crime in the Navy? Over two hundred years of seagoing experience have demonstrated that seniors must maintain a thoroughly professional relationship with juniors at all times. Personal relationships between officer and enlisted members that are unduly familiar and that do not respect differences in rank and grade are prohibited, and violate longstanding customs and traditions of the naval service. Personal relationships including dating, cohabitation, and any sexual relationship between commissioned officers and personnel of the enlisted ranks are strictly forbidden."

"Shit," Hallie mumbled under her breath.

Chief Bernard interrupted Hallie's Google search of the UCMJ—the Uniform Code of Military Justice—the Armed Forces Bible on rules and regulations. "Hey, McCabe, hurricane season started last week. I thought I asked one of you to pull a checklist together and write a piece to go with it. I need to run it tomorrow. Whoever writes it gets the byline."

"Can you get Marini to do it?"

"I thought you'd want the byline."

"Not today. Gina, you want a byline?" Hallie called across the *Blanchard's* Public Affairs office.

"I don't care who does it. Somebody get it done. Need a rough by noon." The chief dropped some notes on her desk and walked away.

The face of Gina Marini, Hallie's other bunkmate and fellow journalist, appeared over the top of Hallie's laptop. "Since when don't you want a byline? I thought everything you published went into your resume."

"I don't want my name on anything on this ship right now." Hallie racked her brain wondering if there were still any newsletters floating around with her byline on them.

Gina's eyes lit up. "Because you don't want somebody to see it?"

Hallie tried to smother her smile, but she couldn't contain it. "Gina. I met the most amazing guy this weekend."

"Wait. From the ship? You got the hots for somebody on the *Blanchard*? What happened to the policy only you seem to follow? Come on. Dish, girl."

"Okay, tell you what. If you'll take this assignment, I'll give you the dirt."

"You got it." Gina grabbed the chief's notes and walked to her desk.

Whereas Trixie slept above Hallie, Gina slept below her in their three-tiered rack in female berthing, when she stayed on board. Since Gina was quietly living off base with her boyfriend, a chief hospital corpsman, she only slept on the ship when she had duty—and she obviously would once they deployed.

Gina might have some insight into Hallie's situation. Like Hallie, Gina was a Petty Officer Second-Class and it was considered fraternization for her to be getting it on with a chief assigned to the same command. Had he been attached to some other unit, fraternization wouldn't have been an issue. Unfortunately for Hallie, there were no such exceptions permitting intimate relationships between enlisted personnel and commissioned officers. Ever. Of course, once they deployed, anybody getting it on with anybody was verboten aboard ship.

Hallie loved the camaraderie she shared with the other Mass Communications Specialists—the MCs—in the Public Affairs office aboard the ship. They worked well together, gathering news about the *Blanchard* and disseminating it to the military and civilian communities via newsletters, email, and social media. She was glad her mom had talked her into joining the Navy as a way to finish college and receive on-the-job training as a news journalist.

Although her job at *All Hands* magazine in Washington had been a plum assignment for an MC, she did not feel she was doing her part in the war on terror. She preferred the nitty-gritty, day-to-day life aboard ship. And she knew it was where she'd find the real stories once they deployed.

Hallie had gladly exchanged her dress uniform and heels for combat boots and the blue and gray camouflage shirt and trousers, nicknamed "aquaflage." Apparently it was doing its duty of camouflaging her or the men on the *Blanchard* were either exceedingly polite or not too smart. Because so far she'd escaped being called, "Babe McCabe" or "The McBabe," monikers that had followed her since middle school. Going without make-up and perfume apparently helped, too.

Despite the lack of privacy in the Public Affairs office, Hallie had the use of her own laptop. This benefit would pay off once they deployed since she could stay connected with the outside world. As an MC, she had far more access to the Internet than any other enlisted person on the ship—and even more than a lot of the junior officers. As long as the satellite feed was working, she could log on.

Her current research was digging through the UCMJ for a loophole so she could continue to see Philip without them getting into trouble. The following sentence did not help:

"Any violation of this rule will subject the senior member to disciplinary action."

Ouch. She pictured Philip being led from the *Blanchard* in handcuffs. Blackballed. Stripped of his brass buttons and drummed off the ship. Hallie thought it sucked that the junior member could get away with a slap on the wrist—not that she wanted a major punishment if caught. It just seemed like a double standard.

But she couldn't help smiling at that "senior member" part when she thought about that senior's member stabbing her in the stomach in the rain yesterday during those mind-blowing kisses. Kisses that had been more tantalizing than flat-out sex. Never had she been kissed with such passion and tenderness at the same time. Long and slow, but deep and hungry. She couldn't believe he was the same guy from the beach on Saturday night. He'd obviously felt more confident on his boat. A flush of warmth curled low in her belly and she squirmed in her chair reliving those kisses. She reached up and touched the stubble burn on her chin.

She and Philip hadn't talked in the car on the way home from the river. Just held hands and listened to classic jazz. His mouth tipped up at the corner now and then, as if he had a secret tucked away. Probably the same one she had, with her heart thrumming like it was. Every glide of his thumb on her hand sent shock waves through her.

She liked that he was a good driver. So many guys tried to prove their manhood behind the wheel of a car; speeding, taking chances, letting the world know they were in charge. He did things like use his turn signal to change lanes, even when there was no one around. When she mentioned it to him, he shrugged and said, "Laws and rules are there for a reason, Hallie."

Just her luck to fall for a rule follower.

All the way home, she worried about what she'd do when he invited her to his apartment. After those kisses and the way she'd responded, she didn't know a guy who wouldn't push for more. Deep down Hallie wanted to go to his apartment, but no way was her sweet little enlisted ass going to do it. For starters she hadn't even known him twenty-four hours and more importantly, she couldn't get that involved with him. She'd use schoolwork as an excuse. But he never asked her to go to his apartment. He'd walked her to her door, took off his sunglasses, put his hand up against the wall, and leaned close. He gave her a slow, sexy smile and said, "Thanks for going today. It was..." He paused, his eyes shining as he searched for the word.

"Magical," she said finishing his thought.

He'd leaned down and kissed her quickly and sweetly on the lips, then his eyes narrowed with confusion. Putting his finger under her chin, he tipped it into the light. "Did I do that? I'm sorry if I hurt you."

He rubbed his stubble. Then he freaking planted a kiss on her chin and said goodnight. The kiss on the chin was even more of a turn-on than the kisses in the rain.

Oh, she was in deep. Philip was a perfect gentleman.

And an officer.

Gina interrupted her daydreaming. "Okay. Who is it? What department?"

"Don't ask."

"I know. And don't tell. Okay, let's work our way down. I'm going to assume it's not Captain Amerson." That brought a laugh at the thought of Hallie and the *Blanchard*'s new CO—the Commanding Officer. He was good looking, but he was an old guy.

"No, but he *is* an officer."

"Okay, here's what I know about fraternization. Since Steve made chief, we have to be careful. We quietly do our thing off base and rarely see each other on board. I'm up here and he's down in Sick Bay. Once we leave on the cruise, we'll only meet to talk in the library or the coffee shop once in a while and only..." she winked. "...you know...get busy together in liberty ports when we can. And even then, we'll have to watch ourselves."

"No frigging in the rigging?"

"He would get so busted if we got caught fooling around on the ship. But there's lots of it going on—even some between officers and enlisted. As long as people are discreet, it's not a huge problem unless they're in the same chain of command. Like it's your boss or something." Gina looked toward the office door of the Public Affairs Officer. "You're not getting it on with Commander Scott are you?" More laughter. "So, you didn't tell this guy you're on the ship because, why?"

"He doesn't even know I'm in the Navy."

"Oh, this is good. What are you going to do? Hide from him?"

Hallie glanced down at her aquaflage. "Well, I am camouflaged." Another chuckle from both of them. "Look, I didn't actually lie. I said I was a student, which I am. I'm not sure what I'm going to do. All I know is this guy is really sweet, not like most of the jerks I end up with. And he's pretty hot, but he's not full of himself. I feel comfortable with him, but he's a major rule follower. His words. And you know what? I like that about him, but I'm pretty sure he'd dump my ass in a heartbeat if he knew I was enlisted. Please don't say anything to anybody—especially Trixie. It'd be all over the ship in five minutes."

"I wouldn't tell that hussy what I had for breakfast," Gina said as she walked away.

Hallie glanced back at her computer screen. When she read the next sentence her heart skipped a beat, her breath quickened, and her lips curved into a dangerous smile.

"A commissioned officer can only be found guilty of fraternization if the accused knew the other person to be enlisted."

But what if he didn't?

Tooling around the engineering spaces that Monday morning in his navy blue coveralls, hardhat, and BCGs, Lieutenant Philip Johnston could barely concentrate on watching his men—and woman—fix a pump. And he could not stop smiling.

"You're looking especially happy today, sir," piped up one of his hull techs.

"It's a beautiful day."

"And you would know that how, sir, since you've been stuck down here since zero-dark-thirty?"

"I don't think Mr. Johnston's talking about the weather, Bulldog," Trixie chimed in. The guys stopped their work and walked over to check out their boss grinning like the Cheshire cat.

"Good weekend, sir?" she asked.

"The best." His mouth quirked up in a smile.

"Mr. Johnston, I think you're in luuuv!" Trixie never had a problem getting right to the point, even with officers.

"Could be. Who knows?" Certainly he bantered enough with the guys in his division, but never when Trixie was around. Not PC, even though she had a saltier mouth than most of the men on the ship. He also knew she called him Bill Gates behind his back. At least his men had the decency to refer to him as Mr. Gates when they called him that.

Philip gradually guided them back to the reality of pump maintenance and reminded them that the next step, the alignment of the pump shaft to the motor coupling, was the most critical part of the job. He tried to concentrate, but flashbacks from the day before—Hallie in a bikini, the sunscreen, the feel of their hands on each other's bodies, and those kisses in the rain kept flooding his mind. Finally he left the chief in charge of supervising the pump and went to his office, tipped back in his chair, propped his boots on the desk, threaded his hands behind his head, and thought about those kisses in the rain.

Kisses that had him wanting to take her right there on the deck outside the marina. After spending the afternoon with her in that bikini, with that curl draped down over her laughing blue eyes, and that wicked bottle of sunscreen. A spike of heat hit him in the gut just thinking about having her pressed up against the wall, feeling the hungry response from her lips, her tongue, her body. It had taken all of his restraint and control not to grind into her. A smile tugged at Philip's mouth. He wondered if it would still be called "dry humping" if both parties were soaking wet.

No way were they going to his apartment after that kiss. He was not going to mess things up by trying to take her to bed last night, even though she seemed to give him a green light. He did not like feeling out of control and he'd never gone to bed with a woman he had known for less than twenty-four hours. Okay, so the opportunity had rarely presented itself.

Anyway, Hallie deserved special handling, but oh, how he wanted to handle her.

His brain fast-forwarded to saying goodbye at her doorway, when he'd taken off his sunglasses and seen her chin. Talk about out of control. Her chin was scraped pink and raw from his stubble. What kind of animal had done that to her? Yeah, good thing he hadn't invited her upstairs.

But then he went back to the kisses and smiled broadly. Since he hadn't dogged the door to his office, he could still hear snippets of conversation out in the engine room and he was certain he heard Trixie say, "Yes, sirree, I do believe our own Bill Gates is gettin' some."

Operations Specialist Second-Class Randy Davis sat at his computer terminal in the Combat Direction Center—CDC, or simply "Combat"—on the O-3 level of the USS *Blanchard*, contemplating another boring day at his job. When the ship was in port, the OS's job pretty much consisted of mustering in the morning, tidying up their personal area, cleaning off a couple of radar screens, and then playing online solitaire for the rest of the day. The fun stuff—operating the radar systems and identifying friend or foe was only done underway. Not a lot of bogeys in port, but he knew that would change once they arrived in the Middle East.

While the *Blanchard* had been in overhaul for almost a year, it had sucked a big, wet one. Randy thought he'd spend the whole time attending schools, completing refresher courses, and studying for his next rating exam. Instead, he and most of the OS Division had been assigned to paint teams and fire watches, which was bullshit for a second-class petty officer. The little bit of training he got was a couple of simulation exercises done in classrooms on shore.

Randy had planned to use the year they were in dry dock to go to school. He and his wife had been talking about starting a family and he had truly wanted to do whatever it took to improve their circumstances. Getting some college in seemed like a good start. He really had wanted to do something important with his life. Leave his mark.

But then the problems had started and now she was gone. And gone were his dreams. Nothing mattered anymore. So fuck those goals and dreams. They were all crap now. Although he still liked the idea of leaving his mark. Oh, yeah. He was taking a crash course in becoming famous now. The Navy wouldn't be forgetting OS2 Randy Davis for a long, long time. He'd make the fucking headlines. He could just see it in print. Well, he wouldn't actually see it in print. He'd be dead. But it would be there for every other one of these assholes to see. Actually, he didn't really like what they would see in print, because they'd use his real name.

Ralph.

The memories of being called Ralphie socked him in the stomach and fire spread through his veins as he wiped down radar screens. Maybe it had been funny in elementary school, but many of those kids had teased him all the way through high school—about that and other things. Wouldn't he just love to get his mitts on a couple of those pricks today with the power he now held in his hands.

Thank God the jerk-offs he worked with here in Combat didn't know his real name because he'd never hear the end of it. They already gave him enough crap about everything else.

"Randy" worked just fine and had gotten him through the last four years. Until now. Because now he wasn't even Randy anymore. He liked that his sadiqs, his new pals in the Middle East, called him Rashid.

That was a man's name.

And that's how he would sign everything he left behind for the assholes in the U.S. Navy to read, which he knew they would do.

Right after they finished picking up the pieces.

Chapter 5

"Cowboy? You had that fucking hat on, didn't you?" Sky laughed so hard he choked on the words. "That why you don't talk much, pardner? Because you're too busy doing other things?" He waggled his eyebrows at Philip, who pretended to blow on a pistol and tuck it back into a holster.

Hallie had invited Philip for dinner on Tuesday, but said she'd be studying the rest of the week, so he was free to meet Sky for a brew.

Bill Gates and the Skylark had met their first day of Plebe Summer at the Naval Academy and had been best buddies ever since, even though they were as different as night and day. Sky was a wild-ass party boy and Philip was, well, Philip. He had always been there to bring Sky back down to earth with his common sense and advice. Sky worked overtime to bring Philip out of his shell, and introduce him to fine—and not so fine—young ladies.

Philip was thrilled when Sky received orders to a helicopter maritime strike squadron across the river at NAS Jacksonville, but even more pleased to learn that Sky's squadron would be deploying with him in July. The two planned to spend their free time during those long days and nights at sea on the *Blanchard* playing cards, watching movies, and working out. And they looked forward to raising some hell together in the liberty ports. Rather, Sky would raise hell and Philip would drag Sky's sorry ass back to the ship before curfew.

"So you had her all day in a bikini on the boat and then?"

"And we sailed. And swam. And..."

"And?"

"We did a little kissing." Philip's lips curved into a self-satisfied smile.

Sky pushed his beer aside and set his forearms on the table, eyes eager. "And?"

"A little sunscreen application." He drew out the words for Sky's benefit.

Sky slapped the table and flashed his signature grin, complete with a space between his two front teeth. He leaned back and slid his fingers through his blond crew cut. "Oh, yeah, now we're getting to the good stuff. Then what?"

"That's it."

Sky jerked back in his seat. "That's it?"

"Yeah, Sky, I'm not an asshole around women like you are. That's it."

"Ah, Lieutenant Integrity speaks. Okay, but let's say her bikini top had, like, fallen off. Would we be talking oranges or cantaloupes or—?"

"You are such a tool." Philip shook his head in disbelief. "Sorry, but Hallie's body is none of your business."

"Yeah, but I bet you're gonna make it *your* business. Okay, forget the fruit, Cowboy, but come on, give me some details. This is the Skylark, king of the skies and the bedroom. Your alpha male wingman, your head coach. I have to know what the playing field's like if I'm gonna give you any pointers."

Philip smiled like the cat that just ate the canary. "I'm doing fine on my own these days, thank you very much, pardner."

"Come on. Use the scale. Give me a number. I can't get a visual on this girl unless I have a number. Just one digit and I won't ask another question. One to ten."

"Thirty-five."

Sky howled. "Damn, I wish you could see yourself sitting there with a shit-eating grin on your face. You got it bad, Billy Boy—or is that 'Billie the Kid' now? When can I meet her—or are you afraid you'll be like yesterday's newspaper once she sees the Skylark in a flight suit?"

"In your dreams, asshole."

"Got a picture?"

"Nope, but trust me, she's gorgeous. With an incredible body to match, and she's..." He drifted off with a dreamy look on his face. "...awesome." Sky rolled his eyes as Philip waxed and waned about Hallie's virtues. He told Sky about her dreams of being a newscaster and how she handled the sailboat and how smart she was.

"I had dinner at her cousin's last night. And it was pretty funny, because we were kissing on the couch while they did the dishes. And Jeopardy was on, and Hallie kept pulling away to answer the questions. And she got them all right."

Sky whooped and slapped his thigh. "A nympho-brainiac!"

"Shut up, Sky." But Philip laughed right along with him.

"Okay, okay." Sky had to catch his breath. "But why were you watching television and playing kissy face at the cousins' when you could have been upstairs doing the horizontal mambo? That's so seventh grade."

"You were smooching on the couch in seventh grade?"

"I was a gifted student, buddy. In all advanced classes when it came to lovin'."

Philip chuckled in spite of himself. "You are so full of shit. Look, I'm not stupid. I invited her up, but she said she had too much work to do."

"Excuses, excuses. So, Billy Boy, you think you've found the mythical perfect woman?"

Philip sobered a bit. "Pretty much, even though there's something I can't place. She's got an edge to her." He focused on picking at the label on his beer bottle. "She goes somewhere in her head sometimes. She gets this haunted look in her eyes, like she's got some baggage. Some secrets."

"Maybe she's doing a clandestine study of the mating rituals of nerd lieutenants. Was she wearing a wire?" Sky failed to keep a straight face.

"No, seriously. She's got a few issues. Her dad was never a part of her life and she lost her mom a couple of years ago. And she was uber-sensitive about me having a nickname. She even mentioned something about being bullied in high school. I never thought about pretty girls getting bullied. She didn't tell me the nicknames guys called her but it's not hard to figure out. Probably 'McBabe' or something."

Sky spewed his beer across the table. "McBabe!" He grabbed a napkin to wipe his mouth. "I sure hope you get Happy Meals!"

"Shut up, Sky." Philip shook his head again and pulled out his wallet to pay their tab. "Look I gotta run. Hallie said she'd call if she got her work done early."

"Oh, man. Look at you. You are so whipped. But it's nice to see you with that big old grin on your face. I'd like to meet her if we can get together before we ship out." He raised his hand in a stop sign. "And I promise to behave. But remember, once we leave on cruise, I'm your number one date in all liberty ports."

Philip fist-bumped Sky, then socked him lightly on the shoulder. "Until something better comes along, right?"

"Damn straight."

Philip climbed into his SUV. "Keep your powder dry, buddy."

Sky waved as he jumped into his truck. "Giddy-up, Cowboy!"

If Hallie McCabe had balls, Sarah "Trixie" Williams had them in spades. In addition, rumor had it she'd slept with half the Atlantic Fleet—the male half. Naked, she was a work of art. Literally. You'd think a nineteen-year-old girl, who was barely five-feet tall and weighed maybe one hundred pounds soaking wet, wouldn't have the square footage or life history to be the proud owner of six tattoos, but she was. When Trixie walked through berthing in a bra and a thong, it was like an advertisement for Strut Your Stuff, Ink.

There was the snake draped around her neck, with its forked tongue pointing the way down into her cleavage, the twisted vine of red roses and barbed wire around her navel, and the words

"Unplumbed Depths" in fancy script above her soon-to-be plumber's crack. But everybody's favorite was "Your Name" tattooed on her left butt cheek, visible to everyone present when she was only wearing a thong.

Trixie had collected plenty of free drinks in bars after challenging strangers to bet that she remembered them so well "I even had your name tattooed on my ass." Not that she'd ever bared it on the ship, except in berthing, but the entire crew was privy to the stories of her baring it in bars. The sailors always baited her by saying, "Trixie, how well do you know me?"

Trixie was a Navy fireman apprentice from the streets of Lowell, Massachusetts. She'd been in a gang since the age of fourteen and had joined the Navy when a recruiter came to her high school. "He was hot, so I told him I'd join up."

Since Hallie pulled the duty on Thursday that week, she stayed on board for the night. She and Gina happened to be in berthing when Trixie debriefed about her day. "You should see Bill Gates this week. He's so much in love he's, like, walking into bulkheads and shit. The man is definitely getting some. Or maybe he's just taking happy pills because I can't imagine any chick wanting to do it with him. What a geek."

Gina caught the look on Hallie's face—pretending not to listen, but obviously taking in every word—and she put two and two together. Hallie and this Bill Gates were both so much in love they were walking into bulkheads and shit. So were they in love with each other?

She shot Hallie a look across the space and Hallie's knee-jerk reaction confirmed that Hallie was "the chick." She caught her eye and mouthed out the words "Bill Gates?" Hallie blushed crimson. Fortunately, Trixie didn't notice.

"Oh, Hallie. He's adorable!" Gina cried as best she could, considering they were whispering in the female head just outside Public Affairs Friday morning.

Hallie had conceded to letting Gina go down in the hole on the pretext of seeing where Trixie worked. Trixie was only too happy to give Gina a tour of the engineering spaces and an introduction to her geeky boss, Bill Gates.

"She took me into his office and you were right. He did have his BCGs on, but I could tell he was gorgeous behind them. And God, what a build. So he stands up, takes his hard hat off, and shakes my hand. How nice was that? I mean, I'm just a peon second-class."

Gina planted her feet and smiled, just getting started with her report. "So he shook my hand and said, 'Pleased to meet you, Miss Marini. Welcome to Shit Central.' You know how guys look at you when they meet you? Basically look you up and down and check you out? They don't know that we know it's all in their eyes, even when their eyes aren't moving. But he didn't do that. He was very polite and decent. You're right. He's a gentleman."

Hallie nodded approvingly as Gina explained how Philip said Trixie could show her around, everywhere but the nuke spaces.

"So Trixie says, 'Well, I'm not allowed in those spaces anyway. Gee, I wonder why the Navy doesn't want me around a fucking nuclear reactor.' And he said, 'Language, Williams,' like you just knew he tells her that all the time. And she said, 'Oh, sorry, sir. I forgot there was a fucking lady present.' So he sat down and pulled off his glasses and rubbed the bridge of his nose, then the back of his neck, and said, 'See what I endure all day long?' Oh, Hallie, he was so hot when he took his glasses off. I totally know what you're talking about now. I still say you need to tell him the truth before you get yourself in too deep."

Gina stopped, out of breath.

"Thanks for the advice," Hallie said, "but I'm still trying to figure out what to do. The UCMJ says he can't get in trouble as long as he doesn't know I'm enlisted, so at least he's covered while I figure it out. I mean, there's no way I'm going to try to fake it through the cruise. But we could have a month or so of bliss before we leave. Rebecca and her husband have been on me all week to tell him, too. They said they're not going to cover for me. It's just that every time I get ready to tell him, I picture him walking away and he is, like, the greatest guy I've ever met in my life."

"How have you avoided him so far on the ship?"

"Well, first of all I'm hiding in plain sight. He's not expecting me to be here, especially in the same uniform everyone else is wearing, and he's not used to seeing me with my hair up. I'm always on the lookout when I'm in the passageways. And since snipes wear plain blue coveralls on board, he'd be easy to notice. Plus, they stay down in the hole and hardly ever travel higher than the mess decks. And I know his hours. He leaves really early in the morning and uses the Officers' brow to get on the ship."

"Oh, man, this is like a spy movie or something."

"And I make sure I get to the ship after him and sneak on board right before muster. He usually works late, so I leave as soon as liberty is called. Even then, I don't mess around going down the brow or hanging around the pier. I just get off the ship and book it for my car."

"What about on the other end? What if he changes his routine? I doubt you'd want him catching you in uniform in The Towers parking lot. What are you going to do? Start changing in a McDonald's bathroom on the way home?"

"Good idea."

"Hallie, no freaking way. You gotta tell him. He's too nice."

"I know. I know."

"What are you doing about duty nights?" Gina asked.

"I thought it was fortunate we're on the same duty schedule. But even that's a problem, because he asked me to dine with him in the wardroom when he had duty last night."

"So what did you tell him?"

"That I have to study. Which isn't a lie. I've never outright lied to him."

"Just by omission."

"Oh, and I forgot. He invited me to a party at the Captain's house tomorrow night."

"No way."

"Way. Course I'm not going, but I may see him after the party if it isn't too late. Then we're going sailing Sunday."

"And then what? Come on, you gotta tell him. Look I hate to burst your bubble, but this whole thing is just a fairy tale if you can't tell him the truth."

"Yeah, thanks for reminding me, Fairy Godmother."

"I say you tell him and let the chips fall where they may. Because Cinderella, if you don't tell him soon, you're going to turn back into a pumpkin *and* break Prince Charming's heart."

Chapter 6

Hallie closed her computer and checked her watch again. Nine thirty. Guess Philip wasn't going to call or come by. Probably for the best. She had no business visiting his apartment anyway. How much she'd wanted to go up there the other night after dinner at Rebecca's. They'd been like a couple of high school kids necking on the couch. She'd wanted him to kiss her all night and take away all her responsibilities.

But she couldn't quiet the little voices in her head that kept whispering about what she'd read.

"...personal relationships including dating, cohabitation, and any sexual relationship between officers and enlisted personnel are strictly forbidden."

So Hallie came to a decision. She would tell him the truth after sailing tomorrow and if he bolted, as she expected him to do, then so be it. If he wanted to continue secretly off base? That would be gravy. They'd figure out how to handle the cruise later. But somehow she doubted he'd break the rules. That was one of the reasons she liked him so much.

The ring tone of her phone pulled her out of her reverie.

Philip invited her up to watch a movie and have that glass of wine. Her heartbeat quickened at the thought of seeing him tonight. She thought long and hard before accepting, but what could a glass of wine hurt?

After she arrived, he debriefed about the party while she sipped her pinot grigio. She listened carefully when he shared stories of his fellow officers, because she knew some of them. Fortunately he didn't mention her boss.

"Actually, the party pretty much sucked because you weren't there." His brown eyes were so focused on her she hoped he couldn't see into her deceitful soul.

He picked up his phone and asked if he could take her picture, since she was looking so cute in braids tonight. Hallie's heart raced. She reached out and covered the phone. "I'd rather you didn't, Philip. I don't like my picture taken."

He cocked his head, questions in his eyes.

"Sorry," she said. "It's just that somebody took pictures of me in high school and Photoshopped them and they circulated through the school. People called me...'Babe McCabe' and...'The McBabe.' Guys had called me that in middle school, but it was worse after those pictures went around. It's not that I don't trust you, but it makes me feel uncomfortable." Not a lie.

Just what she needed. Her picture on his desk in Engineering. Wouldn't Trixie get a kick out of that? The fact that he might mention Hallie's name to the wrong person—especially Trixie—was bad enough. Hallie swore to herself that she would tell him tomorrow after sailing. Period.

"That's awful." Philip reached for her. "I just wanted to capture how cute you look in those braids. Trust me. I'd never do anything like that."

"I know. But we've only known each other a week—"

"Best week of my life." He tried to smile but couldn't move past the concern for her.

"I have some weird trust issues. Okay, Philip? Please be patient with me."

Weird trust issues? No photographs? Bullied in high school? No parents? The woman had some baggage. There were landmines planted all around Hallie and Philip hoped he didn't step on any more.

"Look, Hallie, I know we just met but I am crazy about you. I hope you know I'd never do anything to hurt you. You tell me what you want me to do—or not do—and I'll do it—or not do it."

Hallie reached out and stroked his cheek. "Thank you."

After putting in a movie, Philip slipped his arm around her on the sofa. He was still mulling over her reaction to photographs when he felt fingers in his hair. Turning to her, he found her smile slow, mischievous, and totally breathtaking.

"Sorry, but your curls are so tempting," she said.

"Well, if you get to do that, I get to play with the golden tendril."

"The what?"

"This." He reached up and pulled it from behind her ear. "This is the golden tendril and it drives me crazy."

"You don't like it?"

"I love it." He curled and uncurled the lock of hair around his finger. "That's why it drives me crazy."

He not only thought of Muslim women covering their hair but visions of military women in uniform came to him as well. How many times had he sat in boring staff meetings imagining himself letting down some female officer's hair and then...Bound hair showed control, but unbound?

Wait. Why was he even thinking of women in uniform when he had Hallie right here and the golden tendril between his fingers?

And then they were kissing. Philip wasn't sure who started it, but he wasn't complaining. He wrapped his arms around her, and pulled her to him. Desire twisted in his gut as she returned his long, slow, deep, kisses, tongues searching, and finding.

A tiny purr in her throat just about undid him. She was liquid in his arms, tasting him, threading her fingers through his hair, kissing him deeper. He had no idea what kind of trust issues she might have, but he was powerless over her kisses. Heat curled inside him, threatening his control. True, he kept getting mixed messages from her, but her mouth was so hot. If she wanted him to stop, he would.

And if she didn't? He most definitely would not.

Leaving her mouth, he worked his way down to her neck. He buried his face in the hollow of her throat where he could breathe in her essence. Her fingers played in his hair as he tasted her skin, under her jaw line and behind her ears. When Hallie moaned, liquid heat shot through him. He laid her gently down on the sofa and returned to her mouth, leading with his tongue.

Lust chipped away at his ability to reason. His hand caressed her neck and slid down to her breasts. She shuddered and moaned, which kicked his pulse into overdrive. He cupped her breast, molding the fullness. Traced it. Over. Under. Around. First one. Then the other.

He gently stroked the centers and felt her nipples tighten through her blouse. She made a noise and he stopped, but his hand stayed put. He only left her mouth long enough to whisper into it, "Okay?" She made another noise, but it wasn't a stopping noise.

He deftly unbuttoned her top button. Then the next. And so on. He left her mouth to watch himself stroke her, her nipple puckering to his touch under purple lace. Hallie arched her back, meeting his hand. Unclasping the front hook of her lacey bra, her breasts spilled into his hands, slamming his heart into an even higher gear, something guttural in his throat. His thumbs scraped lightly over her nipples, gently fondling and stroking them. Her soft skin driving him wild.

Philip's mouth left a trail of kisses down her neck and worked its way to a taut nipple, which he bathed with his tongue. He buried his face between her breasts, certain he had died and gone to heaven.

Then he kissed each goodbye, her nipples still shining wet from his mouth. Although he wasn't sure if he was capable of speech, Philip brought his mouth to her ear. Without an ounce of coercion, he whispered, "Stay with me tonight. Let me love you."

No begging. No pleading. Just an invitation.

Hallie bolted upright and pulled her shirt around her. Face flushed, stray hairs loosened from her braids. "I can't." She fought to catch her breath. "I'm so sorry, Philip."

He dropped his forehead to the back of the sofa. "No, Hallie. I'm sorry. Just give me a minute." His primal brain told him to say, "Belay my last," meaning "forget my request, delete what I just said," so he could go back to exploring her breasts for a couple more hours, but he didn't listen. Especially since peripheral vision reported that she'd already hooked her bra and was buttoning her shirt.

While she pulled herself together, he gathered his wits, figuring out how he was going to function. She continued to apologize, but Philip raised his hand to quiet her. He didn't have the strength to do anything else.

"I can find my way home." She rose from the couch.

"No way." Somehow he stood, held her briefly, and kissed her hair. She felt stiff in his arms. "I'm sorry, baby. Come on. I'll take you home."

Hallie smoothed down her blouse and finger-combed the golden tendril. "It's really okay, Philip."

He wanted to take her hand on the way down the stairs but he didn't dare touch her. He'd overstepped his bounds. How many fricking steps did this staircase have anyway? Each step echoed *awkward*.

At her door, she tried to apologize again, but he put his finger to her lips. "Shhh. It's okay. Are we still on for sailing tomorrow?"

She nodded a yes, and then hesitated as if thinking about something important before she spoke.

Uh oh, here it comes. Fuck off, dude?

"Philip...Thank you. For bringing me home. And...for being you."

He kissed her quickly before she slipped through the doorway. Once she was safely inside, he rested his forehead against the wall, gathering the strength to walk back upstairs.

Go to bed, dumb ass.

* * *

Hallie couldn't sleep. Over and over again, she relived lying in his arms, feeling his mouth on her. Wishing that the world, and her enlistment, would go away so she could have stayed with him and loved him all night. She drifted off to another world. A place where there were no words such as commissioned officer, accused, and violation of a written order.

And the only senior member that mattered was the one at the end of his happy trail.

All she knew was her breasts had never known such tender, teasing, trusting, hot kisses before. His fingers tweaking her nipples had electrified her. And when he'd drawn circles around them with the tip of his tongue she was certain she would explode. No way had she wanted to stop.

She wanted to make love with him.

She wanted to stay all night.

She wanted to stay with him forever. But she couldn't.

And it wasn't just his kisses that turned her on. It was him. The courteous way he'd behaved all week was so refreshing and new to her. She'd always had a problem with men hitting on her, so she'd learned to be careful. The few times she'd gotten into situations like tonight, men had tried their damndest to get her into bed. She'd never met a man who respected her wishes and respected *her* as much as Philip did. It wasn't like they were sixteen-year-olds behind the bleachers. This was a twenty-seven-year-old man who had a woman in his apartment who had given him every indication she wanted to make love as much as he did. But instead of talking her into staying, he'd taken her home without an argument.

This was the man of her dreams. But he deserved better than what she was doing behind his back. No question about it. She'd tell him the truth tomorrow night. Right after sailing one last time.

And she'd better be prepared to sail off into the sunset.

Alone.

Chapter 7

Rashid was pissed. He arrived at the mall when it opened at noon, but his favorite restaurant was closed. He'd looked forward to his meal of pancit and lumpia all week. Yeah, like the food court at this dump was going to cut it. Oh, well. At least it was better than the chow on the ship. First he'd see if his sadiq, Ibrahim, was working today.

A trip through the mall was always an enlightening experience. He liked to people watch, and some of the merchandise was always good for a laugh as well. Especially some of the crap sold in the kiosks. Rashid asked himself: Who buys this shit?

An oversized gold-filled charm saying "Favorite Grandmother," caught his eye. Yeah, his drunken grandma would get a kick out of that one. The merchant said, "You name it. We got it. And if we don't, we'll get it for you. Good price. Just for you."

This booth had everything from gold Harleys to Stars of David to fake diamond rings, for Christ's sake. A rhinestone-encrusted Jesus medallion caught Rashid's eye. Funny, he'd never thought of Jesus as a rhinestone kind of guy.

His mind flashed to his new friends and their commitment to their god. Allah? Jesus? Hell, throw in Buddha for good measure. None of them had ever done a fucking thing for Rashid when people were screwing him over. But if the tangos wanted to do their thing in the name of some god, then more power to them. He sure wasn't doing this for a religious belief. Or wait. Maybe he was. Sticking it to the Navy would be a certain kind of heaven for him.

But he sure wasn't going to shout, *"Allahu Akbar,"* when he detonated. Maybe "Fuck you, Uncle Sam" would work. The dumb rag-heads on the fishing boat could yell whatever they wanted.

"Peace be with you, my friend."

Rashid turned to find his contact had joined him. "Back atcha, Ibrahim. What are you doing over here? Checking out the competition? Who's minding the store?"

"My brother is with me today. Perhaps you and I could go sit down and talk. Have something to eat, some tea. I have news for you."

Rashid's heart rate kicked up a notch.

They followed the cacophony of video games and pinball machines to the food court, ordered, and settled at a corner table. His new buddies had kept him apprised of details on a daily basis, but he didn't dare access his personal email on the ship. He popped down to the Single Sailor Center on base most nights to check it.

"Remember, Ibrahim. Once I deploy I can only access my Navy email address. So be sure to remind our friends to watch what they say."

"Yes, we are all aware of that. Thank you for the list of code words to use. We like the idea of pretending we are a girlfriend or lover."

"I'm serious, man. It'll all fall through, if they write anything that smacks of danger. All ship's email is scrutinized by security. Especially on deployment. And be sure to tell them there will be times when I won't have access to it at all. In a crisis the ship will just cut everyone off. Hopefully, we'll be able to communicate all pertinent information before we get to K-Day though."

Ibrahim cocked his head. "K-Day?"

A grin blossomed on Rashid's face. "Yeah. For Kaboom."

Ibrahim's face reflected Rashid's smile. "Go ahead and check your mail, sadiqi. I believe you will find some messages from our friends."

Ibrahim stirred three packets of sugar into his tea and sipped it while Rashid connected to the Internet. How could he drink that sweet shit? There were two messages from hotmama-lovesrandy@gmail.com. "Have I told you how much I like the email account they're using? Once they start writing to my navy email address, the security guards will never get suspicious about messages coming from such a loving address."

"We study Americans to find the best ways to blend in. Some of our people have spent their whole lives here. They know the culture and details that a foreigner never would. What does Hot Mama have to say today?"

Rashid opened the first email. He glanced around the food court. There was no one close enough to hear. And the electronic sounds from the game room made for good cover noise, so he read it to Ibrahim. "The holy month of Ramadan ends on Eid al Fitr, which occurs on September ninth this year. Eid is a day of gift giving and fireworks. Think of it as a combination of your Christmas and Independence Day. Thank you for your part in helping us give the Americans a gift of fireworks on Eid this year." He looked up questioningly at Ibrahim. "Does this mean what I think it means?"

"Yes, my friend. They are giving you the date. September ninth, because Eid is a very special day in our calendar."

Heat rushed through Rashid's chest. "It's perfect because we'll definitely be in the Gulf by September." He paused, a triumphant grin on his face. "But it's even better than perfect. It's brilliant. Because Uncle Sam will be so focused on security for September 11, they'll be caught off guard by an early surprise."

"That is good to know, my friend. What else do they have to say?"

Rashid clicked on the other message. "Send proposed schedule as soon as possible. Be sure to include liberty ports. It would be our pleasure to have friends meet with you. We have sadiqs everywhere." He glanced up at Ibrahim. "Whoa. They want to meet me?"

"You are doing us a tremendous favor, Rashid. I believe they will want to thank you in person if the opportunity arises."

"Even if I have a schedule of ports, not everyone gets to go ashore every time."

"Certainly you will go ashore at some point. And like he said, they have friends everywhere. Just stay in touch and email Hot Mama if you find yourself visiting a port along the way—using the code of course. Do they say anything else?"

Rashid continued reading. "We have a faithful servant with fishing boats in several locales. As long as you are somewhere in the pond on the designated date, we will find you."

Adrenaline rushed to every corner of his body. This was really going to happen.

The pond. The whole fucking Persian Gulf.

"This is awesome, Ibrahim. I can't guarantee anything, except that we will most likely be in the Gulf on September ninth. Just remember, plans could change at any time."

"No problem, my friend. Our man with the boats owns many dhows and will have five boats in two different ports."

His heart stuttered, skipped a beat. He grabbed Ibrahim's wrist. "Did you say five?"

The merchant nodded. Rashid's heart kicked into high gear. Five? He'd expected them to send one dhow to compromise the carrier. But, five? Holy shit, these fuckers were serious.

"Currently we plan to have five boats in al-Jubayl and five more further south, closer to Dubai. The dhows will be pre-staged, but the fishermen and explosives can be transported easily by truck. Our extensive tribal contacts will ensure that border crossings anywhere on the Arabian Peninsula will not be an issue."

Rashid's orange chicken and iced tea sat untouched. His blood hummed with excitement. This was going to be so fucking easy. The sadiqs were going to take care of everything— everything except for CDC. The Combat Direction Center on the ship was all his. He wasn't going to let somebody else have all the fun. He would be personally involved in his cause. No way would he be a pussy like Timothy McVeigh had been in Oklahoma City.

Rashid was going down with *his* ship.

$Chapter\ 8$

Although Hallie and Philip had planned to set sail early Sunday morning, it was hard to stick to a schedule when neither of them had slept the night before. Both were still on physical and emotional tenterhooks. It was after noon before they cleared the marina. When Hallie parked herself on the bench seat and pulled out the bottle of sunscreen, Philip stopped unfurling the sails.

"Please don't ask me to put that on your back." A corner of his mouth lifted in a half smile. "I don't think I could bear it today."

"I'm sorry about last night, Philip. I just didn't feel right about staying."

Philip knelt down in front of her and took her face in his hands.

"No, Hallie, you call the shots. I don't want to push you into anything you don't want to do. I'm just...I don't know... I've been out of my mind this past week around you. I haven't been able to function, just thinking about you. And it's not just, you know, kissing you. It's you, Hallie." He put his finger under her chin and tipped her face to his.

"I'm in a state of shock that I've met a woman who is smart and fun and cares about the world and doing the right things and..." He took the bottle from her. "And sunscreen."

Warmth spread through Hallie's chest, a flutter in her heart.

"You're genuine, Hallie. And I want to be with you all the time." He kissed her gently on the lips, just once. "And although my mind wants to treat you like the gentleman you deserve, I can't seem to get my body to behave. So no, I won't put sunscreen on your back. You'll have to put on a shirt."

Hallie burst out laughing and reached out to hug him, but he raised his hand to stop her. "And I'll put a shirt on too, because there is no way you're going to put me through what you did last Sunday with that lotion. I thought I was going to die. So come on, sailor." He hoisted the mainsail. "Anchors aweigh."

They sailed up Turtle Creek, an estuary of the St. Johns, enjoying the lush jungle on both sides, altering course for a manatee mother and baby. Surprisingly, there weren't many boats on the creek so they had this paradise all to themselves. Hallie parked herself and handled the jib while Philip worked the mainsail and the tiller. Neither felt the need to talk.

But no matter how beautiful the day and how natural she felt in Philip's presence, Hallie could not enjoy it. A clock ticked away inside her. A bomb that would eventually go off and destroy this delicious slice of heaven she had found.

Hallie McCabe had seriously fallen for Philip Johnston. She'd spent the past ten years fighting off guys with a stick; and somehow this thoughtful guy had slipped under her radar and stolen her heart. She'd liked him well enough until last night, but when he took her home without one word of argument, it was all over but the shouting.

As she worked the jib, Hallie thought about how angry he would be when she told him the truth later that night. No, worse. He'd be disappointed in her. She strongly doubted he'd bend any rules and agree to an illicit relationship off base. And definitely not, once they deployed. She'd have to agree with him there. That would be way too dangerous for both of them.

She'd even try reminding him that life was uncertain, nobody knew what tomorrow would bring, grab for the gusto, and all that crap. But she knew he wouldn't fall for it. Because he lived and breathed integrity. And that's what she liked about him. Maybe he'd come into her life simply to show her there *were* men out there like this. Men she could depend on. Feel safe with. Trust.

He'd blown her away with that little chat about the sunscreen. Most guys would have welcomed the sunscreen action today and picked up where they left off last night. If she'd thought taking her home last night was the ultimate in gentlemanly behavior, his refusal to put lotion on her back this afternoon was the cherry on top. No way was she going to let him walk away. Not quite yet.

Suddenly Hallie knew it was time to act. What good was having a set of balls in her seabag if she didn't take them out and use them once in a while? Looking around to ensure there weren't any other boats in sight, she knew it was time to go on a treasure hunt.

And she knew exactly where to find the map.

Philip felt her sneak up behind him as he trimmed the sail. She put her arms around him and hugged his back.

"Hallie," he cautioned.

She kissed his neck. "Thank you for a wonderful day. And thank you for being you." He turned around to protest her hug, but didn't get the chance. She removed his sunglasses, locked eyes with him, and said, "I want to make love with you. Right now. Right here."

Heat slammed into him, along with stunned silence. Had he heard her right? His mouth didn't work, except to fall open.

"I'm serious." She flashed him a do-me smile while lifting his shirttail and running her finger from his navel down the line of hair to his shorts. "I'm dying to know what's at the end of this happy trail."

He grabbed her hand to stop her, his mouth frozen, his brain on fire. Mixed messages. The hell with mixed messages. Sails? Anchor? Damn the torpedoes. Full speed ahead.

Shit. No condom.

"You bring in the sails and I'll make the bed," Hallie cooed.

"But—"

She put her finger to his lips. "Shhh. Love now. Talk later."

He was dying here. "No. We need to talk now. I wasn't prepared for this. I mean, I'm not prepared for this. I don't have a condom on board."

He told Sky's voice in his head to shut up before it even got started. No way was he expecting this in his wildest dreams. Not even if they'd already been intimate would he have thought of making love on the sailboat. Like where? There was just enough room in the well between the bench seats.

The cockpit.

Whole new meaning.

"It's okay. I'm on birth control," Hallie said.

"No, it's not okay. I'm sorry, but that's just how I do things."

Damn it anyway.

"Did a paper on STDs once and got an A on it?" She challenged him with a smile.

"Something like that." He grinned slyly and cleared his throat. "That's not to say there aren't other ways to pass the afternoon, if you're still interested."

Hallie pulled her T-shirt over her head, threw it on the deck, reached into her bikini top, and extracted a condom package. "What's the matter? Flunk boy scouts?"

Philip was dumbstruck. She put her finger to his lips and repeated her command. "Love now. Talk later." She pulled his shirt over his head. Then continued her exploration of his happy trail.

Her finger burned him. He grabbed her hand. "Don't. Please."

"Don't or please?"

Philip couldn't breathe. He knew if she did that again, there was no way he'd be able to bring in the sails or make it to the cockpit.

"I thought you said you had control over your destiny when you were out on the water." She teased him with a sexy half smile.

And he gave one right back to her. "Not if you touch my happy trail again, I won't."

Her bikini top hit the deck. Philip filled his hands and mouth with her. He somehow managed to bring in the sails, when his hands weren't on her breasts. He blindly found the anchor and threw it overboard. They somehow managed to slide the cushions down into the cockpit, along with a couple of life jackets for a mattress.

Their kiss was uninterrupted. A wicked gleam lit Hallie's eyes as she again trailed her finger down his abdomen, but this time he let her reach for him through his shorts. Philip's eyes glazed over as if in pain and he was certain his knees were going to give out. She unlaced his shorts and drew him out as she pulled him down onto the cushions.

He had no choice but to lie on top of her. That was all the room they had. His mouth returned to hers. Still slow, but deep. His tongue filling her mouth. Then to her breasts. Licking them, making her arch her back toward him. He taunted her with each of his slow, deliberate actions. And then went back to her mouth, while trying to shield her face from the sun as best as he could.

Philip slid his left hand into her bikini bottoms, finding her hot and wet and more than ready for him. He rolled right and braced himself with a hand and a foot, so he could peel down the bikini.

Hallie's hungry eyes invited him in, as she raised her hips. This was really going to happen. He deftly used a big toe to hook her bikini bottoms and slide them off. How he removed his shorts he had no idea. All he knew was he was naked with this incredible, equally naked woman who had just said, "I want to make love with you. Right now. Right here."

And Philip Johnston had always been one to comply.

After tearing the condom package with his teeth, he put it in her hand and closed her fingers around it. Hallie reached for him and slid along his length, slowly driving him almost to the brink, before covering him.

Inch by painful inch.

He wasn't sure he'd make it inside her.

Philip broke the kiss. Bracing himself on his elbows, he took her face in his hands, and while looking deeply into her eyes, he slid home. Just like his kisses. Slow and deep. Filling her.

Hallie moved first and he matched her stroke for magnificent stroke. In perfect rhythm. Gazes locked in sizzling intimacy.

She pulled his head down, begging him to kiss her as she arched her hips up to meet him. Their pace quickened, until they were grinding and pounding, rocking the boat. Despite the intensity, they fought to keep their eyes open, lost in each other's ecstasy.

She grabbed hold of his hips and rocketed from side to side.

Her eyes slid shut and she cried out her release as wave upon wave of pleasure ripped through her. And the combination of her orgasm pulsing around him and hearing his name being screamed to the heavens above, took him right over the edge to join her in oblivion.

Their eyes closed briefly as they enjoyed each other's aftershocks. The waves rocked them gently, cradling them in the cockpit. They couldn't move, except to take little nips and give baby kisses to each other's faces, cheeks, and shoulders. Still loving. Not talking. There was no need to say anything.

Slowly coming back to the world of the living, Philip squinted against the sunlight and reached for his hat to shield their faces. He kissed Hallie's mouth, her neck, her hair. His eyes returned to hers between each kiss. Was it possible for Hallie to be more beautiful than she'd been before lovemaking? But now bathed in a satisfied afterglow, her face was angelic. An extremely sexy angel, but an angel nonetheless.

Hallie broke the silence first. "Well, no wonder you don't talk much, Cowboy. You don't need to." She giggled. "I'm sorry I screamed like that, I've never—"

"Sorry?"

"It wasn't very ladylike of me."

"Men don't want a lady in the bedroom. Or in the cockpit." He kissed her again. "I'm guessing you don't know that having a woman scream during sex is like the highest compliment a man could ever receive?"

And somebody owed him a beer, but no way in hell would he ever tell Sky that.

"It is?"

"Well, why did you scream?" He nuzzled her neck.

"I totally lost control. God, you were amazing."

"I rest my case." He knew that scream would echo in his head for the rest of his life, reminding him of a sultry June afternoon, lying naked with this woman on a sailboat in the middle of nowhere. A woman who he hoped would be around for a long, long time. "Let's just be glad there weren't any other boats around, because somebody might have called in the Coast Guard."

Philip pulled her tight and rolled them onto their sides. Seeing her fully naked, tracing the path of her bathing suit tan lines with a forefinger, had him practically ready for another round. He cursed himself for not having a condom, but he vowed never to be unprepared again. Not with Little Miss Full of Surprises.

"I have a question," he said.

She smiled. "Do I always carry a condom in my bathing suit?"

"No, that would be question number two. Why did you stop things last night when we could have made love in my perfectly comfortable bed, and then seduce me on the sailboat today? Not that I'm complaining."

She turned serious. "Because you took me home last night."

"I like your reward system."

"Because you refused to put sunscreen on me today instead of trying to pick up where you left off last night. I am so charmed by you. Your standards, and the way you have a condom policy."

He laughed. "A condom policy? Never heard it put like that before."

"And you actually tried to turn me down when you didn't have one. I mean that really turned me on. I take care of my own birth control, but I always carry a condom, because I don't take chances with STDs. You're such a good person, Philip. You make me feel safe. Do you know the moment I fell in love with you?"

Warmth flooded his chest. She was in love with him? He was toast. And completely hard again.

He knew if he lived to be a hundred years old, he'd never get enough of this woman. "When you first met me in my BCGs while I was elucidating you on sewage?"

"No, when you took my chin in your hand and asked, 'Did I do this? I'm sorry if I hurt you.' Instead of talking me into going to bed with you after those kisses in the rain, you took me home and then you were concerned that you'd hurt me. You're different, Philip. Most men live in the moment and try to take whatever they can get."

"They think with their dicks." He nuzzled his way up her neck to her ear. "As a matter of fact, it's what's thinking for me right now. Sorry to sound so crude, but I'm in the Navy, remember?"

Hallie suddenly sobered. "And Philip?" She paused long enough that he brought his head back up to hers, shielding their faces from the sun with his hat. "I've never made love with my eyes before."

"You mean with them open?"

"That too."

Desire shot through him all over again. He knew exactly what she meant. "Me either."

Her blue eyes were hypnotic. For a nanosecond, there was something familiar about them. But then it was gone and they were just Hallie's deep blue eyes. Beyond cobalt and almost into purple.

"My grandmother's got these dishes," he said. "You know for Thanksgiving and stuff. I wasn't allowed to eat off them until I was, like, ten. She calls them the good *cornflower* dishes. And they are the exact color of your eyes." He shook his head. "Sorry, that was cheesy. But true."

"That's something else about you. You don't tell me I'm pretty or anything like that."

"And that would be a good thing because?"

"Because boys have told me that since I was in the sixth grade. I want to be more than that. I want people to like me for me."

Philip went back to exploring her neck with his kisses. "I was just trying to get in your pants—or get you out of them. You know how we cowboys are."

Hallie laughed.

Philip continued. "And since I did get you out of them, how about we take this new relationship for another ride. You don't need a condom for everything. Unless you happen to have a back-up in that purse of yours."

"Well, actually..." She paused so long, he looked up at her. "I thought about throwing in another one." He continued to look at her hopefully as the faintest trace of humor lit her eyes, "But I didn't have time to open a new package and get one."

Damn.

She reached for her beach bag and flashed him a sexy, wicked smile. "So I just threw in the whole box."

God, he loved this woman.

"Philip, it's getting late."

Hallie glanced up at the vermillion sky in the west as Philip raised the anchor. They had made love all afternoon, but now the sun was settling low and it was time to sail back to the marina.

As Philip unfurled the sails, he said, "I guess we better head home to my nice, comfortable bed, if we can walk, that is. But do me a favor when we get there, okay?" A bad boy grin shined in his soft brown eyes. "Don't scream too loud. Don't want the neighbors calling the cops."

Hallie socked him in the arm. "Come on, we better head home. It's going to be dark soon."

Philip glanced at the horizon. "Check out the sunset. You know what we say about the sky in the Navy?"

Hallie's heart missed a beat but she managed to reply, "They say it on sailboats too. Red sky at morning, sailors take warning. Red sky at night..."

"Sailors' delight," they recited together.

Hallie thought about her plans to sail off into the sunset alone. Suddenly it didn't sound like such a good plan. She belonged here with Philip. And he belonged with her. They should be able to sail off into the sunset together. However, this boat was not their real world. The USS *Blanchard* was. And the longer she drew this lie out, the more she jeopardized his career.

But what about their hearts? Didn't they count for anything?

Apparently not in Uncle Sam's Navy.

Chapter 9

They say a guy is in a serious relationship when there's a box of tampons in his bathroom cabinet. A woman's toothbrush is one thing, but tampons signify a Category-Five relationship. Several weeks after sex on the sailboat Sunday, Philip charged out of the bathroom brandishing a wrapped tampon. "These damn things are the bane of my existence!"

"Tampons?"

"Do you have any idea how much damage one of these can do to the sewage system on an aircraft carrier? Don't they have shots for that kind of thing now?"

Hallie found that amazingly humorous. "Wait. Are you suggesting all the women on your ship get shots so they won't have periods?"

"I'll pay for 'em." He joined her in mirth. "I've got this girl who works for me. Everybody calls her Trixie. She's a real piece of work. I love having her in my division, because she's a real hard ass, so I made her responsible for all the female heads. She's planning to go to plumbing tech school when she gets out of the Navy. She tells the men she's only in the Navy so she can get some mentoring while she's working on her plumber's crack."

Hallie snorted with laughter, because she could just hear Trixie saying that.

"She came to me the other day and asked if there was anything else she could do to speed up her advancement. I told her, 'Williams, I'll promote you to captain if you can get those ladies to read the freaking signs and stop trying to flush tampons down the hoppers."

Weak with laughter, Hallie collapsed against him. She'd witnessed Trixie walking through berthing announcing "No plugs in the shitters, girls. You do and I promise they'll come back to bite you in the butt. And if they don't, I will!"

"Actually, it's kind of funny. The guys hate it that she's got head duty in all the female berthing compartments now. They used to count on going into those spaces and fixing things. Apparently when we're deployed the enlisted ladies string up clotheslines in their berthing areas to dry their unmentionables. But with Trixie on the prowl, there's no chance of the guys checking out the girls' skivvies on the lines anymore."

Hallie knew the clothesline well. It was strung up right under the 1917 recruiting poster of a woman in a sailor suit, with the caption, "Gee I wish I were a man. I'd join the Navy." Hallie would be using the clothesline herself once the ship deployed and she could no longer avail herself of Rebecca's or Philip's washers and dryers. Guilt gnawed at her.

The cruise. The days were ticking by. This fairy tale was going to end soon.

"I still think you made Hallie up. How come I can't meet her?" Sky said over a pitcher of beer.

"I don't know. She's always got some excuse. And I'm really busy these days too. I shouldn't even be here tonight."

"Oh, come on, Bill, all work and no play. Bet you're getting plenty of play time at night with *Hallie*." Sky's mouth curved into a roguish smile.

Joy lit Philip's tired face. "Never too tired for that."

"You got a picture of her?"

Philip turned serious. "No, I don't. She's funny about that. I went to take a picture of her once and she put her hand over my phone. Said she didn't like her picture taken."

"Oh, she's ugly! I get it now. Billy Boy keeps his woman to himself because she's a dog."

"Trust me. She's no dog."

"Course you'd say that cuz she's ringing your chimes. I bet she's a double bagger. No double bagger wants her picture taken." A double bagger was a woman who was so ugly she'd need to wear two bags over her head in case the first one fell off.

The dreamy look was back on Philip's face. "And she's no double bagger."

"You still watching Jeopardy and necking on the sofa?"

"Yeah, cuz you know what?" He paused for emphasis. "The winner gets to be on top."

Sky roared with laughter. "Told you she was a nymphobrainiac. No wonder you can't meet me for a beer. You got to get home for Final Jeopardy every night. You're not only dating a dog, but a smart dog. Nerd meets nerd. I love it!"

Philip chuckled with him, but guilt stabbed at him from sharing too much about Hallie. This was his best buddy and even though Sky teased him mercilessly, he loved him like a brother. They had a deal whereby they owed the other one a beer any time they made a woman scream during sex. However, there was no way Philip was collecting that beer by telling Sky that Hallie was a screamer. Okay, he wasn't going to collect that *case* of beer, even though he'd never been on the receiving end of the deal before. He'd keep it his own little secret. He didn't need his ego stroked when he had Hallie.

"Time for truth. Have you done the dirty deed?"

"Many times."

The dirty deed had nothing to do with sex. Well, not really. It was saying, "I love you" to a woman—and meaning it.

"You used the L word?"

"Many times." He gave a self-satisfied smile before taking a sip of his beer.

"And meant it?"

Philip could not contain his smile. "Every time."

"Swear on John Paul Jones' crypt?"

The body of the Revolutionary War hero and Father of the American Navy had been disinterred in Paris in 1905, and brought to the United States, where it lies today in a sarcophagus beneath the Naval Academy chapel at Annapolis. The Holy Grail for Academy graduates.

"Swear on John Paul Jones' crypt."

Sky whistled. "You mean?"

"Yeah."

"Holy shit, Batman. The One?"

A broad grin split Philip's face. "Yup."

They'd used the term, The One, to mean the perfect woman that each of them would meet and marry someday, if and when they ever grew up. Neither of them had ever used the term seriously thus far. It had only been used as a negative, as in "Well, she sure as shit ain't The One," when discussing the lesser talent that frequented their local watering holes or hookers in liberty ports overseas.

"Yeah, I've met The One. Now I just have to make sure she wants to be The One."

"Roger that. When do I get to meet her? You know, some night after Final Jeopardy."

"Sorry, I'll be busy."

"Maybe Saturday. No Jeopardy on Saturdays."

"That might work. I'll give you a call."

"Okay, and be sure to let me know when it's time to get my mess dress pressed and polish my brass buttons for a wedding."

"I wouldn't hold your breath. I've only known her a couple of weeks and I'm hoping we can keep this thing going after we ship out. It's going to be hard to leave an awesome woman like this on shore when I go on cruise, but I do feel safe about one thing."

"What's that?"

Philip smiled wickedly. "You'll be on the cruise too."

Sky huffed out a laugh. "No, Billy Boy. The official rules state that once you find The One, nobody else can touch her. But I do have one request."

"Shoot."

"Promise me none of the bridesmaids will be double baggers. Okay, Cowboy?"

Philip and Hallie settled into some semblance of a routine, stealing time together at Philip's apartment whenever he could get away from the ship. Hallie ramped up their sex life when she presented him with her clean bill of health statement. Philip followed suit and condoms became a thing of the past, as did sailing.

They rarely ventured out on the weekends after that. She wanted to spend every waking moment with him, knowing this dream would end soon.

The weekdays were grueling for Philip, and Hallie's heart ached for him. Engineers on a ship rarely see the light of day, and poor Philip was exhausted since he was doing double duty: being an engineer and being in love.

His job became even more hectic as they neared the deployment date, with several short trips out for sea trials to test engines, propulsions, weapons systems, catapults, and arresting gear. Hallie tried to give him time to rest, but he kept telling her he could sleep for the next six months. Fat chance, but it sounded good. He said he wanted to spend every free minute with her.

Sea trials hadn't been a problem for Hallie because they both went to sea. She just laid low on board. Except she made a mistake once, knowing the exact time of day he'd be back, when he hadn't specifically told her. He'd even questioned her about it. She'd gotten a wicked gleam in her eye and said she'd consulted her crystal ball so she'd know when to be ready for him.

Philip left for the ship at 0600 on the mornings he slept at home. Hallie followed thirty minutes later and always beat him back to The Towers, since his job was more demanding than hers. Meals at home were catch-as-catch-can. Hallie ensured they rarely dined out. Jeopardy was a special bonding time for them whenever he made it home on time. She loved challenging him and she could tell he was impressed with her knowledge of intellectual trivia. Since they were on the same duty schedule, duty nights weren't a problem either. And, of course, she never joined him for dinner in the wardroom on those nights, or for a tour of his ship. She always "had too much schoolwork."

There was rarely time to dine out or socialize with friends. Dinners with Rebecca and her husband were about it. Philip offered to take her out, but she always said, "I'd rather just stay here," and then she'd smile seductively at him, and that was all she wrote. Philip was like putty in her hands. This pattern continued quite smoothly until the night he asked her to meet Sky.

Chapter 10

"We met our first day at the Naval Academy," Philip told Hallie as they sat on the couch. "There are three of us who are still close. We call ourselves 'the Highwaymen' after a rainy night of drinking illicit beers under an overpass in Annapolis when we were midshipmen. Nick is on a ship out of Norfolk right now, but we keep in touch by email. Sky is here in Jacksonville, over at the air station. He's actually the one who named me Bill Gates. He's a real cut-up. And okay, he's kind of wild and a total player, but he makes me laugh. What's really cool is he's going to be on the cruise with me." Philip looked at Hallie. "So do you want to meet him for dinner on Saturday?"

"Wait. He'll be on the *Blanchard*? For the cruise?"

"Yeah, his squadron's deploying with us."

"I don't think so, Philip."

"Why not?"

"I don't like military pilots."

Philip's gut registered another freaking landmine. He was getting a little leery of Hallie's weird trust issues.

"That's quite a blanket statement," Philip said. "You haven't even met the guy and you already don't like him. I'm really surprised to hear that coming from you of all people, Hallie. Make the world a better place, don't call people names, don't judge people, and all that. And yet you're prejudiced against pilots?"

"They remind me of those guys in high school, with their cocky arrogance."

"Oh, come on. Some aviators are kind of wild. They have a dangerous job. They work hard and play hard. But there are lots of pilots who are mature and responsible guys. My *dad* was a pilot and he's a good guy. You're not being fair."

"You just called this Sky a player. Are you now telling me he's one of those responsible, mature guys?"

"Well, not exactly. Okay, no." And then he knew there was something else. He could see it in her face. Something big was coming. She didn't say another word for the longest time. She just looked at him. And he just looked back at her. Had he done something wrong?

And when she said, "Sit down, Philip. I have something to tell you," he did what she asked, because those words were almost as bad as *we need to talk*, the four scariest words a woman can say to a man in love.

Hallie sat on the end of the sofa, staring straight ahead. "When I turned fourteen, my mom told me something I've never shared with another soul, except Rebecca. Mom waited until a week after my birthday because she didn't want to spoil my special day. I give her points for that."

Hallie looked at him and continued. "One night I came home from a friend's house and Mom was sitting in the living room waiting for me. She had an open bottle of wine and I could see most of it was gone. She said she needed it to get up the courage to say what she had to say. I could see she'd been crying and was very upset."

Philip moved closer and stroked her arm. Hallie turned to him. "I loved my mom, Philip, and she loved me. I miss her so much, but she made me very angry that night and I stayed mad at her for a couple of years. Now that she's gone, I feel bad about that. I know she did her best."

Hallie tucked that loose tendril of hair behind her ear, and then wrapped her arms around herself as if to hold herself together. "She said it was time I knew the truth about my father. I couldn't imagine what she was going to tell me, because Sam McCabe disappeared from my life after their divorce when I was six. I mean it really hurt that I never saw him again and he never called. Even divorced kids get to see their dads sometimes. And then she told me Sam McCabe wasn't my father."

Philip put his arm around her shoulders and pulled her to him, kissing her gently on her temple. Hallie didn't respond in any way, simply stared at the opposite wall.

"Mom said she had to tell me everything because I was getting attention from boys and she didn't want me to make the mistakes she had." Hallie absently swiped at her hair again, folded her hands and worried her thumbs against each other, then turned and looked at him. "My mom was in the Navy in the mid-eighties."

Philip's mouth dropped open.

She went back to drawing figure eights with her thumbnails. "She was a weather girl—an aerographer's mate, in Atsugi, Japan. She told me my real father was a Navy pilot who she met when she was stationed there. He flew F-14 Tomcats. His name was Rick. She'd never tell me his full name because she didn't want me to find him. It's not even on my birth certificate, which I hadn't seen until that week." Hallie turned to him.

Philip made sure his face showed he was listening, but his brain was churning.

"Mom said he was handsome and exciting and a very smooth operator. That's why I was upset when you told me about your friend. Naval aviators have left a bad taste in my mouth since that night."

Philip pulled her to him and kissed her on the forehead. Then she turned back to look at the wall. He was stunned by the information, but touched that she would share this painful part of her life with him.

"He was on an aircraft carrier that pulled into a shipyard in Japan for repairs and apparently the planes flew off to the air base at Atsugi, where they met. They had a blazing love affair for a couple of weeks. She'd had too much wine and told me things, details, that she never should have."

Hallie looked down, then back at the wall again. "Her name was Suzanne. Apparently he called her his 'Little Suzie Q' and she called him 'Her big, strong Irishman.' When she popped up pregnant, she wrote him and you know what he did?"

She turned to look Philip in the eye. "He sent her five-hundred dollars and told her he was sorry, but she 'needed to take care of it.' She wrote back asking him if he'd consider marrying her, at least until the baby was born. And that's when he informed her he was already married."

Philip pulled Hallie into his arms and stroked her back. Didn't say anything. Just held her. And rocked her gently. But he was thinking that if her mother had been enlisted and her father was a pilot, they couldn't have gotten married and remained on active duty because fraternization between an officer and an enlisted member was illegal.

"I knew the word, but I'd never used it. I understood the meaning though, so I said, 'You mean I'm a bastard?' and I'll never forget how she answered me: 'No, Hallie, your father was.'"

"So she raised you by herself?"

Hallie nodded. "She gave birth to me and when her enlistment was up she moved back to the States to live near her sister. She named me Hallie, which is Greek for 'thinking of the sea,' which is pretty ironic. She didn't meet Sam McCabe until I was almost two years old. They married and he adopted me, so I got his name. I never knew any of that. I thought Sam was my dad. And that's why it hurt so much when he left. Thank God I had my Uncle Pete in my life."

Philip wrapped his arms around her and kissed her hair. "I'm so sorry to hear all this. I mean, about your dad. And Sam. Everybody should get to have a dad."

"I'd always wondered where I got my blue eyes, because Mom and Sam had brown eyes. And neither of them was particularly tall either. Mom told me that night that Rick was six-foot-three and that's where I got my height. Oh, God, she kept telling me about his eyes. The wine was talking and she said it over and over. She just kept looking at me and saying, 'You have his eyes.' I've wondered since that day how hard it must have been for her to look at me and not think of him. She held that secret for fourteen years. Not being able to say anything."

Hallie turned to Philip, curled into his embrace, and wept against his chest. He held her, rocked her, and muttered soothing words into her hair.

"I didn't fully forgive her until she got sick. I had to. I learned that life is short and you have to forgive someone you love, so you can move on with your life. So at least we were at peace with each other before she died."

Philip continued to hold her close, stroking her back rhythmically. But, Hallie pulled away.

"Anyway, learning that at fourteen was hard to deal with, but when I started high school that fall, things got worse because that's when those pictures started floating around and the older guys started hitting on me. And now I knew this secret. I felt like I was being punished for something when I hadn't done anything wrong."

Her eyes pleaded with him. "I tried hard to blend in at high school and stay away from those kind of boys, like my father had been. Why do you think I'm here with you? Because you're not like them. You're like an anchor for me."

Philip's heart ached for her, but his ego soared. His mother had been right: "Just be yourself, Philip. Be your sweet, wonderful self. The smart women will be looking for a nice guy, someone they can count on." And the fact that Hallie was allergic to anything in a flight suit gave more Surface Warfare guys like him a fighting chance. Most chicks glommed to the jet jocks.

Aw, hell. Hallie was hurting. This wasn't about him. So he just rocked her. "Shhh. It's okay. I'm right here."

"I know it's a sore spot for you, but can you please be patient with me when I get all weird about things? I've been working on this for years, but I'm not there yet. And I really don't want to meet your friend right now." She attempted to smile through her tears. "See? There are still things you don't know about me."

Philip held her for the longest time. His mind raced. Major landmine. Doesn't trust aviators. F-14 pilot named Rick. Richard? With an Irish last name? Mid-eighties.

Did she want to find her father? He could tell by her angst that she hadn't let anything go. Should he put his dad on this? The aviation community was pretty close-knit, especially as they got older and attended reunions so they could re-live some of their youth.

He just wanted Hallie to be happy, and he was more than willing to keep dancing around landmines and red flags as she worked this stuff out. He knew Sky would tease him that this woman had more secrets than Colonel Sanders had recipes, but he didn't care. He figured it was a small price to pay for the rest of her that was utter perfection. So he continued to comfort her and snapped the red flags in half and buried them in the sand, along with the landmines, as soon as she kissed him.

The guilt of deception deepened its hooks in Hallie. Philip was too decent a person to deceive, but she loved him too much to put him in jeopardy, or lose him. Once she told him the truth, he would be honor-bound to walk away. How could she willingly push this wonderful man out of her life? He was a tonic for her soul.

She'd managed to avoid all get-togethers with his shipmates, pleading too much homework, but she could tell he was tiring of her excuses. The clock continued to wind down and a week before the deployment, Philip arrived home with an invitation that nearly knocked her socks off.

"Hey, good news. My parents are driving down for a couple of days to visit and see the ship off. I can't wait for them to meet you." His face beamed with pride.

Hallie felt the blood drain from her face. "Your parents. How nice."

He rubbed at the back of his neck. "Yeah, I'll try to get away a little earlier on Wednesday so we can all go out to dinner. Maybe

Thursday, too. What do you say? Or are you too busy with homework again?"

Hallie straddled his lap, dug her fingers into his shoulders, slid her thumbs up under the base of his skull and hoped her nervous laugh covered her trepidation. "I'm not too busy to do this." Then she kissed him. Gently and tenderly, tracing his lips with her tongue, murmuring what she was going to do to him, all the while digging at his aching muscles. She hoped he'd think her pounding heart was due to passion, not anxiety.

There was no way she deserved to meet his parents.

Philip groaned, kissed her back, and pulled away long enough to ask, "So what about dinner?"

Hallie kissed her way down his neck. "Plenty of time to figure it out. What you need right now is a little appetizer." She pasted a smile on her face. "Come on, skin down and I'll give you a backrub."

"Well, I'm sure not going to turn that down." Philip pulled his shirt over his head and lay on the carpet.

Hallie retrieved lotion from the bathroom and lathered her hands. She knew he thought this was about loosening up his muscles, but it was more about loosening him up before spilling her guts. This had gone on long enough. The parent thing was the last straw. She would tell him today. And if he was going to ask her to leave after she told him, she was going to make damn sure it was after a lovemaking session that neither of them would soon forget.

"Nope, pants too," she said.

"I need my pants off for a backrub?"

"You know, your buddy, Sky, would probably say, 'Don't ask stupid questions.'"

"You got that right." He stripped off his jeans and lay back down in his briefs. "Okay, honey, have at me."

Hallie started at his feet. She knelt down and bent his knees, then dug her slicked-up thumbs into his arches, her fingers massaging the small bones on the tops of his feet and the joints of his toes. He grunted in sweet pain and she knew she'd found the right spot.

"Reflexology says your feet rule the rest of your body. If your feet are relaxed, then you should be relaxed all over."

He answered with another guttural sound.

Hallie thought about the first time she'd seen these toes, thinking them sexy as the "Geek god" dug them in the sand on the afternoon they'd met. Here it was more than a month later and she was madly in love with the man. Not just in love with him. She *loved* him. Deeply and fully. A dull ache echoed in her chest at the thought of what she was about to do.

Not the lovemaking part. The soul-baring part.

She banished it from her mind and focused on his pleasure. The moans that escaped him told her she was successful. She slid her hands down the backs of his calves, then traced the trail of his sciatic nerves up the sides of his legs to his increased groans.

"Surely I've died and gone to heaven," he mumbled, face in the carpet.

"Not yet you haven't," Hallie said, laying his feet back on the rug and sliding up to sit on his rump. She leaned down and kissed the side of his neck, then whispered in his ear. "Not even close, Cowboy."

Hallie drizzled lotion on his back and rubbed it in, both hands working in tandem, thumbs tracing his vertebrae from butt to skull. She started at the bottom and, digging deeply, slid her way up, ending behind his ears. After kneading his shoulders, she went back to square one and glided her way back up again and again. Mumbled sounds of ecstasy were her reward.

She switched to tracing his spine with her left thumb and forefinger, so she could unbutton her blouse. Slinking out of the right sleeve, she switched hands and shirked off the left sleeve too. It only took one pop of the front clasp of her bra to loosen her breasts and she slipped out of that as well. Now naked from the waist up, she resumed the upward slide of her thumbs, but leaned over and let her breasts follow the trail her thumbs forged.

"Mmmm," he mumbled. "This must be where the heaven part starts."

She slid her thumbs up his back once more, but this time she lay down and kissed his neck while her hands worked his biceps. "We're almost to the pearly gates. Turn over."

Philip rolled, eyes still shut, a lazy smile sliding from one side of his five o'clock stubble to the other. Hallie slipped off her jeans and straddled him again. He obviously was enjoying more than a backrub. She leaned down to kiss his mouth, trailing her nipples across his bare chest. Philip took a breast in each hand, sliding his thumbs over the centers.

She kissed him again then pulled away and nuzzled his neck. "You don't smell like ship tonight. Did you shower before you left work?"

"I did."

"Good." She scooted down and began to lick his toes.

Philip exhaled a rush of air.

When Hallie finished with his toes, she kissed her way to his ankles. She loved his toes and his ankles and his knees and every square inch of this man. She loved the curls in his hair. She loved his smile and his muscles and the way his body worked when he swam butterfly or made love to her. She loved the way he thought, the way he cared, the way he laughed, the way he loved. She treasured everything about him and she could not bear to let him go.

Without warning a dam burst inside and tears came out of nowhere. She grabbed him behind the knees and lay her head down in surrender.

Philip bolted upright. "Hallie? What's wrong? Are you okay?"

She shook her head gently from side to side. No. Not okay. "I can't do this."

He scrambled to his knees, wrapped his arms around her. "You don't have to do anything, honey. Talk to me. What just happened? Did I do something wrong?"

She rocked back on her knees. Avoiding his eyes, she reached for her clothing. "No, Philip. Trust me. You've done nothing wrong. Ever. I just—"

She hooked her bra, reached for her shirt, then finally looked at him.

"We need to talk."

Holy shit. Philip's heart slammed in his chest. Cold fingers of uncertainly clutched at his gut. He grabbed his jeans. A man doesn't want to get caught with his pants down, or off, when there's a chance his ass is about to get dumped. "Honey, what's wrong?"

"I'm sorry. I can't meet your parents."

Relief flooded him and he blew out the breath he was holding, but his hands still shook trying to get his foot into his jeans. "Is that what this is about? Don't worry. They'll love you."

She threaded her arms into the sleeves of her shirt. "I'm not what you need, Philip. You're too good for me."

"What are you talking about? Is this about your parents not being married? It doesn't matter. Times have changed."

Hallie continued, nonplussed. "And besides, you're leaving next week. Maybe we should, you know, back off a little."

"What? After what we've shared for the past month you think we need to back off a little? Is this about your dad abandoning you or something?" He tripped over his pant leg, hopping around trying to get his physical and emotional equilibrium. "Hallie, I'll be back. I've fallen hopelessly in love with you and I want you to wait for me. You know, write me. Email me. Send me care packages. Think of me while I'm gone. Come on," He laughed self-consciously. "Every man in a foxhole needs a good woman to come back to."

"What?"

"It's just something my dad used to say to my mom when he deployed. Every guy needs a girl to think about when he's deployed, Hallie, and I want it to be you." He joined her on the sofa, but she wouldn't look at him. "I've never felt this way about anyone in my life. I love you. I want to marry you."

He hadn't really intended for that to come out of his mouth, but he damn well wanted her waiting on the pier when he returned from the cruise. If needing to propose to her would guarantee it, then he was not adverse to the idea. He'd feel more comfortable leaving Hallie McCabe with a ring on her finger than just sailing away and hoping no one else took his place while he was gone. So if proposing would do it, he was game.

She continued to button her shirt, stoically looking straight ahead. "No. We can't do that."

"Why not?" His pulse raced. His stomach churned. Jesus Christ, what was wrong?

She slipped on her shoes, staring pensively at the floor. "Because I'm..."

"You're what?" He hoped he didn't sound as desperate as he felt.

"I'm...I'm...We just can't."

And then Philip knew she wasn't done. Because she turned to him, intensity radiating from her eyes, stabbing him point blank in the heart. "There's something else, isn't there?"

She shook her head affirmatively, took a deep breath, and continued. "There are still things you don't know about me...You see, I'm in..." She swallowed hard.

"In what? Are you in trouble? In debt?" What the fuck was she trying to tell him? He'd fix it, whatever it was.

Her tears erupted again and all the words flew out in a rush. "I'm in love with you but as much as I've tried to figure this thing out we just can't be together anymore!"

And she walked out the door.

And out of his life.

Leaving him in a minefield with red flags flapping everywhere.

Chapter 11

The tugboats had begun the workhorse job of pushing and pulling the USS *Blanchard* from the safety of her berth, and were now turning her toward the center of the harbor channel on her path to the river and the open sea. No small feat considering she measured over a thousand feet and displaced close to ninety-thousand tons fully loaded.

Many of the wives, husbands, girlfriends, boyfriends, parents, and children crowding the pier on that hot July morning were in tears as they waved goodbye, bidding farewell to their loved ones for the next six months. Probably more.

The *Blanchard* would operate twenty-four seven at sea. Crewmembers would hold down the fort in the fully staffed hospital, one of the six galleys, the four workout centers, the two barber shops, chapel, bank, post office, library, two general stores, brig, television studio, water purification plant, or two nuclear reactors. All designed to support the airport on the four-and-a-half acre flight deck on her roof.

The *Blanchard*'s primary mission was to provide a facility for aircrafts to launch and recover at sea in order to provide combat air operations while forward deployed.

Although only five percent of the crew would actually fly the aircraft, the jobs of the remaining ninety-five percent were there to support them with fortifying troops on the ground, protecting friendly shipping, deterring aggression, and defending freedom worldwide.

Along with her five thousand trained sailors and airmen, the ship would soon embark about seventy aircraft with price tags of up to sixty million dollars each, making the USS *Blanchard* an example of the most complex and expensive fighting machine in the world.

No other country possessed a vessel of this magnitude.

The United States had ten.

Eight hundred crewmembers, looking crisp in dress white Cracker Jack uniforms, their black neckerchiefs fluttering in the summer breeze, manned the rails of the flight deck as the tugs turned the carrier's bulk one-hundred-eighty degrees before nosing her eastward toward the Atlantic Ocean. Two of the sailors did their best to keep their lips from moving while they talked in ranks. Petty Officers McCabe and Marini stood at parade rest: feet twelve inches apart, hands clasped in the small of their backs, chins high, chests out proudly. Lips barely moving.

"Look at her. See the pregnant one on the pier who looks like she's going to deliver, like, yesterday? I can't believe they wouldn't let her husband stay behind for the birth."

"Needs of the Navy, Gina. Needs of the Navy. At least he'll get to be first off the ship when we return. I've always found that to be the most poignant Navy tradition, that the new dads are the first to disembark after a cruise. Makes me cry to see those guys meeting their children for the first time on a Navy pier. But I love that they get reunited with their families even before the Captain does. I guess rank doesn't always have its privileges. And yay for that."

Gina tried to stifle her smile. "Yeah, but that guy's kid will practically be walking when we get back. I still say it sucks."

"I wonder how many of those women out there won't be on the pier when we return. Stuff can happen in six months."

"You're one to talk. When are you planning to spill the beans to lover boy that you're living on his ship in a sailor uniform?"

Hallie's overworked adrenal system kicked into an even higher gear. Maybe her head knew Philip would be down in the hole this morning, but her gut hadn't gotten the memo. "I know. I know.

I'm going to explain everything in a letter and send it through ship's mail as soon as we're truly underway. I wasn't going to stress him out this week while he was getting the ship ready to leave."

"And smacking into you in a passageway wouldn't stress the crap out of him? Let alone the poor guy thinking he's done something wrong. Come on, girlfriend, you're running out of excuses. If you really love the guy, you'll do what's best for him and write that letter ASAP."

A fist closed around Hallie's chest making it difficult to breathe when she thought of him. Then it tangled with the guilt that rolled around in her gut. She was still kicking herself for chickening out that last night and not telling him the truth. But she was so ashamed, and couldn't bear to see the hurt and disappointment on his face. Yeah, like he hadn't looked hurt when she said it was over.

She'd moved on board the ship that very night. Knowing his job would be uber-stressful until they pulled out, she did not want to upset him further by telling him until they got underway.

Paranoid all week, she had rarely left the safety of Public Affairs, except to sleep in berthing or eat on the mess decks. She had simply performed her job, worked on her courses, and laid low. Hallie's only foray to the outside had been to purchase some hair color. Her new light brown hair bought her a few more days before telling him the truth, but she couldn't put it off forever. She felt like a selfish child after what she'd done to him.

Trixie kept the berthing area informed of how Bill Gates had been a real pill lately—"because he obviously wasn't getting any." But it was way more than that. Hallie knew how empty she felt without him. She could only imagine what it was like for Philip, who didn't even know why she'd walked away.

And there was no way she could let him find out by accident. He deserved better. To just bump into her somewhere on the ship or for Trixie to casually mention her name one day was unacceptable.

She would write the letter and explain everything.

Tonight.

Then he could go off by himself to read and digest it, and she wouldn't have to witness his disappointment in her.

The crowd continued to wave their flags and posters, but many of the well-wishers were disbanding. Probably headed home to start marking off days on the calendar until the *Blanchard*'s homecoming.

Hallie flexed her knees inside her dress whites, a little trick she'd learned in boot camp to keep her circulation going. She turned her head ever-so-slightly to see the last of Naval Station Mayport. "This is pretty weird. Exciting, but weird, to know I'm not going to see U.S. land until after New Year's."

Gina snorted in an attempt to keep from laughing. "Honey, you're not going to see hardly *any* land until after New Year's. See that big blue thing out there? That's an ocean and that's your new home. Welcome to haze gray and underway."

The crew didn't know where they were headed. They assumed it was the Persian Gulf, but they never knew for certain. It depended on the whims of the President and the Secretary of Defense, and whatever was going on in the world on any particular day.

Hallie knew in case of a natural disaster, the *Blanchard* could be at the scene in record time with her floating hospital, SAR and Med-Evac capabilities, water purification system, and the electricity from her two nuclear reactors. It boggled her mind that, aside from fuel for the aircraft, the *Blanchard* needed little to no fossil fuel to travel or perform all these tasks. Or fresh water either, since her Evaps could purify four hundred thousand gallons of seawater a day.

Philip had told her he would be in charge of the plumbing and air conditioning systems for what was essentially a small city, with all the occupations needed for that small city to function.

But most small cities didn't need intelligence specialists, weapons handlers, bomb disposal teams, catapult experts, jet mechanics, search and seizure personnel, and checkers who walked around the town checking people's living and working spaces to ensure nobody was using drugs or having sex.

Having sex. Ha. Something Hallie McCabe wouldn't be doing for a long, long time.

"Now hear this. Now hear this," called the Executive Officer over the 1MC communications system. "This is the XO. Very impressive departure. Thank you for setting such a professional tone on our first day at sea. Secure from manning the rails. All hands get in your working uniforms and turn to. That is all."

Gina reached for the sky, then bent and touched her toes. "Man, I thought he'd never release us."

The tugs were now guiding the *Blanchard* into the St. Johns River. Hallie watched the jetties slide by as she stretched. With a pang she realized it was the same river that she and Philip had sailed.

"You're thinking about him again. I can tell."

"Am not."

"Never bullshit a bullshitter. It's written all over your face. Either go tell him you can't live without him or cut him loose for good, but either way you gotta come clean with him."

It only took a few minutes for the carrier to clear the mouth of the river and head out into the open blue. Hallie looked back one more time to bid a silent goodbye to home.

No. The USS *Blanchard* was her home now.

She reached under the hem of her blouse and turned on the "brick" she had clipped to her waistband.

The handheld radio squawked immediately. "McCabe, Marini," said Chief Bernard. "Where in the hell have you two been? Go change and head up to the Admiral's Bridge. You've been assigned to cover the aircraft fly-on. Commander Scott wants you to collaborate on a story for the ship's Facebook page. And hurry up. The helicopter squadrons are already airborne and due to land in thirty minutes."

* * *

Philip had grieved for Hallie for the past week. For what they'd had, or what he thought they'd had. He'd been miserable most of the time, and then he'd switch to steaming mad. His parents had come and gone, but his despair stayed put.

He'd texted and emailed her but received no response. He had even dropped by Rebecca's to talk with Hallie in person, but was told she'd moved. After a few days that's exactly what he did too. There'd been so much to do on the *Blanchard* before they got underway, it was simpler to just move on board. And it helped to be out of that apartment where he and Hallie had shared so much together.

A clean break.

For the past week Philip had poured himself into his work, often taking his frustration out on his entire division. Trixie became so fed up with him that she called him on it. "Am I doing something wrong, sir?"

When he told her no, she continued. "Well, you've been riding my ass lately like nobody's business and I don't know why. If I'm not performing like you want, then feel free to tell me. But if you're on me just because you're in a bad mood or something, then I have a right to be pissed and come in here and tell you."

He had to admit he admired this little pistol. She didn't mince words and she knew how to take care of herself.

"I'm sorry, Williams. You're doing fine. I have no complaints. I had some bad news. That's all. And I'm sorry if I've been taking it out on you. I appreciate your coming in here and bringing it to my attention."

Trixie almost blew him away when she suddenly turned all soft. "Everything okay? Anything I can do, sir?"

He would never have guessed Trixie had an ounce of maternal instinct down there under all that crust. But she was still a woman and he was none too enamored with women these days. Who the hell could figure them out? He just wanted her to leave.

Leave him alone and let him wallow in his misery. "No. But thanks for the offer, Williams. I appreciate it."

"Well, if you ever want to talk about it, I'm here. I'm a chick. I know how they think. But I'm on your side."

That left him smiling. Yeah, like he'd talk to *her* about it, but it was a tender gesture on her part.

Trixie went back out into the spaces and, thinking she was out of his earshot, debriefed the working party. "He apologized for biting my head off. Said he got some bad news. And you can bet your sweet ass the bad news has something to do with not getting any."

No matter how hard he worked, by the time Philip crawled into the rack in his stateroom at night, all the memories were waiting for him. The good, the bad, and the beautiful. He'd lie awake nights, staring at the underside of his roommate's bunk, reliving the good times, and then trying to figure out what the hell "we can't be together anymore" meant.

Philip Johnston held a mechanical engineering degree from the United States Naval Academy. He was experienced at taking things apart, analyzing the pieces, repairing the broken parts, and then putting them back together again. And although this worked on the job and he could fix most of the problems in his corner of the Engineering Department, he was not always as adept at fixing problems in his life.

Every night when he crawled into bed, he dissected their relationship and reexamined it. Piece by piece. Trying to figure out what the hell had gone wrong.

He had loved Hallie enough to tell her he wanted to spend the rest of his life with her. And it wasn't just about the most incredible sex in the entire world. It was about the intelligent conversations, talk of the future, their shared joys in a sailboat, the same sense of humor, and not needing to talk to communicate with each other. But he'd always end up fast forwarding to that last night.

How had he fucked things up?

What was it she had to figure out? Why couldn't they be together? Besides him deploying. Was it personal, something wrong with him, or were there circumstances he didn't know about?

"There are still things you don't know about me," she had said.

Was she already married? Maybe legally separated from an ax murderer? Did she have a couple of children tucked away somewhere? Maybe she was a vampire. Or an alien.

He knew she would have thought that humorous, but he couldn't even laugh any more.

Wait. Maybe she was a peacenik.

Eventually, "we can't be together anymore" morphed into "I don't love you anymore." That was simpler and easier to process for Phillip. She had gotten tired of his nice guy ass. He was boring. Didn't talk enough. Worked too hard. Never wanted to go out and have fun. The kinds of things other women had kindly tried to tell him.

Then why would she have continually told him that that's what she liked about him? That he made her feel safe.

That he was her anchor.

So he tried to move on. Planned to work hard during this deployment, just put one boot down in front of the other every day. And then maybe when they got back to the States, he would look around again for a good woman who his mom swore was out there looking for somebody just like him. Although he knew for sure that he'd have a snowball's chance in hell of ever finding someone he would ever love as much as Hallie McCabe.

Dear Hot Mama: I was sad leaving you today. I'll miss you while I'm gone, but I know you'll be strong. I'm sorry I'll miss our anniversary on September 9, but I will have a surprise for you. I have everything I need to make it, so I promise it will be ready on time. I love you, Randy.

Rashid clicked send and knew his sadiqs would understand the pre-coded message he'd sent them. "I had to leave you today" meant that the *Blanchard* did indeed get underway as planned on the date of the email. "I have everything I need," meant that he was successful in getting the necessary explosives and a gun onto the ship. He couldn't believe how easy it had been. He'd just carried a little on board each day and stowed it in his locker. Only random screenings on the quarterdeck, and even if they'd checked his stuff, he had everything sewn inside the lining of his gym bag.

You would think they'd have better detectors these days, but no. The powers-that-be apparently knew everyone on board had a security clearance, so there was little risk from a member of their own crew. Rashid's clearance had been completed four years ago when he finished OS "A" School and a lot had happened since then. He wouldn't be due for another until he re-enlisted.

Fat chance of that happening.

The rest of his message was self-explanatory, although the sadiqs would find a different meaning in it than the ship's Information Systems Techs who monitored all electronic communications. A fictional wife or lover wouldn't even get a second look by the ITs. They would assume he was planning a sweet surprise for his woman.

Though he had been assigned to man the rails, Rashid did not go topside for the send-off. He had no one on the pier to say goodbye to anymore. Nobody blowing a kiss or waving a flag in his honor. Besides he hadn't slept well lately and figured he could grab a power nap while nobody was looking.

The OSs would be working Port and Starboard shifts: twelve hours on, twelve hours off. It was the price they paid to play Solitaire in port. Starting tonight, his life would become one long cycle of monitoring radar screens and naming unidentified vessels and aircraft. He wasn't worried about working too hard these days though. He was the lone member of the *Blanchard* who knew there were only forty-eight days left of this deployment.

Once they arrived in the Middle East there would be plenty of fish lighting up the radar screens for him to detect, or miss, since he was planning to be the duty OS on September ninth. He'd make sure of it. Wouldn't be a problem since he wrote the watch bill. Oh, fucking Commander Haggman, the Combat Direction Center officer, would sign it off, but Rashid would write it. And his name would be on it. Using the Identification Friend or Foe function of the surveillance radars, he'd be the first to know when his sadiqs came to visit. And left their calling card. Correction. Cards. Their last communiqué had confirmed there would be five at each location.

Allahu Akbar.

Nah. He decided he definitely wasn't going to yell that Arabic shit when the time came. Maybe some kind of a toast to Rosie? He had plenty of time to think about it. A sweet little nugget he could tuck away in his seabag and take out and mull over every night in his rack. Whatever it was, it would be the last thing he said in this lifetime. And what he wanted to see? The look of horror on Commander Haggman's face right before he blew him to kingdom come.

Chapter 12

Hallie and Gina exchanged their dress whites for camouflage and high-tailed it to the Admiral's Bridge, where the commander of the entire Carrier Strike Group would be watching the fly-on with his minions. Getting there was no small feat, considering they had to ascend eight ladders inside the island to get there from the flight deck.

Commander Scott assigned them to do more than just take notes for the ship's Facebook page. If they got any face-time with the Admiral, he also wanted them to use their youth and charm to talk him into making a daily Facebook announcement and opening a Twitter account. Apparently they were tasked with bringing him into the twenty-first century.

Once everyone was aboard, the population of this floating city would be roughly five thousand. Two thousand airedales, members of the air wing; and three-thousand ship's company, those responsible for the functioning of the ship itself.

The *Blanchard* would be joined by two thousand more sailors and officers on two destroyers, two fast frigates, and a cruiser, from both Mayport and Norfolk. These ships would make up the rest of the Carrier Strike Group and would form a distant perimeter around the aircraft carrier, protecting her from enemy ships, submarines, or aircraft. The Admiral would be responsible for all of them.

All the glamor of the send-off was gone. The crew now wore practical working uniforms. Administrative types had changed into aquaflage, while engineers and others performing dirty work below decks wore navy blue coveralls. Airedales seemed to wear whatever they wanted.

Hallie glanced down at the colorful scene below as the flight deck crews prepared for the aircraft recovery. She knew the pilots and flight crews would be wearing flight suits, but the enlisted airedales who'd arrived yesterday were scuttling around below looking like a motley crew. They were a virtual kaleidoscope of colored jerseys and matching flotation vests, all worn with camouflage pants bloused over combat boots.

"Do you know why they call the flight deck workers Skittles?" Gina asked.

"Because of their different colored shirts?"

"You got it. The colors allow everyone to know who does what without having to ask in that deafening environment. See those guys in the green shirts? They work catapult and arresting gear. We call the guys in purple shirts Grapes. They handle aviation fuel. You don't see any yellow or red shirts yet because yellow is for plane shooters and we're not doing any launches today, and red shirts are ordnance. Doubt we'll be loading any bombs for a few days."

A shiver worked its way up Hallie's spine. This was really happening. They were going to war.

"Ladies," said a nice-looking officer with salt and pepper hair and a welcoming smile. "I'm Commander Taylor, Ship's Safety Officer."

He radiated confidence and offered his hand in greeting. But his smile and the desert tan flight suit put Hallie off. She barely raised a sweaty palm before he grabbed it and gave it a firm shake. She reminded herself the ship would be crawling with aviators within a few hours. She decided to suck it up, but to never let her guard down.

"All my flight deck personnel are serving as safety observers for the fly-on. So when your boss asked for an escort for two of his best and brightest, I volunteered."

"Thank you, sir. We appreciate it," Gina said.

"Since the Admiral's Bridge is packed with observers jostling for a good view, I thought we'd begin up one level on the Navigation Bridge. Follow me."

Oh, well. During a fly-on was probably not the best time to discuss Facebook with the Carrier Air Group Commander anyway.

The Safety Officer extended his arms. "Ladies, this is 'The Bridge,' where the Officer of the Deck drives the ship. And anytime we're involved in a high risk evolution you'll find the Commanding Officer up here."

"Hello, Buck, how's it going?" asked Captain Amerson, the *Blanchard*'s CO, turning to welcome them.

Hallie's gut registered *wolf in sheep's clothing*. Although he wore a blue camouflage uniform instead of a flight suit, the embroidered wings over his breast pocket, the aviator sunglasses, and his come-on smile tipped his hand as a pilot. She greeted him respectfully, then turned away and looked through the windshield at the flight deck below. She better toughen her resolve, because there were more pilots than she could shake a stick at winging their way to the ship this very minute.

"I'm escorting a couple of sailors from media, sir. They're covering the fly-on and I'm their official tour guide. This is Petty Officer McCabe and her fellow paparazzi, Petty Officer Marini."

"Excellent," Captain Amerson said, joining them at the window. "We're landing Helicopter Combat Support Squadron Seven, the Dusty Dogs, right now."

Like a well-orchestrated dance of dragonflies, one by one, five gray Seahawk helicopters passed left to right just aft of the stern, then turned and flew up the port side. The first one getting almost to the bow before sliding sideways and landing on Helicopter Spot Number One. The second turned into Spot Number Two and so on.

By the time number five had landed, the first two had shut down their engines and their rotor blades had stopped turning. Like giant damselflies, the helos began folding their blades back along their fuselages. Then crewmembers approached and manually folded the entire tail section toward the folded blades.

"Wow. I've seen Navy helos folded up like that stowed on board ship, but I've never watched them do it before," Hallie said. She wondered if one of the helo pilots was Philip's friend, Sky.

Philip.

Her heart skipped a beat. She was so involved in watching the fly-on, she forgot what her priority was today. Finish that letter.

"We always keep a couple of helos on the flight deck, so they're ready at a moment's notice. And we'll keep one airborne all day to fly Search and Rescue in case of an emergency. The rest of the helos will be taken down the elevator to the hangar bay, so the next squadron can start landing."

Since this was her first cruise, Hallie had only seen the hangar bay empty. Located directly below the flight deck, it was the size of two football fields and stood three stories high. It would be a busy place for maintenance and repair of aircraft—when it wasn't being used for full-court basketball games or all-hands meetings.

"You know you two could get a better view and better photos from Vulture's Row above us."

"That's our next destination, sir," Commander Taylor said.

"Thank you for your time, Captain," Gina said.

"My pleasure, ladies."

When the last of the helicopters had landed, Commander Taylor pointed out the four cables stretched tight across the deck about fifty feet apart.

"Those are what the jets and propeller-driven planes will catch with their tailhooks. Each of those wires is capable of stopping a fifty-four-thousand pound aircraft traveling a hundred-fifty miles an hour within three-hundred-fifty feet." He smiled proudly. "In about two seconds. See how all the Skittles are taking their places? The recovery will be fast and furious once the jets come aboard. They have to come in at top speed in case they miss the wires and have to take off again. The ship has to be steaming at thirty knots to launch or recover the planes."

Even with double ear protection, the first thing Hallie noticed as the first FA-18 Hornet approached was the noise. It turned into a thunderous roar as the aircraft touched down under full power. Just two seconds after the jet snagged the number three wire, the Hornet was at a complete stop. It rolled backward a few feet as the pilot raised the tailhook and then taxied out of the way so the next aircraft could land. This would go on all afternoon.

Gina pulled up Hallie's hearing protection and spoke in her ear. "I once asked a jet pilot what it felt like to land on a carrier. He said to imagine having an orgasm while being hit by a bus. And being launched by the catapult was like climaxing while being shot from a cannon."

Hallie couldn't get over how quickly the planes landed, stopped, and taxied before another came in right behind it. Like clockwork.

"If you think this evolution is busy, you two should come back when we're doing launch and recoveries at the same time. Then you can witness the world's most dangerous parking lot."

Commander Taylor smiled at the look on Hallie's face. "And feel free to come by and watch night ops as well. It's really amazing in the dark."

Once they had witnessed all the different types of aircraft landing, they thanked the Safety Officer and headed below decks for a late lunch. They would write up their observations about the recovery of aircraft and the next day they would observe launches from the catapults. Flight ops would begin first thing in the morning and would continue daily, or nightly, until they pulled into their first port.

But Hallie McCabe was more concerned with something else she needed to write. She had avoided the pain of sharing the truth with Philip for far too long. They were now utterly and totally haze gray and underway.

And she'd run out of excuses.

* * *

OS2 Randy Davis plunked his tray down with several of his colleagues on the aft mess deck for evening chow. He wasn't planning to bond with his shipmates, but he didn't wish to draw attention to himself as a loner. He'd make polite conversation if he had to, all the while seething at the assholes around him. He knew he had power over everyone at the table. Hell, every person on board the ship.

"So who's running the Anchor Pool?" one of his tablemates said.

"What's an Anchor Pool?" asked an OS3 who had recently reported aboard.

A man named Rogers sneered. "Don't you know anything?"

Rashid shot Rogers a menacing look, challenging him with his eyes. "Hey, lay off the new kid. He just got here."

"Well, excuuuuse me, Davis," Rogers rolled his eyes and Rashid caught a smirk out of the corner of his eye.

Davis turned to the newbie. "It's a matrix of possible dates and times when we drop anchor or moor pierside. You pick your date and pay. We'll do one in Combat for five bucks a pop, but if you want in on the real action, see Jackson in Supply."

Rogers jumped in again. "Hey, did you hear who Jackson's got the hots for these days?"

Rashid tuned them out. It was all scuttlebutt. Gossiping would be the top downtime activity on the cruise. He chuckled when he thought about the word, scuttlebutt. Since it was the word for water fountain in the Navy, he always pictured sailors of old gathered around an oaken water barrel, sipping from a dipper— most likely exchanging gossip.

And didn't scuttlebutt just fly on a Navy cruise. It could be the truth, a partial truth, or totally false. Regardless, rumors spread at light speed. One chick on his last deployment laughed her ass off when she found out she was engaged to some guy she'd never met. Christ, these cruises were like high school. The average age of the freaking crew was twenty-one years old. Half of them were leaving home for the first time in their lives, lots with sad stories about how this was their only chance to succeed in this world. At nineteen? What the fuck was wrong with them? They clearly didn't use a fraction of their brainpower to think most things through. And all of them were horny as all get out.

"I hear she puts out like nobody's business," an OS named Dixon said.

"Yeah, but only because she's a five-nine-five," Rogers said. "A five before and after the cruise, and a nine at sea."

They all had a good laugh over that. Rashid even smiled, but not at what they'd said. Let these assholes have their trysts at sea. They were all going to die soon anyway.

"Hey, check it out," one of the men said, indicating the TV. "This should be good. It's the annual 'Don't Fuck Your Shipmate' lecture."

"Perfect timing too. Maybe we can find out all the good spots on board."

"And who's available."

That brought another round of snickers from the men. All except for Petty Officer Davis who did not find it the least bit humorous.

The crew quieted when the senior chief in charge barked, "Quiet down and listen up!" He cranked up the volume on the flat screen monitors positioned around the mess deck.

The Command Master Chief, or CMC, filled the screens and began his speech to the crew. "I'm gonna make this short and sweet. This ain't the Love Boat. If you think it is, you may very well find yourself at Captain's Mast or headed to the beach on your way out of the Navy. This ship has a zero tolerance policy for fraternization—and while we're at sea that means anybody fraternizing with anybody.

"We are on our way to break things and kill people, not to pro-vide you with a social network to hook up with a shipmate. So no screwing around, literally or figuratively. This is a warship and you are warriors. Behave accordingly. If don't think you can do that, let us know and we will help you find another line of work."

"The CMC sipped from his water bottle and continued. "And while we're on the subject, there will be zero tolerance for sexual harassment in any way, shape, or form. I'm talking about your shipmates, folks. Treat them with courtesy at all times and report anything that appears suspicious or makes you feel uncomfortable. All of you should have completed the required hours of awareness training and signed off that you understand the consequences for crossing boundaries."

Dixon whispered, "I feel uncomfortable when Petty Officer Stroud wears that perfume that gets me all hot and bothered. She sure knows how to bring me to attention."

Every man at the table had to stifle his laughter. All except for one. Assholes, Rashid thought to himself. This was exactly what the Master Chief was talking about. These dickheads had no respect for anybody.

It was going to be a pleasure killing them.

"And remember, even permissible dating can get you in a lot of trouble on board this ship," the CMC said. "Let me clarify. Keep your distance, folks. No PDA is ever allowed. That means never. No holding hands, no sitting closer that a butt-width apart, and no inappropriate touching of any kind. And I get to decide what is and is not appropriate, so just don't do it. Because I'm always gonna be right and you're always gonna be wrong. I know half the complement of this ship is under twenty-one. I know what it's like to be that age, even though most of you think I was born a master chief." Laughter rippled across the room. "But keep your distance and focus on the mission."

"Yada, yada, yada," the man to Rashid's left mumbled. The man's cheeks threatened to erupt in smiles that became contagious around the table.

These were the same kind of idiots who had teased Rashid in high school, laughing around the lunchroom table. At least they were making fun of the Master Chief this time, but who knew what would happen if Rashid turned his back on them. His pulse began to pound. He already knew what they'd done behind his back. Another round of muffled laughter broke out around the table. When the hell were these guys going to grow up?

Oh, that's right. They were never going to grow up.

"Just so you know," the Master Chief continued. "If you decide to disregard what I'm saying and break the rules, we will throw the book at you. I'm talking loss of privileges, loss of pay, loss of stripes, and possibly separation from the Navy. It's a small price to pay to keep your shipmates safe.

"People, I'm not doing this to spoil your fun. I'm doing this to save your lives. We're dealing with life and death situations on this deployment and we don't need no lovesick, hormone-crazed sailors mooning over shipmates while trying to launch or recover a jet on the flight deck. That goes for every other department on this ship as well. You hold people's lives in your hands. Think of it this way: Loose hips sink ships."

The crew groaned over the Master Chief's little joke. It was all a fucking joke as far as Rashid was concerned. He pushed away from the table, picked up his tray, and cleared out. He had bigger fish to fry than worrying about a bunch of immature teenagers who were lonely and homesick and thought with their genitalia. Hell, he was lonely too, ever since he'd lost his Rosie, but he wasn't going to make a fool of himself, or get busted by getting it on with some sailor chick. And the hell with the assholes giggling like a bunch of girls at everything the Master Chief said. The guy was trying to save their fucking lives.

Oh, well, it wasn't going to make a hell of a lot of difference in the long run. Let them laugh now.

He walked off the mess deck while the Command Master Chief prattled on about Captain's Mast and Non-Judicial Punishment for getting caught with one's pants down. Let the CO, XO, and CMC worry about how the crew behaved. Let them all play good cop and bad cop. Rashid knew they'd do their damndest to make sure everyone obeyed the rules and coexisted as best as possible because they were responsible for all five thousand on board: Four-thousand-nine-hundred-ninety-nine men and women, sailors and officers.

And one pissed-off soon-to-be terrorist—who was going to beat all of them at their game.

"Reveille! Reveille! Reveille! All hands heave out and trice up. Reveille!" called from the 1MC. "Sweepers, sweepers, man your brooms. Give the ship a good, clean sweep down both fore and aft. Sweep down all lower decks, ladder backs, and passageways. Dump all garbage clear of the fantail. Sweepers!"

Hallie now understood the old saying that life aboard a U.S. Navy ship at sea had been equated to being in prison, but with a chance of drowning. She doubted she'd slept a wink last night, between planes landing through the night and a berthing compartment seemingly filled with snoring women. My God, she didn't know women could snore like that. For the first time since she'd arrived on the *Blanchard*, every female assigned to the ship slept on board.

Hallie, Gina, and Trixie were fortunate to be in a berthing compartment with just thirty-six females. Some women had sixty in theirs. She felt especially sorry for the male sailors on the lower end of the food chain who shared living quarters with up to one hundred fifty roommates.

Gina had the best deal, sleeping in the bottom rack, or maybe Trixie did, sleeping in the top one, since she could sit up in bed. Hallie climbed down from her middle rack and made her bed as best she could without stepping on Gina's hands.

"Come on, Geen. Get up."

Gina rolled over and grunted, then pulled her privacy curtain closed. "Just five more minutes, please. I did not get any sleep last night. How could there still have been planes landing in the night?"

"Those weren't planes landing. Somebody said it was the flight deck crews testing the catapults for today's flight schedule.

And I hear it gets a lot worse when they do night ops and launch and recover while we're sleeping.

"Speak for yourself," a woman called out. "Some of us just got off the night shift and are trying to sleep."

"Sorry," Hallie said.

Trixie scrambled down from the top rack and whispered, "Welcome to your new home beneath an airport, McCabe. Actually, it's worse. Airports don't have catapults. Hopefully you'll also enjoy the sound of aircraft tie-down chains being dragged across the roof at night. Don't worry. You'll get used to it. And you'll be able to sleep through anything after this cruise."

The racks stood in groups of three, each with a sleeping space six feet long, two feet wide, and twenty-two inches of space above each mattress, except for the top bunk. That space varied from rack to rack, depending on the piping and overhead equipment.

The privacy curtains might block out some of the visual world, but not the noise. Hallie thought it charming how the women made their twenty-four cubic feet of personal space homey: matching bedspreads and throw cushions, stuffed animals, and posters plus photos of loved ones stuck in the bottoms of the racks above them and on the bulkheads next to their sleeping spaces.

Beneath the racks, each sailor had a drawer, called a coffin, in which to stow her gear; in addition to a high school sized standing locker for her uniforms. Adding the coffin and the locker to the space within her rack, each crewmember had about fifty cubic feet to call her own for the next six months.

Because Hallie would never be able to display pictures of her boyfriend, especially since she didn't have one anymore, she hung a mural of a Japanese garden to remind her of land and serenity on the bulkhead. And tucked pictures of her mom in uniform, her aunt and uncle, and photos of Hallie and Rebecca soaking up rays on Jacksonville Beach in the underside of Trixie's rack. She would have to content herself with the mental images of Philip, such as that first day on the sailboat. The Ralph Lauren ad with the day-old beard and the cowboy hat—the Marlboro Man-goes-to-the-

America's-Cup. And looking into each other's eyes while making love on the sailboat.

Stop.

It was over.

She showered and dressed quickly, deciding to skip morning chow and duck into the ship's store to buy some good stationery for that letter she'd started the night before. She'd finish drafting it on the computer at work, then copy it on to pretty paper. Writing it in her own handwriting was the least she could do, giving him a little piece of herself. Anything to help Philip see it came from the heart.

A heart that now raced as she scoped out the gray passageways, lined with miles of wires and cords strapped to the bulkheads. She figured Philip would be getting ready to hold quarters for the morning shift at 0800, so it would be a safe time to shop. After a quick scan, she darted into the ship's store and grabbed writing paper, granola bars, and a boxed juice for breakfast. She exhaled a sigh of relief as she got in line to pay—eyes peeled for the door. Almost done. But what was taking the cashier so long? This felt so *public*. And she still had to skulk her way back through the passageways to Public Affairs. Why, oh, why was the cashier so slow, and why, oh, why couldn't she and Philip have just continued the way they were?

Shit.

Her gut registered *tall* and *dark* before her brain could even identify the man who entered the store. But the glasses were a dead giveaway. Her heart jump-started. She hadn't seen Philip in his BCGs since she first met him, but she now remembered he wore them at work. She froze to the spot, heart pounding. Her eyes took charge, darting around to find the best escape. Her feet followed, how they worked without her knees buckling, she had no idea.

Hallie sidled up to the card racks, heart rate racing out of control, her breaths short and desperate.

Had somebody sucked all the oxygen out of the store? She stood with her back to the cashiers and opened a card to hide her face, glad she'd changed her hair color. From the corner of her eye, she watched him walk to the front of the store. She gauged the distance to the door. Not yet. She turned her head millimeter by millimeter. Peeking around the edge of the card, she caught him looking in her direction.

Double shit.

Hallie snapped her head back and slid around the display, bending her knees slightly, hoping Hallmark would keep her secret.

She counted out the heartbeats, then shielding her face again with the card, she peeked over the top row of greeting cards to discover his back to her. The image slammed into her. The back of his neck, curls threatening the back of his military haircut. Those shoulders. God, she missed those broad, strong shoulders.

Unshed tears blurred her vision. His long back, tapering down to his tight, little ass. Long legs in coveralls. How she wanted to stay and drink him in. Every detail. How she wanted to run to him. Throw her arms around him. Hug his back. Stay with him forever.

Forget the stationery. She needed to get that letter in the mail this minute. What if he'd caught her just now? How devastating for him to discover her with no explanation to soften the blow?

Hallie hauled ass out of the store, feet racing as fast as her heart rate. She double-timed up the ladders and leapt over the raised watertight doorways, trying not to bang her shins. Reaching her desk, she caught her breath and fired up the computer. She'd finish the letter and get it in ship's mail. ASAP.

> *Dear Philip,*
>
> *This is Hallie writing. It is very painful for me to share the truth with you this way, but here goes:*
>
> *I am a second-class petty officer in the Navy and I am stationed aboard the* Blanchard. *With you. Right now. Right here.*
>
> *I'm an MC2 in Public Affairs on your ship. I am so sorry for deceiving you. Words alone cannot say how sorry*

I am. When I first met you, I thought it would be fun to go sailing and then I would quietly disappear. I figured the ship was big enough that I could get away with never seeing you again. I hadn't planned on falling in love with—

But that's all she wrote before Chief Bernard interrupted. "Hey, McCabe, Commander Scott wants to see you in his office. You too, Marini."

Chapter 13

"You want me to *what*?"

"Take over *Blanchard* News Tonight," the Public Affairs Officer said. "We've taken some polls and it appears nobody was watching Emmanuel on the in-port broadcast."

Mass Communications Specialist First-Class David Emmanuel was the anchor each evening on *Blanchard* News Tonight, the on-board evening news that essentially read tomorrow's Plan of the Day. Nobody watched it because it was boring. And so was Petty Officer Emmanuel. There was no background. Just Emmanuel in his aquaflage uniform. Big whoop.

Hallie looked from one person to the other, trying to comprehend what they were asking of her. Commander Scott sat at his desk. Chief Bernard and the Deputy Public Affairs Officer, Lieutenant Junior Grade Latimer, flanked her and Gina.

Commander Scott glanced down at some notes, then continued. "We want to revamp the whole approach. Move away from essentially reading the Plan of the Day to maybe fifteen minutes of national news that pertains to the mission. You know. What's going on in the Middle East that day.

"Then maybe the second fifteen minutes would be ship's news. Safety measures, risk management practices, cool ideas on making shipboard life easier, and even security reminders. Oh, and maybe some historical background on some of the ports we're scheduled to visit. Maybe a piece on the Suez Canal before we go through. Go over customs and culture in the Arab cities we'll be pulling into. The Muslim holy month of Ramadan starts soon. Give the background and share how people are supposed to behave. That sort of thing."

Lieutenant Latimer jumped in. She was a petite, young blonde about Hallie's age, but because she had a college degree in journalism, she was a commissioned officer and Hallie was an enlisted petty officer. "We're thinking service dress uniform, McCabe. You know. Jacket and tie, fix your hair, make-up. New backdrop. The whole nine yards. As if you're on a national news network. We're looking for CNN meets 'Navy News This Week.' And we think you're the perfect person for the job."

Hallie wanted to answer yes. This was a dream come true. But she had difficulty because all the words were tangled up with another word: Philip.

The Deputy continued when Hallie showed no reaction. "When I thought about this, you were my first choice. Hallie, I know this is your dream. We've talked about it. This would look awesome on your resume when you're discharged from the Navy. This could be your ticket to the big time. With an audience of five thousand, this is almost as good as anchoring 'Navy News This Week' or 'Armed Forces Television and Radio' in Europe."

Hallie bought time as she continued to wrestle with the Philip problem. She was certain Gina knew why she stalled. "It would be a huge responsibility, ma'am."

Commander Scott took over. "The staff would write your copy. All we need you to do is go before the camera and deliver the news—good and bad. You'll be able to use the teleprompter of course. We know you'd be a natural. You've studied this for years and we know you've had a lot of practice in school. You've told me you wanted to do your part in the war on terror, McCabe. So here's your chance. Be the person who gets this info out to the crew."

"I thought I was just going to write about things, sir."

"You're welcome to write any copy you want. As a matter of fact, we were talking about you putting in some of those little Hallie-isms you're always sharing with us. Hell. Talk about sunscreen. Especially when we get to the Gulf and the temperature hits a hundred-and-thirty on the flight deck. Throw in those big words you're always using—basal cell carcinoma and all that. I'm sure the folks working on the roof could use a reminder now and then. I have a feeling the men will listen to whatever you tell them."

"Actually, it would be more important to remind the people below decks to get topside and get some sunshine." Hallie suggested. "I understand some of them never see the light of day. They're probably not getting enough Vitamin D."

"See, you're a natural," said Chief Bernard, smiling.

Hallie's heart raced with excitement and trepidation. "When do you need an answer?"

"We'd like to run the first broadcast on Monday night. Give me an answer by Saturday. Because if you don't want it, it's all yours, Marini."

"Me?" Gina looked stunned. "Are you kidding?"

"We know you'd be excellent too, Gina. And it would be your ticket to promotion," Lieutenant Latimer replied. "If Hallie takes it, we want you as backup."

Hallie and Gina turned and looked at each other. Gina was grinning. Hallie was a little more reticent. This was her big break, if she took the job. It was a win/win for Gina either way. She was going on the air regardless.

"Give us a definite by noon on Saturday, McCabe," said Commander Scott. "You ladies talk it over and let me know. I'll have the staff start working on any filler we might need. We'll pull the latest news highlights on Monday afternoon for the lead-in."

The Public Affairs Officer and the chief rose and left the office, closing the door. Lieutenant Latimer turned to them and spoke confidentially. "I took this idea to Commander Scott myself. As a woman I was hesitant to approach him with the idea of putting a female on camera. We don't want you to think we're using you as a sex symbol here. But let me be blunt here. We've got over four thousand, five hundred males on this ship and who knows what one detail they might hear that could possibly save their lives or the lives of their shipmates. I feel you two would be able to get their attention. If either of you find this offensive in any way, we totally understand – we totally understand."

Okay, at least they admitted they were going the sexual attraction route. And Lieutenant Latimer was the one who had approached them, because her priority was making sure the crew stayed safe. Who knew? If more people were watching because of her, maybe something she said would end up saving somebody's life.

"Oh, and McCabe. If you decide to do it..." she reached out and indicated the no longer golden, but still wayward, tendril. "You're going to have to make sure your hair stays secured. We're not actively going for the sexual angle. I know you'll keep it professional." Hallie did her unconscious swipe of the tendril, which slid right back down over her eyebrow.

"Yes, ma'am." Hallie thought of all the times Philip had told her how crazy it made him. No way would she let it fall in front of forty-five hundred guys. If she decided to take the assignment.

"Talk it over, ladies, and let us know by noon on Saturday. That is all."

Gina jumped up and down in the Public Affairs spaces after the lieutenant returned to her office. Hallie was quieter, but smiling nonetheless. This was her big break. But she had a letter to finish first, and she needed to caution Gina not to say a word to anybody about the show, especially Trixie. At least until Philip received her letter.

And then it wouldn't matter anymore.

When there was no response from Philip, Hallie agreed to anchor the show, starting with Monday night's broadcast. She had placed her letter in ship's mail on Wednesday morning, so he'd had plenty of time to respond.

Besides telling him the entire truth, she told him if she didn't hear back by Saturday noon, she'd assume he didn't care. It would hurt, but only what she deserved considering what she had done to him. And then she would be able to move forward with her life and her career.

And since he apparently didn't care, she might as well show him what he was missing.

Saturday night became beauty parlor night in female berthing. The word was out. Everybody pooled their hair and make-up products and gave Hallie a makeover. Starting with a highlighting kit, they managed to pull her brown hair almost back to blond. They practiced applying make-up. Enough to show up on camera, but not too much to make her look gaudy. Gina took Hallie's service dress blues down to the ship's laundry to get them pressed and she buffed up her patent leathers, not that they were going to show, but she knew Hallie wanted to be squared away from head to toe.

This was not about looking pretty for the guys, including one hot Engineering Officer, however. This was about getting people to listen to important information. If looking good was a part of that, so be it. She hadn't worn make-up in so long, she was surprised at how really nice she looked. Hallie checked her email and ship's mail the rest of the weekend, but her mailboxes remained empty.

So there was nothing left to do except sit there looking pretty, practice the script, and wait.

Monday was a ball-breaker. Philip slammed the parts to the seawater regulator valve on the workbench. "No, no, and no!" he yelled at them.

"Sorry, guys." He pulled off his hard hat and ran his fingers through his hair. Took his glasses off and rubbed the bridge of his nose. "I didn't mean to raise my voice."

Trixie jumped in. "Sir, how about we take a break for chow?"

Philip glanced down at his watch: 1740 hours. Where had the time gone? Oh, right. Up in smoke with the fucking valve. He reached back and massaged his aching neck. "Yeah, go ahead, men.

You too, Williams. Bulldog, you got the watch. Can you keep working on it while we eat?"

"Aye, sir."

"Williams, spell him after chow. Okay?"

"Sure thing, sir."

"I'll be back down to check on it after the news." Philip was expected to be at officers' mess in the wardroom by 1800, so he'd better hurry up. He slipped into his office and changed into a clean uniform.

Damn it. There was that stack of brown ship's mail envelopes.

He'd planned to go through it today, but the regulator had distracted him. Maybe after dinner.

He climbed the ladders headed for the wardroom. Why was this valve such a problem? There were hundreds of them throughout the ship and he'd never had this much trouble with one. His gang could usually do an Indy Pit, tearing down and rebuilding regulators just like this one in no time flat. So focused on the valve, he smacked his head on the hatch opening and while cringing to hold his head, managed to smack his shin on the knee-knocker.

"Shit. Just plain shit." Then realizing he'd said it out loud, chastised himself and mumbled the rest. "This day totally sucks."

Actually every day had pretty much sucked for Philip Johnston lately. Ever since Hallie McCabe had walked out of his life—taking his heart with her. He was usually adept at compartmentalizing personal stuff once he arrived at work, but it was like she owned his soul. So there was a constant pall over him, suffocating him, locking in all his anger and frustration. Lately it didn't take much to push his buttons and let out the steam. And it wasn't fair of him to take it out on his men, and woman. He really needed to get a handle on this before he yelled at the wrong person.

And Hallie hadn't just *taken* his heart with her. She'd ripped it from his chest, stomped on it, then repeatedly backed over it with her car for good measure. Sky wasn't any help at all. They'd been having dinner together since he'd flown on board. It was nice for

Philip to have someone to debrief about his day again, because he missed doing that with Hallie. But Sky just kept telling him, "Come on, I'll buy you a beer when we get to Palma. Find us a couple of women. Get your mind off what's-her-name. You need to get brewed, screwed, and tattooed. Okay, hold the tattoo. But you do need to get brewed and screwed."

"Forget it." Philip had replied. "I just got royally screwed." And as to getting drunk? There wasn't enough alcohol in all of Spain to dull this ache.

Get a fucking grip, he told himself. She's just a woman.

Yeah, right.

Maybe some dinner and a half hour of news would clear his head so he could figure out what was wrong with the regulator. Maybe he could eat fast and sneak out before the crappy ship's newscast came on and get back to his office and watch CNN. He never had time to catch up with the news and at least CNN gave him some world news instead of just who the duty section was for tomorrow.

Philip stumbled into the wardroom, alternately rubbing his head and his shin, which caused him to smack his shoulder in the doorway.

Fuck. Could this day get any worse?

Chapter 14

"Good evening, this is MC2 Hallie McCabe with *Blanchard* News Tonight. Reports from Afghanistan indicate..."

The din in the wardroom quieted as the officers nudged each other and pointed to the screens. Nobody had heard the opening, since they rarely paid attention to this broadcast. But they were paying attention now.

Philip chose that moment to return to the wardroom table with his coffee. He looked questioningly at Sky, who had heard the introduction and now stared at him open-mouthed.

"What?"

"Didn't you say Hallie's last name was McCabe?"

Philip's heart went to red alert. "What of it?"

"She isn't, by any chance, in the Navy, is she?"

"*What*?" Philip screwed up his face like that was the most ridiculous thing he'd ever heard in his life.

Sky turned and looked at the screen. Philip's eyes followed. His heart froze.

Hallie.

Her hair was a little darker. But it was Hallie. No question.

What was Hallie doing on the TV? In the wardroom? On his ship? In a uniform?

Hallie?

What the hell?

Philip tried to ignore the anguish shooting through his system so his engineering brain could do its thing. This was being broadcast from shore. She was doing something for one of her classes. And it was being shown here.

In the middle of the ocean. On the USS *Blanchard*.

Hallie.

In a Navy uniform.

He turned and looked at Sky. Speechless.

Sky bit back a smile. "How come you didn't tell me she was a squid?"

"What the hell is going on?" Philip whispered. He collapsed into his chair transfixed, his coffee forgotten.

Sky huffed out a laugh and punched him on the arm. "You sly dog." But when he realized this truly was a big surprise to his buddy, he had the decency to back off and watch how things played out.

Sky spent the entire broadcast looking back and forth between Philip and the screen, torn between compassion and outright envy. This was no double bagger. No wonder she hadn't wanted her picture taken. Her photograph on Bill's desk would have spread around the ship faster than a bad case of clap after a liberty port.

Philip remained glued to the screen. His mouth hanging open. What had she said? "There are things you still don't know about me?"

Holy shit.

He broke the trance momentarily to glance around his table.

Grins radiated from every male officer as they craned their necks to catch the news tonight. He was dumbfounded. Why was Hallie on the TV? It couldn't be Hallie. Hallie was in Florida. Wasn't she?

But then he knew for sure that she wasn't.

The woman on the screen looked down at her notes and a single lock of hair fell from behind her ear. When she looked up, it lay there curling down her forehead over her right eyebrow, punching him in the gut. She didn't miss a beat in her report by brushing it away.

The guys at his table smirked at one another, giving thumbs-ups and fist bumps. Anything more would grass their asses for sexual harassment.

Good thing the CO didn't hear the guy to Philip's right say, "Oh, baby, permission to lay alongside." The reference to how one captain would ask another if he could tie up his ship next to his, brought more stifled laughter around the table.

The XO must have picked up on the newly heated atmosphere because he grabbed the microphone and reminded the men they were gentlemen and that there were ladies present. It grew quieter, as the officers now hung on the newscaster's every word. Philip had to admit she was good, whoever she was. Professional. But it couldn't be Hallie.

Hallie was a college student.

In Florida.

So why was she wearing a uniform that sure as shit had a rating badge with two red chevrons on the left sleeve? Why was she dressed like a Petty Officer Second-Class in the United States Navy? A petty officer with the golden tendril draped over her eyebrow?

Philip watched, frozen in time and place. His coffee grew cold. His mind raced. His heart raced. What the hell was going on?

"The duty section for August..." When she read the highlights for tomorrow's Plan of the Day, the entire male faction of the wardroom was transfixed, never knowing the POD could be sheer poetry.

She closed the broadcast with, "This is MC2 Hallie McCabe signing off for *Blanchard* News Tonight, saying goodnight and stay safe."

Each syllable stabbed him in the gut. There was no doubt about it now. This was no long-lost twin sister. Hallie smiled sincerely and professionally at the camera until the screen turned blue. The wardroom erupted with applause and cheers.

Surprisingly Sky behaved, mostly in deference to his buddy, but also because he was in shock. Holy shit, The One was a sailor—and truly a McBabe.

As Philip pushed away from the table and stormed out, heading for his stateroom, he heard the first mumbled reference to "Babe McCabe."

It all made sense now. That last night when she kept saying, "I'm in...I'm in..." She wasn't in debt. She wasn't in trouble. She was in the fucking Navy—although that was trouble enough.

An enlisted sailor in the Navy.

On. His. Ship.

Sky was hot on his heels. "Are you telling me you honestly didn't know she was a swabby? I'm guessing she didn't wear her dog tags when you were...you know...doing it?"

"Shut up."

Philip slammed open the door to his stateroom, glad that his three roommates were out. He opened his computer and banged out an email, and then hit send.

> *From: philip.johnston@navy.mil*
> *To: hallie.mccabe@navy.mil*
> *Subj: What the...?*
> *YOU'RE IN THE NAVY???*
> *WHAT THE H. IS GOING ON???*

He stared at his in-box waiting for his email to come back undeliverable—no such addressee.

But it didn't.

Philip felt like he was going to puke. He dropped his head into his hands, elbows on the desk. He shook his head from side to side.

Sky started babbling. "No wonder you couldn't meet me for a beer. I'd give up drinking too if I had that waiting at home for me. I'd have sold my soul to al-Qaeda for just one night in the rack with her. Hell, I'd resign my commission just to hang the McBabe's wet skivvies on the clothesline."

Philip whirled in his desk chair, grabbed Sky by his shirtfront, and yelled, "Don't you ever call her that again!"

Sky shook him off. "Okay, but she has to have a nickname. Come on. We all have nicknames." He nodded his head in disbelief. "I still can't believe that every swinging dick on board is lusting after her and you're going to tell me that sweet, innocent, little Billy Gates is the one who bagged her?"

Philip collapsed back into his chair, tried to roll the tension from his shoulders. "I didn't *bag* her."

Sky lay down on Philip's bottom rack. Clasped his fingers behind his head and made himself at home. "To think that my protégé, little Billy G. is the proud owner of that? I hope you told her who taught you everything you know. I'm in awe of you, man. You've added a whole new chapter to 'still waters run deep.'"

"Shut up, Sky!" he yelled. Then mumbled, "She lied to me."

"Aw, don't get your skivvies in a twist. Did she ever say, 'Oh, by the way, I'm not in the Navy and I'm not on your ship?'"

"No, but she never said she was in the Navy." And then he had to think. He'd spend the entire night trying to remember everything she'd ever said to him. Had she lied to him, or just not told him everything? Didn't matter. That was lying by omission. He swiveled in his chair, hit refresh on the computer, hoping a response that explained everything would appear. "A second-class petty officer. I was fraternizing and I didn't even know it."

"Oh, I believe, Billy Boy, that you're not technically fraternizing if you don't know you're fraternizing. I've had a little experience with this myself."

"You have?"

"Any port in a storm, buddy. I've been known to put my helicopter down in foreign territory a time or two. Nothing like a little forbidden fruit to whet the old appetite. Yours truly was fully aware he was fraternizing however, and he enjoyed every minute of it. But trust me, I never treated any of them like my brother."

Philip turned to him in disbelief. "What the fuck are you talking about?"

Sky sat up on the bunk with a shameless grin on his face. "There was this hospital corpsman that had a pair of lips on her _that could cure anything that ails you. And that musician's mate? Oh, man, could she ever blow Reveille on me. Morning, noon, or night. She never had a problem getting me up."

"Shut. Up. This is serious." Philip stood and paced as best he could in the small stateroom.

"So was that piccolo player. She caused me to have PTSD." He put his hand to his heart and feigned distress. "The flashbacks are killing me. To this day I can't hear 'The Stars and Stripes Forever' without popping to attention. Even when I'm sitting down."

Philip turned, incredulous, hands out in supplication. "Sky, I'm dying here."

"Oh, come on, Bill. Don't ask. Don't tell. It's not a problem unless you're both in the same chain of command and you're expecting favors and shit. It goes on all the time. You think all these horny bastards are afraid of a little fraternization? Hell, this is war. If you gotta go, might as well go with a smile on your face."

"But what about ethics?"

"I think I missed that class."

Sky had gotten over the shock of Hallie being so beautiful, and realized he better tone things down because as far as he knew Hallie was still The One. The unwritten rules strictly stated that you didn't say anything sexual about your best buddy's One. You could say it about your own, but not your best friend's. It would be like talking dirty about his mother.

Philip resumed checking his computer. Nerves danced in his stomach and his fucking neck was killing him. He reached up and rubbed it.

"I saw a woman in the ship's store the other day that reminded me so much of Hallie, except her hair was different. Hallie has gorgeous, long blond hair. This girl was the same size as Hallie and had the same figure, as best I could tell in uniform. I don't know. She just carried herself the same way, but her hair was darker. I bet it was her. Why'd she dye her hair?"

"Probably because she's hiding from you."

"Then why'd she go on the TV like that? Did she think I wouldn't see her?" No reply on the computer. Maybe if he paced some more that would hurry things up.

"What if she had to? It's her job."

"Then wouldn't that have been the time to tell me? Before she went on? Come on, Sky. We were *so* close. We talked about everything."

"Well, apparently not *everything*."

"Why did she think she couldn't tell me?" Philip continued to walk from bulkhead to bulkhead, anything to break the tension. "Was it all a lie? Wait. Did I mention following the rules too many times? I don't know what to do."

"Well, if you don't get your smart ass up to Public Affairs this very minute and talk to her, you're not only a dumb ass, but a fucking moron. Sweep her off her feet. Beg for forgiveness, even if you've done nothing wrong. Profess your undying love. Do whatever it takes, because I got news for you, Billy Boy. There's going to be a line forming at that door real soon, and if you don't get at the head of it, somebody else will."

"I can't do that, Sky. She lied to me."

"That's bullshit. I bet she didn't have any other way to keep you from finding out she was a sailor before we deployed. And because you're such a paragon of integrity, with your holier-than-fucking-thou attitude, she probably thought you'd say *sayonara* if she told you, which is probably the truth because you *are* a dumb ass sometimes. Look, if she's The One—"

"She's obviously not The One, you dumb shit. Aren't you listening? She lied to me and she doesn't love me anymore."

"Tell me the exact words she said. Did she say, 'Fuck off, dude. I don't love your ass anymore?'"

Philip stopped pacing. He bounced his knuckles against his mouth. A glimmer of hope invaded his muddled brain that she had not, indeed, said she didn't love him anymore—even if he'd interpreted it that way. "She said, 'as hard as I've tried to figure this thing out, we just can't be together anymore.'"

"Shit!" Sky cried.

"We can't be together because..."

"She's enlisted, dumb ass! Look, buddy, you told me what it was like with you two. I could tell it was something special. It was written all over your dumb face. You've never acted this way over a woman before. And it sure as hell sounded like she felt the same way about you. If it's the real deal, man, go talk to her. Work it out. Don't blow it. Don't lose this one. And, Bill?"

"Yeah."

"See if she has a sister."

Rashid sat alone at his table on the aft mess deck, watching the news while he finished chow. He saw not only the newscast, but also the reaction to McCabe. He'd seen her around. Of course she probably didn't know he existed—or that he watched her from afar. She was pretty and popular, even though he could tell she usually tried to downplay things. Because he'd never seen McCabe looking like this. Tonight was New York shit. This was Hollywood. She was gorgeous and the response from the crew verified his opinion. Many of these people were her friends, so mixed among the cat calls tonight were words of encouragement, such as "Yay, Hallie!' and "You go, girl!"

Hallie. Never knew her first name before.

He also saw how everyone was completely entranced with the news tonight. Usually nobody watched it after dinner. What was that jerk's name? Manuel or something. They were definitely doing something right in Public Affairs by using this babe to bring them the news. That's right. Put a beautiful woman up there and all the guys would drop what they're doing and watch her.

God, men could be so stupid when a woman was thrown into the equation. Like any of them would ever have a chance with a chick like this. But he did like the idea of them watching her. And if this babe was going to be doing this every night, she might get a real following. Maybe everything would stop on the ship during the newscast. Might be a good time for a ship to be attacked. If you're the bad guys.

It had to be after dark, so the dhows would be less likely to be seen, even though the lookouts topside had night vision capabilities these days. But pretty much, they still relied on the OSs down in Combat to alert them of possible threats approaching the ship. Yeah, after dark was a must and since they'd be off daylight savings in the Middle East, it would be after dark. When everyone was busy. Watching the news.

While he was *making* the news.

And wouldn't it be nice to have this chick be a part of the plan. She was almost as beautiful as Rosie, with that butter-wouldn't-melt-in-her-mouth, sexual innocence look on her face.

So McCabe was probably a whore too. Probably screwing the other half of the ship.

The guys Rosie missed.

Hallie waited for the camera's red light to go off before she leaped from her chair. The production team had been smiling, silently cheering, and giving her thumbs up during the entire broadcast. Everybody jumped now, screaming and hugging each other once the light clicked off. "You rocked!" MC3 James Hall, the cameraman, called out as he high-fived her.

Gina gave her a big hug and danced her around, "'Goodnight and stay safe?' That was brilliant!"

"It just came to me at the last minute and popped out of my mouth."

Commander Scott remained professional, obviously restraining from hugging her, but he was grinning from ear to ear. "That was exactly what we were looking for. I felt like I was watching the national news."

Lieutenant Latimer joined the celebration. "It was fantastic. You're a natural." Then she pointed to the tendril, ready to chastise Hallie.

"I know, I know. I'll take care of it, ma'am."

Hallie was ecstatic. She knew it had been good. What if Philip had watched it? Or worse, what if he hadn't cared to watch it? She couldn't worry about him. It was obviously over and the sooner she got that through her head, the better. He'd probably gotten royally pissed she'd deceived him and he wanted nothing to do with her. It cut deep, but she'd gotten what she deserved. However, this show on her resume would help ease the pain. It was time to move on.

To the world of broadcast.

"Come on, girl. Let's go celebrate. I'll buy you a mocktail on the mess decks," Gina said. Everyone was gone but the watchstander. It had been a long day getting ready for the show.

"No, I'll secure. I want to check my mail before I go." And she wanted to be alone to do it, just in case there was a message. Or in case somebody special dropped by the studio. Her mailbox held twenty-four emails from crewmembers. More popped up as she scanned through the addresses. All from unknown names.

Except one.

> From: philip.johnston@navy.mil
> To: hallie.mccabe@navy.mil
> Subj: What the...?
> YOU'RE IN THE NAVY???
> WHAT THE H. IS GOING ON???

All in caps. No salutation. No signature. Just two questions. Each followed by three question marks.

Did he not receive her letter? Is that why he hadn't responded?

She typed her response:

> "Explained all in ship's mail. Did u not receive??? I am SO sorry. Can we talk? Can't use email. H."

Then she sat and waited.

Chapter 15

Philip couldn't wait one more second for Hallie's reply. He grabbed his sweats and, after checking on Trixie and the valve, headed for the gym. Funny how the sea water regulator didn't seem quite as important any more. He'd deal with it tomorrow. He had to keep moving, pump iron, do something, or he was going to take out a steel bulkhead with his bare fist.

Betrayed. That's how he felt. She'd lied to him. Lied all along, from the moment she'd met him. She was in the Navy? And on his ship? How could she? He had loved her. Trusted her. Given his heart to her. Professed his love for her. He'd opened up his soul to her and she'd been lying the entire time.

As he pounded away on the treadmill, his words came back to him from the day they met. She had stood there on the beach and let him explain snipes, down in the hole, and BCGs for God's sake. No wonder she knew how many lives were lost on the *Cole*. "No, I can't meet the guys from the ship," she'd said. "I have to study."

And she'd sat there and let him tell her all about the laundry line in women's berthing. She knew about that clothesline. Probably had skivvies hanging on it right now. And Trixie. Oh, God, she probably knew her too. No wonder Hallie knew when they were getting back from sea trials. She was out on the same damn sea trials.

Fucking crystal ball, right.

Next he lifted weights, sweat pouring off his body, wanting to wrap the barbell around her neck. No, he'd never do that. He'd never hurt Hallie. He loved her—or he *had* loved her. He didn't know anymore. All he knew was he'd trusted her and she'd betrayed him. Now he just wanted to punch the living crap out of something.

He showered and dressed in clean coveralls before he checked his email, stalling for time. Afraid to check it. What if there was still no response? What if she cared so little for him that she didn't reply? What if it had all been a game to her?

Let's see if we can snow the nerdy lieutenant.

She probably knew the enlisted person wouldn't get in trouble for her part in fraternization. "We just can't be together anymore." Did she really mean "we can't be together" or did she mean "I don't want to be together with you anymore?" It was hard to tell with a liar.

He inhaled deeply, exhaled just as hard, uttered a silent prayer—for what, he wasn't quite certain—then glanced down at his laptop.

It was there.

> *From: hallie.mccabe@navy.mil*
> *To: philip.johnston@navy.mil*
> *Re: What the...???*

With his heart pounding, he clicked on it:

> *"Explained all in ship's mail. Did u not receive??? I am SO sorry. Can we talk? Can't use email. H."*

The fucking ship's mail.

Philip tore out of his stateroom for Engineering, jumping over the knee knockers and sliding down the ladders. He knew he should have at least perused it and pulled out anything important. He never let work mail pile up, but he'd been so distracted by—

There it was. He should have opened anything that was addressed to "Philip Johnston" instead of "AUXO."

Dumb. Ass.

He ripped the manila envelope open to find a smaller envelope inside, with the following words written on the front: "*LT Philip Johnston—Personal. Read in private.*"

She was smart at least. Emails were monitored by security. An old-fashioned, handwritten letter was probably less likely to be read by the wrong person.

He shocked Bulldog and Trixie by telling them to leave everything until tomorrow, and then he raced back up the ladders to his stateroom. Philip certainly wasn't going to read it in his office with the duty section hanging around. Thank God he hadn't found it in the middle of a normal workday. Philip locked the door and stood with his back against it, breathing heavily, his heart pounding. He took a deep breath and dove in.

> *Dear Philip,*
> *This is Hallie writing. It is very painful for me to share the truth with you this way, but here goes:*
> *I am a second-class petty officer in the Navy and I am stationed aboard the* Blanchard. *With you. Right now. Right here.*

Just like she'd seduced him on the sailboat. Right now. Right here.

> *I'm an MC2 in Public Affairs on the USS* Blanchard. *I am so sorry for deceiving you. Words alone cannot say how sorry I am. When I first met you, I thought it would be fun to go sailing with you and then I would quietly disappear. I figured the ship was big enough that I could get away with never seeing you again. I hadn't planned on falling in love with you.*

His heart started beating again.

I didn't know you'd end up being the man of my dreams and then I didn't know what to do.

Holy shit, it wasn't all a lie.

I knew I should tell you, but you would have ended it. You'd have to. It would have been too risky for you to date me. It would hurt your career, and I know how important that is to you. But I just couldn't let you go. I was too selfish. I loved you too much.

Philip's heart damn near pounded right through his chest.

I tried so many times to tell you, but I lost my nerve every time. The UCMJ says the senior member is not committing fraternization if he doesn't know the junior member is enlisted. I kept thinking about that as I kept my secret, because I knew you'd probably stop seeing me if you knew. I thought since the Blanchard is so big, I could get away with being on the ship by keeping a low profile, but I knew I couldn't do it through the cruise. It just wouldn't be fair for you to bump into me. I saw you in the ship's store this morning and I knew it was time to tell you everything.

It had been her in the store.

Philip leaned his head back against the door, sucked in a deep breath and exhaled just as deeply—at least he could breathe again.

Today my boss asked me to take over Blanchard News Tonight on Monday. It's a big break for me, and I want to do it so much, but I won't if it will hurt you in any way. I mean, I know it will hurt when you find out I'm in

*the Navy and on the ship, so I'm writing and telling you
everything now—in advance, so you won't be shocked if you
watch the news. But also I didn't know if you'd mentioned
my name to colleagues, etc. so if there's any reason you
don't want me to take this assignment, please let me know
by noon on Saturday and I'll give the job to someone else. If
you want to talk about any of this before Monday, please let
me know. I will do anything for you. Email is not a good
idea for anything detailed, however.*

*I may not have told you the whole truth about myself,
but I never blatantly lied to you. Even when I left, I told you
the truth, that we couldn't be together. It doesn't mean I love
you any less, though.*

I don't think I'll ever stop loving you.

Relief flooded into every cell of Philip's body. He was certain
that his heart was going to give out with the abuse it had taken this
evening, but now the adrenaline spikes were from relief.

*I'd do anything you asked, if I could just know we
might be together again, maybe when I get out of the Navy
next spring. I know your answer will probably be no. I
deceived you and I doubt you'll forgive me. You're such an
honorable man, which is one of the reasons I love you. And
you deserve an honorable woman.*

*If I don't receive a response to this letter, I'll assume
you don't care that I do the news – or you just don't care.
You not caring is only what I deserve, but at least I'll know
it's OK for me to move on with my career and my life.*

*Again, I am sorry I've hurt you. You are the sweetest,
kindest, most loving and perfect man I have ever met and I
miss you terribly.*

Love, Hallie

She loved him.

That was the truth. He'd known it. He wasn't sure what he was going to do about it, but he'd needed to know that he hadn't been wrong about her loving him.

His hands shaking, he hit reply and typed:

Library 2130 hours

Then, because he was an officer and a gentleman, he grabbed a handkerchief and stuffed it in his pocket. There was very likely going to be tears. Philip glanced at his watch: 2100.

These were going to be the longest thirty minutes of his life.

Hallie was appalled at the emails popping up on her screen. Most subject lines said something to the effect of: Good Job; U were great; and Way 2 Go! But others read: Hey, Baby; Good job, McBabe; I think I love you; I'm hot 4 U; and Will you marry me, McCabe?

But none that said: re: What the...??? From one philip.johnston@navy.mil. How could he not have received her letter? She'd sent it five days ago. She read his email again.

YOU'RE IN THE NAVY??? WHAT THE H IS GOING ON???

The words made her cringe. She couldn't imagine what it must have been like for him to be blindsided like that. Probably just turned on the TV and Whammo! There she was, in a second-class petty officer's uniform.

On his ship.

She hoped he'd been alone so he hadn't embarrassed himself.

Guilt continued to roil through her gut. Hallie rose and paced the Public Affairs Office. So far the watchstander had paid her no mind, too busy proofing tomorrow's newsletter. Now he glanced up. "You okay, McCabe?"

"Yeah. I'm just waiting for a message. Sorry if I'm bothering you."

"No bother. You were good tonight. I think the show really needed that shot in the arm."

"Thanks." She sat back down. Pacing wasn't going to work. She did not want to talk to anyone. Well, there was one person she would love to talk to, but apparently he wasn't interested in talking. She glanced back at her computer: Another proposal of marriage and...ewwwww. That one was so nasty, she stuck out one finger and hit the delete button. And it felt so good, she hit all the ones with suggestive subject lines. One by one.

They popped up as fast as she could delete them.

Pop. Delete. Pop. Delete. Pop. Delete. Pop.

philip.johnston@navy.mil. re: What the . . . ???

Her heart stopped. Fingers flew away from the keyboard as if burned. She found herself paralyzed, too afraid to open it. What if he—?

"You sure you're okay?" She hadn't even seen the watchstander walk over to her desk.

"Yeah. I'm okay. Sorry, I just..." She tried to laugh it off.

"All right." He walked away. "Let me know if you need anything."

She took a deep breath against panic. Her finger snaked toward the keyboard to click on his reply.

Library 2130 hours

Hallie's chest tightened. She swallowed, attempting to keep her throat from closing up. He wanted to see her.

Tonight.

She glanced at her watch. 2100. She had just enough time to run to berthing and change, but these were still going to be the longest thirty minutes of her life.

* * *

Philip thought the ship's library would be a quiet, unobtrusive place at 2130, but it wasn't. This was an aircraft carrier, and it operated twenty-four seven. This was where the computer banks were housed for the folks who didn't have access to a computer in their daily jobs. Email was checked at all hours of the day and night. And he didn't feel unobtrusive because he was apparently meeting with the newest celebrity on the USS *Blanchard*.

Everybody recognized her.

He watched while men stopped Hallie to congratulate her on her debut as a newscaster, and to try to worm their way into her inner circle. Several others gave her a thumbs-up as she passed. Some just nudged their friends and pointed as Hallie walked toward his table in the corner.

God, she even looked beautiful in baggie camouflage— complete with enlisted insignia on her collar.

His brain registered that he had repeatedly had sex with a second-class petty officer.

Without a condom.

A new pang of anxiety shot through his gut. He hadn't even thought about the fact that he'd trusted her with the birth control. Hopefully she wasn't lying about that too.

"I'm so sorry, sir," she said, on the verge of tears.

"Sit down, Petty Officer McCabe."

"I brought a clipboard. We can pretend I'm interviewing you—about your job or something."

"If you like. I happen to know you're very good at pretending."

But he was impressed that she'd thought of it because people were watching them. Fortunately, she had her back to them when her tears started.

"Philip, I'm sorry," she whispered.

"It's Lieutenant Johnston," he snapped at her.

She flinched. "I'm sorry, Lieutenant Johnston."

"Now, what would you like to know about my job, Petty Officer?" he began in a harsh whisper. "How the heads work on the *Blanchard* or would you rather hear about how I can't keep them running smoothly because there is too much other crap in my life. How about how hard it's been to concentrate on my job because some conniving little sailor broke my heart? Maybe you would like to hear about how I find the time to get away from work for a few minutes to grab a bite to eat and catch up on the news, only to find that the woman I thought I loved and respected is now the heartthrob of the entire wardroom? The part where I sit and listen to the guys cheering on the new McBabe in the newsroom? Is that the part you want to hear?"

Hallie's shoulders shook as she tried to stifle her sobs.

He glanced around and handed her the handkerchief. "Don't make a scene. People are watching you. You made your bed," he said, then laughed. "And mine. What were you thinking?"

Hallie blew her nose, dabbed at her tears, and pulled herself together. She sat up straight, locked eyes with his, and said soberly and respectfully, "Lieutenant Johnston, I apologize for not being completely honest with you. I apologize if I hurt you in any way. I apologize for jeopardizing your career. I apologize for everything except for loving you...*sir*."

Philip took that one to the gut and softened. "What did you do to your hair? I loved your hair. I loved you. Do you have any idea how hard it was to see you on that TV? To have to put two and two together and keep coming up with nine? I didn't know. I know you tried to warn me, but I didn't see your letter until just now. The guys. Jesus, the guys went crazy. The things they said about you. I wanted to hit every one of them. They were talking about *you*. *My* Hallie.

"And then when you looked down and that fucking piece of hair fell, guess I can swear around you now, since you're a *sailor*. When that golden tendril—*my* golden tendril—fell down and you looked so sexy and they saw it and they loved it, I just went into shock. I guess that's good, because I would have torn them limb from limb otherwise." He shook his head in disbelief. "First you stabbed me in the heart by saying you didn't love me anymore and then you twisted the knife by being in the Navy. Or do I have that backwards?"

"I didn't say I didn't love you. I said we couldn't be together."

"Same thing. You fucking slayed me," he hissed, looking around to see if anyone had heard him.

Hallie winced. "Do you think it was easy for me?"

"No, I guess you had to be pretty busy, sneaking on and off the ship and coming up with stories for why you couldn't meet my friends."

"No, it was hard because I loved you and was trying to protect you. As long as you didn't know about me, we were safe. And it hurt to my very core to know that one way or the other, as long as I was still in the Navy, I was going to end up hurting you. I knew that if I told you, it would be our death sentence. And I loved you so much. I still do."

"Well, don't. Okay?" He felt torn in half. Did he want her to love him or not?

"Would you rather I'd never come into your life?"

Philip recoiled when she hit that nerve. "I would have appreciated it if you'd been upfront with me from the start."

"So you could have told me to take a hike? I can just see you saying, 'Sorry I can't get involved with you, because you're enlisted and I'm a major rule follower.'"

He dropped his head, and shut his eyes. She was probably right. That's who he was. And he would've walked away from the best thing that had ever happened to him.

Hallie continued to whisper. "Do you remember that Saturday night at your place? The night before we made love for the first time on the sailboat?"

Philip lifted his head, eyes wide at her audacity. Then he nervously glanced around the library, looking anywhere but at her, all the while wondering if anybody else in the room could possibly be privy to this whispered conversation.

Did he remember it? It was seared in his brain, along with every other second he'd spent with her.

He could feel himself getting aroused under the table at the mere mention of that night. The night he'd first met her breasts. Taken them in his mouth...Damn it. He was torn between wanting to throttle her and wanting to drag her to the closest fan room and take her right on the deck. Or over there behind the DVDs.

"Hallie, don't. You're not fighting fair."

Philip couldn't believe they were talking like this in the ship's library, especially when two hours ago he hadn't even known she was on board. He continued to look anywhere but at her. He couldn't even get up and walk out of there now.

"I bring it up for a reason."

Well, don't because all kinds of other things are coming up with it.

Somebody walked close to the table, looking on a shelf right behind Philip. Hallie didn't miss a beat in the current charade. She looked down at her notes and the tendril slipped out so that when she looked up to ask a professional question, there it was, draped across her forehead. She swiped at it, but it didn't stay put.

Philip thought he was going to die.

She raised her voice to a stage whisper, so the interloper could hear her. "So tell me how hard it is to control the air conditioning system? I mean it just gets so hot here. Do you ever have problems keeping up with the demand?"

The patron moved on and Hallie went right back to her original conversation.

"That night. Tell me if the words, 'Belay my last' ever entered your brain after I said I couldn't stay?"

How had she known?

"Because if you hadn't said anything and I hadn't turned you down, we might have continued like that for who knows how long."

She knew him so well.

"Did you almost wish you could take it back so we could've gone back to what we were doing...you know?"

He didn't answer though. Just looked at her. Because he was still trying to find any kind of possible control he could. And because he couldn't get over how she had gotten into his head like that. It was exactly what he'd thought.

"Every time I came close to telling you the truth, I found myself seeing you walking away from me, and me running behind you saying, 'Belay my last. Belay my last. Just pretend I didn't say that. Delete button. Let's go back to five minutes ago.' And so I very selfishly chose to let us enjoy every single moment together until the last possible day. And yes, it was probably not the right thing to do, but it felt right being with you for the time we had together. And yes, I have no excuse for not coming clean before we left, but I was just so ashamed of deceiving you because you're such a good man. And there was no way I deserved to meet your parents. I just flat-out panicked, Philip. I loved you so much. You are everything I've ever looked for in a man. You stripped away my ability to reason."

She seemed to have forgotten they were in the library, so lost in his eyes and his pain. "Look, Lieutenant Johnston—"

"Fuck Lieutenant Johnston," he hissed.

Her mouth curved up in a smile. "Oh, I'd like that."

"It's not funny, Hallie."

"Can I call you Philip?"

"I don't know. I don't know anything right now. My whole life just changed in the last two hours. I need time to digest all of this." He bowed his head to absorb it all and remained quiet. "Give me some time to think. We can't meet like this again. Too many tongues will wag. I have a feeling you're going to be a very popular girl and everybody will be watching you. They're watching you right now. All I know is I need to go lick my wounds for a few days. Let's just leave it at that. Okay?" And he damn well hoped she didn't take up with someone else while he was doing that.

"Okay."

"And I mean it. Do not contact me in any way. Give me some time. As somebody recently said, I have some weird trust issues."

"Ouch."

Philip pushed back his chair because it was finally safe to stand up. He reached across the table to shake her hand, squeezing it against his better judgment.

Then said loud enough for the benefit of the other sailors, "You're welcome, McCabe. Hope that helps. Again, good job tonight."

He pushed in his chair and left her there to gather up her clipboard, her pen, and one linen handkerchief.

But just before he left the space, he walked back to add one more thing. "Oh, and McCabe?"

"Yes, sir?"

"Find a bobby pin."

Chapter 16

Hallie lay in her rack at midnight with the curtain closed, hoping she'd be able to sleep after unloading her burden.

Almost asleep, she jerked awake when her earphones piped in the strains of Eric Clapton's "Bell Bottom Blues." How many times had she and Philip made love to that song? Ha, did she ever have some bell-bottom blues now. She bet most of the kids on board didn't even know bell-bottoms had originated in the Navy, so sailors could roll their pants to swab the decks. She might not be wearing bell-bottoms anymore, but she sure as shit had the blues.

The lyrics reached down now and grabbed her in the gut, but she wasn't going to crawl across the floor and beg. She'd told Philip everything and now the ball was in his court. Shutting off the music, Hallie refused to feel guilty anymore. That had been her M.O. for close to two months now and she was done with it.

Maybe even jets taking off and landing overhead wouldn't disturb this first night of guilt-free sleep. She'd confessed the truth, and although he was noticeably upset, she knew Philip still cared for her. She could tell by the way he'd squeezed her hand and held on to it a heartbeat longer than necessary when he said goodbye.

What he was going to do about it was anybody's guess. He would definitely need time to process everything. She had promised him that she wouldn't contact him, but she would be available to talk if he ever wanted to. Hallie had repeated what she'd said in her letter:

"I will do whatever you want."

The most important thing was that he now knew for certain he'd done nothing wrong. It had torn her up that he might be beating himself up for something he hadn't been responsible for. She also felt lighter because now she'd have free movement on the ship again. She'd been hiding out since mid-June. Now she could go to the gym, the library, the ship's store, and topside for fresh air and sunshine.

Visiting liberty ports was more of an option now and she hoped he'd ask her to meet him somewhere so they could talk off the ship. That's all she expected from him. Talking. They were pulling into Palma Majorca, Spain in a few days and maybe he'd ask her to meet him there.

She was so hung up on the Philip thing, she'd forgotten how awesome the newscast had been. She knew it was good. She couldn't wait to get to work tomorrow to see if anybody had emailed her boss to comment.

Yes, this definitely deserved a goodnight's sleep.

After spending the last hour online reading about fraternization and the UCMJ, Philip climbed into his rack where he tossed and turned for most of the night. There was a lot to digest. He'd found nothing more than what he already knew.

Fraternization between officers and enlisted personnel had torpedoed and sunk many a commissioned officer's career.

And then his mind turned to Hallie and what she'd done. He thought about his sleepless nights trying to figure out what "we can't be together anymore" had meant. No way in his wildest dreams did he ever consider she might be a sailor. What was the first thing he'd said to her when he met her on the beach? "You a sailor?" How was that for irony? And what had been her answer?

"I can find my way around a boat."

It had been right in front of him the whole time. Staring him in the face every day. She'd been in the Navy and on his ship the entire time. Maybe he couldn't see the forest for the trees, maybe because the forest was so well camouflaged. Well, at least she wasn't a vampire. And definitely not a peacenik.

And then he thought about how good she'd been at keeping her secret. She'd pulled it off for over a month while they were on shore. Probably checked the UCMJ the day after she met him. She must've worked overtime to orchestrate all that sneaking around. Actually, he was flattered. She did all that so she could keep seeing him.

No wonder she didn't want her picture taken. Or go to a wardroom party with him. Or have dinner on the ship. But all that sneaking around must have been a lot of work and he couldn't imagine the stress. Why would she go to all that trouble? But the answer just kept coming back and smacking him upside the head.

Because she loved him, and she knew he'd end it if she told him the truth. He'd used the words "rule follower" the night they met when they talked about Rules of Engagement. Okay, so he let her know he followed the rules. She said that's what she liked about him.

But how could she have pulled it off without ever giving him a clue? Okay. One clue. Seventeen dead on the *Cole*. He bet very few sailors could quote that number off the top of their heads. But hadn't her knowing the number seventeen been the thing that had reached in and grabbed him by his beating heart? Wasn't that the moment when he looked past her beauty and realized she was The One? That she cared enough about the Navy to know that? And the Navy was his life. Philip knew without a shadow of a doubt he would be out of his mind to simply throw this away.

Well, he'd give Hallie this. She hadn't said, "Oh, come on. Fraternization isn't such a big deal. It goes on all the time." Because she knew it was a big deal to him. And he was the one whose head would roll if they were caught. So yes, an eventual reconciliation was definitely a possibility. But first he needed time to wrap his brain around the whole deception thing.

But how long? A week? A month? The whole cruise? Sky said there'd be a line waiting for her and Philip didn't want her looking for someone else. He saw the way the guys drooled over her in the wardroom tonight. And these were supposed to be the gentlemen on board. He could only imagine what the crew had been saying on the mess decks, let alone the reviews from the goat locker—the chief's quarters. He didn't even want to know what those old salts were saying about her.

He'd check with Sky tomorrow to see what the reaction had been up on the air wing. Any one of those flyboys would probably risk brig time for a night with Hallie. And the jet jocks? He didn't even want to go there, thinking of her father romancing her mother. She'd probably be receiving emails and proposals of marriage from every Tom, Dick, and Harry on board.

Okay, he wouldn't take too long to think all this over, but he wasn't going to give in right away, because he was still mad as hell.

And he hated not trusting her, but that birth control thing kept niggling at the back of his mind. She was probably telling the truth, considering how she had been accidentally conceived, but you never know. Not that a month ago he wouldn't have given the world to be married to her and father her children. But not like this. Not with deception involved, let alone the possibility of two ruined careers if she should pop up pregnant. How well did he really know her? He started doing the math in his head, but it had nothing to do with quadratic equations.

Philip rolled over and punched his pillow. Yeah, like he was going to get any sleep tonight. Maybe he and Hallie could eventually talk things out and figure out what to do, once he recovered from the shock. But he saw the reception she'd gotten in the library and he knew from the reaction in the wardroom that people would be watching her. Meeting too often with the same man, especially an officer, would spread scuttlebutt faster than gossip in a high school locker room.

So what about a private place? No. Couldn't be. There was no way he would be able to handle talking with her in her office at night, or God forbid, a deserted fan room, because he needed to be able to think with his brain. So what if they agreed to meet in a liberty port? They'd be in Palma in a few days. Get away from the ship for a few hours? Find a restaurant or a park or something? But his primal brain was pretty slick and he knew it would con him into making a beeline for the nearest hotel room. Pronto. Hell, an alleyway if it was dark enough. And although he had conceded that breaking rules might be a possibility in the future, first and foremost, they needed to talk.

Rashid lay awake in his rack plugged in to his K-Day playlist. As Pat Benatar serenaded him with *Hit Me With Your Best Shot*, he couldn't get Petty Officer McCabe out of his head. She had definitely been able to hold everyone's attention on the mess deck tonight. He would watch for the next month and if she continued to be so mesmerizing, he knew exactly when to time the attack: 1915 hours.

Right in the middle of *Blanchard* News Tonight.

Maybe some watchstanders would be too busy watching McCabe to pay attention to their duties. Hadn't that been essentially what the Master Chief had been talking about? Rashid would be more than happy to show the crew just how lust could destroy their lives—just like it had destroyed his. Too bad he couldn't figure out a way to take McCabe out with him. A woman who could draw men like that. Just like Rosie had done.

He had been such a fool about Rosie. He'd trusted her. The way she fawned over him whenever he was home. Cooking him whatever he wanted. Willing to do for him whatever his heart desired. In bed and out of bed. God knows she was amazing in the sack. That should have been another clue. She swore that he had been her only lover, so how did she know her way around the bedroom so well?

He should have guessed. The new big screen TV. The stereo equipment. Her new clothes. Everything she had supposedly bought with the big bucks she was making at her job at the salon. She wasn't making squat at her job. She was making the guys on his ship. Even some from his own division. They were spoiling her rotten. And they all knew she was his wife. How was that for loyal shipmates?

He hadn't caught her with anyone. He found out while having a beer at one of the clubs by the base. Just nursing a brew and minding his own business at the bar. They were a bunch of sailors from another division on the *Blanchard*, laughing at a table, just like the OSs did at chow time. Obviously they had no idea that the guy at the bar was the husband of "that incredible babe, Rosie." It might not have been so bad if they hadn't known his duty schedule and shared what nights she was available.

'Til death do us part? Right. Because first he'd wanted to kill them and then he'd wanted to kill her. But he would have just ended up in jail and not been able to punish anybody. So when Ibrahim had approached him with an offer, it made perfect sense to just take out the whole ship.

He'd show them.

Rashid had decided to bide his time and figure things out after he threw her out and filed for divorce. But then things got really bad for him, because he lost his housing allowance and had to move back on board the ship. Now he was surrounded by those very men who might have slept with his wife. He knew he was the laughingstock of the USS *Blanchard*.

The worst part had been going to his boss, the Combat Officer, Commander Haggman, and putting in for a compassionate transfer. No way would he be able to do his job well on this ship anymore. But did he get any compassion from him? No, he was told in so many words, "Sorry you can't satisfy your wife, but that's your problem, not the Navy's."

Fortunately, that was the very week he met Ibrahim, the only person who seemed to care about him. And within a week or two they'd become close enough to strike a deal. Rashid said he'd do whatever they asked as long as the last thing he saw in this life was the smile wiped off of the OSs' faces. And Commander Haggman's.

Oh, yeah, Haggman would be going down with him for sure.

Chapter 17

"Eat your hearts out guys, because I get to sleep on top of her every night!" Trixie told the boys in Engineering the next morning. Babe McCabe was now the hottest topic on the ship. "My rack is right above hers."

Philip turned to stone, his hands froze on the valve.

Trixie was Hallie's bunkmate? Oh, shit. But she didn't show any sign of knowledge, and he knew for a fact that Trixie wouldn't be able to hide it if she did. Trixie's mouth was that big. Surely Hallie had enough sense not to have shared him with Trixie. Hallie might not have always exercised the best judgment, but she wasn't stupid.

He listened carefully to all the scuttlebutt for the rest of the day.

Especially from Trixie.

His division pushed him to the limit however, when one of the guys asked her what Hallie had hanging on the clothesline. Philip stormed out of his office and lit into all of them. "Will you guys grow up? You are talking about one of your shipmates and it is totally inappropriate. Have a little respect."

He returned to his office but before he could slam the door, he overheard Trixie tell his men, "See, even Bill Gates has the hots for her." Then she laughed. "Wait. Maybe he got so upset because she's the chick that shitcanned his ass!" He was certain the round of laughter came from them picturing him putting the moves on the McBabe.

Oh, God. If they only knew. And thank you, God, that they didn't.

Philip endured more the next day when he heard Trixie debriefing the troops that Hallie had received sixty-eight personal emails from sailors wanting to meet her. Philip focused his eyes on his paperwork, but his ears were glued to her every word.

"McCabe never talks about anything personal. No way would she have shared that. But Marini, our other bunkmate, works with her and she said everybody's been emailing Public Affairs because they love the show. *But* the ones that email the McBabe directly are not exactly for public record—if you know what I mean."

They all laughed—except for one of them. Wasn't Marini that chick that came down with Trixie for a tour? As far as he knew, Sky was the only other person who knew about them, but were there others? He'd have to make a point of asking Hallie.

Once he was speaking to her again.

"She only opened, like, two emails, but she was so offended she block deleted the rest. God, she's such a prude." Trixie grinned. "I'd have opened every one of them and kept my dance book filled for the rest of the cruise. Anyway, all of you losers can forget about her, because Marini said there's only one name she ever looks for when she checks her mail. And it's not one of yours."

Philip stopped breathing.

"Some guy on the ship?" Bulldog asked.

Philip's heart stopped beating.

"Doubt it. She doesn't date anyone from the command. Apparently she's got some main squeeze back home. I think she was living with him or something before we left. Who knows? She never dishes any dirt."

Philip sucked in a lungful and blew out a long sigh of relief.

"Lucky bastard," somebody said.

"Yeah, well, you wouldn't want to sleep with her anyway. She snores."

Oh, God. He knew that.

He didn't like men emailing Hallie, even if she was deleting them unread. And what about all the smooth types, including officers, who would figure out how to chat her up in the gym, the coffee shop, or the store? He didn't want anybody hitting on her. Not only because she belonged with him. Did she? But because he knew how much it upset her. He wanted to protect her from those guys. Yeah, and jealousy had nothing to do with it. Right.

Finally the senior chief got on their case for gossiping, but when he closed with, "Besides, fellas, there's a lady present," he got some laughs over that one.

Philip glanced up and saw Trixie sock somebody on the arm and say, "Fuck you. I am too a lady."

But despite all the disturbing gossip, Philip wasn't ready to talk with Hallie yet. So he watched the news each evening and listened to the scuttlebutt Trixie brought down each morning, as he thought things over. And bided his time.

"I have an idea." Hallie sat with Lieutenant Latimer across from Commander Scott at his office. "What if I move around the ship during the day and tape a two-minute interview with people from a different division daily, then tack it on at the end of the news broadcast? Many people have no clue what goes on in other departments. I'm sure a mess cook in the galley doesn't know what goes on in Combat and vice versa. Obviously we wouldn't broadcast anything classified, but I think the sailors would love the chance to be on the news and learn about each other."

Hallie had presented her idea to the Deputy Public Affairs Officer, who thought it was a great idea, and together they'd approached the boss.

"I like it, McCabe. See, I knew you'd come up with good ideas to spice up this show," Commander Scott replied. "This is like a small town. Let the people get to know a little about the other people and some of the places they don't ordinarily see. Hey, why not start with the Captain? Then maybe the XO, the Command Master Chief, and the department heads?"

Hallie disagreed. "Starting with the CO might be a good idea, but the majority of people on this ship don't care about the lives and jobs of the officers. This would be for the crew, so I think we need to highlight their world. If they think one of their own might be speaking at the end of a broadcast, they're more likely to stay tuned."

Commander Scott turned to Lieutenant Latimer. "Let's do it," he said. "Let me check with Captain Amerson and see when it would be convenient for him to kick this thing off."

"Sounds good. Thanks so much for setting that up, sir." Hallie had only met the CO once during the fly-on. She'd seen him around the ship and heard him over the 1MC giving words of encouragement or relaying the latest information, much of which Hallie reiterated on the news each evening, but that was it.

She spent the next couple of days brainstorming a list of carefully thought-out questions for Captain Amerson and then a list of where she would head next. Air Ops? Medical? The Galley? Maybe Combat? Or maybe she'd go down in the hole to Engineering? She was already envisioning a compilation tape of the best of the interviews by the end of the cruise, which would look awesome in her portfolio. A sampling of everyone from the CO to the newest seaman recruit. What a terrific boost to her career this was going to be.

In the meantime she had to find time to get down to Sick Bay and maybe get some vitamins or something. Her job was exciting, but she felt run down all the time. Probably from working twelve hour days and not getting enough sleep with jets taking off at all hours of the night. Initially she'd slept better after telling Philip the truth, but it had been almost two weeks since they'd talked and he still hadn't made any kind of contact with her. So now she slept fitfully again, worrying.

He hadn't asked to see her and talk in Palma, even though they ended up on the same liberty launch to the beach. He'd totally ignored her. She wasn't able to get off the ship in Greece and wondered if he had, but he hadn't mentioned any chance of talking there either. She missed him with all her heart, but she said she'd do whatever he wanted. And no contact was apparently what he wanted. Maybe he needed more time, or maybe he was truly through with her.

Oh, well. His loss. Just wait until he saw how awesome the broadcasts were going to be with the interviews tucked in at the end. She reminded herself it was up to him to make the next move, so she'd just focus on her job and the new project. With everyone watching all the way through to see who'd be highlighted at the end of the broadcast, she'd have another jewel in her crown when she hit the broadcast world. If only she had a little more energy.

Philip was still furious, but damn it, he missed her. It seemed as if she was everywhere these days. Was it because he still loved her or because she moved about the ship freely now? He cringed each time he saw her, because there were always men with her.

She had to turn guys away while running on the treadmill, browsing in the store, or walking laps on the flight deck. He'd ended up on the same liberty launch with her headed to shore in Spain, but he didn't acknowledge her and she showed no sign of recognition. Hallie seemed to truly be letting him call the shots. She owed him that much after what she'd done. Trixie continued to bring scuttlebutt down in the hole each morning, but it was obvious she knew nothing about Philip and Hallie's relationship. Thank God for that.

One day Philip walked into the ship's store to get a birthday card for his mom. He noticed Hallie across the space, surrounded by three pilots in flight suits—obviously finding something they said to be very funny, because she threw back her golden head and laughed. Jealousy wrapped around his gut and squeezed. So much for her not liking attention from men. And what happened to her being allergic to flight suits? Hopefully she was too blinded by the jet jocks to notice him there. How could he leave without her seeing him? One lone engineer in a pair of blue coveralls and BCGs.

But she did see him. Hallie excused herself and slipped over next to him in the card racks. There were no words as they looked through the selection. Philip's nerve endings tingled when he inhaled her sweet, fruity scent. Lemons? With a side of coconut?

He briefly flashed to that day on the sailboat when she'd driven him insane with the sunscreen. He could never quite put his finger on her scent. All he knew was he wanted bury his face in her neck and hair and smell her up close and personal this very second, but he didn't so much as flinch.

Finally, without looking up, Hallie said, "Looking for something for your sweetheart, sir?"

His hands stilled. He, too, kept his eyes on the card he was holding. "I don't have a sweetheart, McCabe. How about you? Looking for a card for your sweetheart?"

"Apparently I don't have one either, sir." She continued to shuffle through the cards. "But yes, I am looking for something for a guy who I wish was my sweetheart. Unfortunately, they don't appear to make any 'Sorry I fucking slayed you' cards."

The corner of his mouth tried to tip up, but he forced himself not to laugh. "I'm surprised you don't have a sweetheart, McCabe. Seems there are thousands here to choose from."

"But there's only one cowboy I want in my rodeo."

Philip's breath hitched in his chest, but he didn't give in. He was still pissed from watching her laugh so naturally with those aviators. He looked at her now and nodded his chin toward them. "I'm surprised you'd even have time to think about your former sweetheart. Looks like you're pretty busy these days."

Her mouth dropped open and pure, outright hurt radiated from her face. She looked like he'd slapped her. "That's so not fair. I don't invite that."

"You invite it with your very presence, *McBabe.*"

Pain flashed in her eyes right before she executed a perfect about-face and marched out.

Aw, hell. That had been downright rude. Come on. She might have done a huge number on him, but she was never mean.

He selected two cards. One for his mother and another that didn't matter what it said. He didn't care. It had butterflies and flowers on it. He took it to his office, scratched out the printed words, and wrote inside.

Sorry I fucking slayed you with my thoughtless comments.

Then put it in ship's mail to her.

He was certain that she'd find it humorous, but she never responded. Well, what did he expect? He knew how much she hated the name, McBabe, but that damn green-eyed monster had made him say it.

So he was completely surprised when a few days later he received an email from Hallie marked "Urgent."

Something horrible has happened. Same place. 2130. Please. H.

Philip slammed his hand down on his desk. Shit. He knew it. She was pregnant. He'd done the math in his head the other night and now he knew it was true. Not that he didn't love her and want to have kids with her someday, but not like this. She would have to leave the ship but they wouldn't be able to marry until he got home unless he was charged with fraternization and faced charges.

Wait. What if the horrible something was that she'd left his card lying around and Trixie had found it? He knew he shouldn't have used ship's mail since anybody could have opened it. He hadn't signed the card, but what if Trixie knew—no, he was being paranoid.

Maybe somebody else on the ship had done something to her. Had some guy attacked her or something? He'd kill him. Plain and simple. But she wouldn't have done the news tonight if that had happened. No, she was pregnant. He'd noticed how drawn and tired she looked on the news lately, especially tonight. His engineering brain fast-forwarded to what he was going to do, but all he could think about was the way her father had treated her mother—and he wasn't going to do that. He'd made his bed and now he was going to lie in it. What had she said on the sailboat that first time and again on the news tonight when she talked about sunscreen? Something about paying later for mistakes you make in your twenties?

Just plain shit.

Philip grabbed a handkerchief. Yup. There'd be tears. And then he caught his reflection in the mirror and saw his heavy five o'clock shadow. Should he shave? Nah. It wasn't like there was going to be any kissing.

He walked into the library, stomach clenched, jaw tight, heart rate totally out of control. She was already at the table, looking haunted with dark smudges under her eyes. It felt like visiting day in prison as he crossed the room to meet her at a public table. And now she was going to give him the verdict.

Philip pulled out a chair and sat. His mind raced. His heart raced. The next minute could ring a death knell for his career.

Hallie pushed a piece of folded paper across the table.

It was so bad she had to write it down.

He looked at it lying there between them. His eyes flickered up to hers. She nodded toward the paper.

Anxiety coiled in the pit of Philip's stomach as he opened the note.

Captain Amerson is my father.

Chapter 18

Philip's heart started beating again. Hard. His chin dropped to his chest, forcing every breath of air from his body. Then he took off his glasses, laid them on the table, rubbed his eyes, and tried to clear his mind.

Overload.

The initial rush that Hallie wasn't pregnant was quickly surpassed by the impact of her note. His immediate reaction was that she'd nailed it. Not only the Captain's eyes—but the eyes of his son, Andy—popped into his head. And when he glanced up at the woman sitting across from him at the table? Those same eyes stared back at him. He'd never have put it together on his own, but he sure as shit would have gotten it on a multiple-choice test.

He knew he had seen her eyes somewhere before. They had haunted him but he could never put his finger on it. The first time he noticed had been right after they'd made love on the sailboat. Probably because he'd recently chatted with the Captain at a party. They had been talking about his son, Andy, who was Philip's classmate at the Naval Academy. Philip remembered thinking how much Andy looked like his dad, especially his eyes. His cornflower blue eyes, he now realized.

Just like the Thanksgiving dishes.

Philip exhaled another sigh of resignation and held up a single finger telling Hallie to hold on another second. Then he shut his eyes as the facts clicked into place like dominoes. He didn't understand the Rick part because the Captain's name was Andrew, so maybe "Rick" had lied to Hallie's mother, but everything else made perfect sense. Amerson had flown F-14 Tomcats, obviously in the late-eighties. The age would be right. About fifty. He was tall. Well over six feet. And as far as Philip knew, the CO was a classic jet jock type. A player. Handsome, smooth talking, and very charming with the women. Philip had witnessed it at every party at his house, and he knew his son had been. Probably still was.

Assy. That was what he, Nick, and Sky had called Andy Amerson at the Academy. Assy Amerson. Big lacrosse jock, midshipman battalion commander, ladies' man, and now a fucking jet jock himself, and most likely Hallie's half-brother. If Assy was any indication of how the Captain had behaved at that age, well then there you have it. He'd obviously learned from the master.

Big Assy and Little Assy. The all Navy Father/Son Prick Team.

Philip knew what he wanted to do, which was to walk around the table and take Hallie in his arms, but he had to think of what he could do.

Taking out a pen, he curled his left hand around and scribbled a note.

Fan Room 03-181–10Q 5 minutes

He slipped it to her and then walked out of the library. Now he was glad he had scoped out the fan rooms in a weak moment, just in case he decided they needed to talk. No matter what she'd done to him, Hallie needed him now. Once again in her life, she'd done nothing wrong, yet she was being punished.

It seemed like only a minute before she slipped into the fan room and into his waiting arms. Her tears started immediately.

"Oh, Philip, I'm sorry. I know you told me not to contact you, but I needed you so much. I didn't know who else to—"

"Shhh. It's okay. I'm right here. Everything's going to be all right," he mumbled into her hair as he held her tightly. God, it felt good to have his arms around her again. But that's not what they were here for. He pushed back from her, holding her at arm's length, to support her or to keep her body away from his, he wasn't sure which. "What's going on?"

"I found out the Captain's my father. It was awful."

"How?"

"I'm starting a new project, interviewing people for the broadcast each night and we decided to start with the CO. So I went up to his cabin today to chat with him before I interviewed him on camera. I had a whole list of questions, but as soon as I saw his eyes up close, I realized they looked familiar and I thought about my mom saying, 'You have his eyes.' I mean, I met him on the Bridge for the fly-on, but he was wearing sunglasses. You know, those aviator shades. No wonder I didn't see his eyes. I remember thinking about his being tall, but I didn't give it another thought because his first name is Andrew.

"Years ago I Googled all the Ricks and Richards who were pilots in the '80s, especially with Irish names, but they either flew the wrong aircraft or were stationed on the wrong coast. But all of a sudden today, I realized my mom might've made up his name to protect him, because the Captain's eyes were just so...and the whole time I was trying to wrap my brain around that, I realized..."

She started to hyperventilate, barely able to get the words out.

He took her by the shoulders. "Realized what?"

Her lips trembled. "That he was looking at me like the other guys on the ship do. He was..."

Fresh tears.

"Son of a bitch!" he yelled, slamming the bulkhead with his flat hand, not caring who heard them. "He hit on you?"

Philip reached for the door, but she stopped him. Good thing too, because he was so lost in a testosterone fog, he would've made a freaking fool of himself.

Hallie pulled herself together and continued. "Well, he said a few things I didn't like, but mostly it was the way he looked at me that was all wrong. I could have handled it if I wasn't trying to figure out if he was my father at the same time. I was already creeped out about the Rick thing but now my guy-dar was going berserk."

Philip took her in his arms again, rocking her, stroking her back, and mumbling comforting words to her. Then he gently pulled away, his eyes direct and probing. "Are you sure he didn't do anything he shouldn't have besides look at you? Did he?"

She turned and looked at the door. "Shhh. Keep it down. It's okay."

"No, it's not okay. I want to know every single thing that happened up there!"

"It wasn't so much what he said or did, just how he looked at me. Women pick up on that, even when men don't think we know that they're checking us out. Maybe I read him wrong, but I've been dealing with men for a long time, and he gave me the creeps."

"That asshole!" Philip let her go and started pacing in the tight space. It was ingrained in his genes to want to protect her. And the frustration built because he was powerless to do it. He turned to her. "Why'd you go up there alone?"

"Because I didn't know there was any reason not to. Are you saying this was my fault?"

He reached for her again and kissed her forehead. "No, you didn't do anything wrong. It's not your fault." She couldn't help it if every man on the ship was in love with her. Even the CO. "He was the one who was a fool for not having a female officer in there too. Probably wanted to have some private time with the hot new newscaster. And the guy's up for admiral. What an idiot. What did he say to you? I want to know everything."

Hallie's eyes sparkled as she removed some papers from her pocket. "I'm a reporter, remember? I took notes."

Philip shook his head in disbelief at just how good she was.

"As soon as I realized he was being too familiar with me and then, that he might be 'Rick,' I jotted everything down. And when I got back to my desk, I typed it up. Just in case I ever need it."

Hallie opened the papers and told him the story.

* * *

"At ease, Petty Officer McCabe," the Captain had said when she entered his at-sea cabin and stood at attention. "Have a seat."

"Thank you, sir, for granting me this time. I appreciate it."

"No problem. This is a pleasant interruption to an otherwise hectic day. Gives me a chance to tell you what an outstanding job you're doing on the nightly news. Not only have you improved morale around here since you took over the show, but your shipmates look forward to it every night, Hallie."

Hallie?

Her first thought was how inappropriate for the CO to be calling a second-class petty officer by her first name. Especially the first time he met her. Alone in his cabin. While sporting a smile that tap danced damn close to the PC boundary line, with a twinkle in his blue eyes that definitely did not belong there.

"McCabe will be fine, sir." And just as she'd re-established that boundary, she realized his bright blue almond-shaped eyes were identical to the ones that stared back at her in the mirror every morning.

What did Philip call them? Cornflower blue?

Rick?

Wait. The Captain's name was Andrew. No way could this be Rick. Hallie glanced at the embroidered wings over the breast pocket of his blue camouflage uniform. There were lots of pilots that age who were not Rick.

And hadn't her mom called him her big, strong Irishman? Wasn't Amerson Swedish or something?

"Thank you, sir, but I don't do the show alone. There is a dedicated group of MCs in Public Affairs who are behind me, doing most of the work."

How she managed to speak, she didn't know. Buckets of adrenaline dumped into her bloodstream as fight or flight impulses vied with each other: One cried: "Tear the bastard limb from limb," while the other screamed, "Get the hell out of here!" Tendrils of panic curled through her gut like roots in photography. Her mind Googled every detail her mom had ever told her about Rick.

"You got his height too," her mom had said.

The Captain was obviously tall, but how tall? Based on the length of his arms, he could easily stand six-foot-three.

"Yes, but you're the one we see. You've become the head cheerleader on the *Blanchard*, McCabe. You have single-handedly put a spring in every sailor's step lately and I appreciate that."

His cool blue eyes continued to fixate on her cool blue eyes. He showed no sign of recognition and why should he? This couldn't be Rick and even if it was, Rick didn't even know she existed.

Did he?

"We all like having you bring us the news every night, even when it's bad news. So I'm glad I got this chance to tell you how much I've been enjoying watching you." A disarming smile seemed to lock in those last five words.

Her body and soul went to high alert, double time. Either the fact that he was looking at her the same way the younger pilots did or the fact that he could possibly be her father was bad enough. Trying to process both thoughts at the same time was over the top. The "Get the hell out of here" voice was currently winning, but Hallie couldn't move. Panic had now turned to paralysis. She acknowledged this as shock. It was the body's way of caring for itself when it can't process something horrific and simply shuts down.

But then Philip's words came back to her: "I happen to know you're very good at pretending." And her mother's: "I have a daughter with balls." And then she almost burst out laughing because now John Paul Jones was in the mix: "I have not yet begun to fight!"

And as quickly as panic had overtaken her, a sense of calm and peace washed through her, as if her mom was hugging her and reminding her she could handle this. Besides, he couldn't be Rick. He just couldn't be.

"I beg your pardon, sir?"

The leer factor slid from his face and he looked away before responding. "Well, I'm just saying that the crew likes hearing what you have to say, McCabe. They're all watching every night and that's important, because you have valuable information to share."

He sounded like a freakin' politician because that was not what he'd said. But by calling him on it, she felt a shift in the balance of power. She now knew that he knew she did not tolerate harassment. And no way was she leaving, not yet. Not until she verified he was not Rick. And while she was asking, she'd better write down every single thing that transpired. Because whatever did happen, it would be her word against his.

Nobody took the wind out of Hallie McCabe's sails.

"I try to do my job the best I can. I have some questions for you, sir, if you have the time. This won't take long."

They proceeded with the interview, discussing the current mission and his background. When he described his former flying days in F-14 Tomcats, Hallie swallowed hard, but realized there were lots of former F-14 pilots out there and although her father had been one of them, it probably wasn't this one named Andrew.

This tall man. With her eyes.

"You know the F-14 was a helluva jet. Though landing one on a pitching carrier deck could be a little like wrestling an elephant. I enjoyed flying them. Guess I'm getting old now." A slow smile tipped up his mouth. "The Navy retired them in 2006. The F/A-18 Super Hornet, which can practically fly itself, totally took over. My son's flying those now."

"Your son? Oh, sir, you couldn't possibly have a son old enough to fly F-18's."

Flattery would get her whatever information she wanted. Because if he had had a son flying F-18's, he would have to be older than her. And certainly Rick hadn't left a baby at home with his wife while he was romancing Suzanne.

"Oh, Andy's twenty-seven. With the Flying Jacks out of Miramar."

So if he was Rick, he was a double bastard.

"Oh. Well, I wonder if you'd mind helping me out with something while I'm here, sir. I'm taking an online course in international diplomacy and we're discussing U.S. relations with Asia over the years. Did you ever go on a West Pac cruise? Maybe see some action near North Korea?"

"Yes, when I was with the Salty Dawgs. We were attached to the *Kitty Hawk*. We did fly some sorties, checking out things along the DMZ and near North Korea's borders. We were flying..."

She let him talk, but just as he seemed close to finishing, she interrupted. "Did you ever visit Japan, sir? I've always been fascinated by Japan. I even tried to get stationed there." Hallie pulled out her most enthusiastic "head cheerleader of the *Blanchard*" smile.

Amerson chuckled. "Yes, lots of good times in Japan." His mouth curved into a slow, lazy smile. "Beautiful country. We spent a couple of weeks there. The *Kitty Hawk* needed some emergency repairs so we pulled into the shipyard. Good liberty in Japan."

Amusement lit his face as he waxed and waned about the good old days in Japan: flying over Mt. Fuji, trips to Tokyo, sushi, summer festivals, all she could think about was her mom waxing and waning—over too many glasses of wine—about meeting Rick when he came ashore for liberty. Just long enough to woo her and get her pregnant.

"Oh, so you were at the shipyard in Yokosuka, sir?"

"No, the *ship* was in Yokosuka, but we flew the aircraft to the air base. Didn't want the planes sitting there in the shipyard."

"You mean the air facility at Atsugi?"

Another good humored grin as he tripped down Memory Lane. "Yeah, we were in and out of Atsugi a lot that summer."

"And what summer would that be, sir?"

"Let's see. That was the cruise when...so that would be..."

Let's see. The summer you were screwing Suzie Q. Andy Junior was two...so...1986?

"1986."

Hallie scribbled away as the puzzle pieces clicked into place.

She flew on autopilot, getting everything down in black and white so she could peruse her notes later while she put the rest of the puzzle together. She ended the interview and came to attention, clutching her clipboard. "Thank you, sir. I'll pick out a few questions for tomorrow. Please let me know when would be a good time to come back with my camera crew and we'll film for the broadcast. Permission to depart, sir."

He stood up and that's when she saw he was clearly six-foot-three. "Tomorrow's fine. Feel free to come up and see me anytime, McCabe. Just call ahead. Keep up the good work on the news." And then looking her right in the eye and smiling one more time, he said, "If there's ever anything you need, you know where I am. Carry on."

It hit her like a ton of bricks just as she reached the door. Out of the blue. As if a voice whispered in her ear. Philip had never called Sky anything but "Sky," although it wasn't his given name. It seemed everybody in the Navy had a nickname, especially aviators. So maybe?

"Excuse me, sir, but I have one more question for you, if you don't mind."

"Shoot."

"What was your call sign when you flew F-14's? Pilots always have interesting call signs, usually with a funny story behind them. Care to share?"

Captain Amerson laughed. "Well, now that is an embarrassing story, and no, I don't care to share its origins with you. But since my call sign is probably well known within the air wing, I guess I can share it with you. It's 'Ricochet.'"

Rick O'Shea.

My big, strong Irishman.

Game. Point. Match.

Chapter 19

Philip folded her in his arms again. "You're going to make one hell of an investigative reporter." He'd only interrupted her twice. When the CO called her by her first name and when he said that he was enjoying watching her.

But damn if Philip wasn't proud of her for calling him out on both occasions. Hallie had never told him her mom's line about having a daughter with balls and he thought it described her perfectly. And John Paul Jones? Only Hallie could find humor in a situation like that. Hallie McCabe could take care of herself. Another reason he loved her so much.

But her bravado was fading fast and he saw the pain return to her face. "I held it together while I was in there, but once I left I fell apart."

Hallie had wanted to vomit. Her own father flirting with her. Wasn't verifying that he was her father bad enough? But to have him come on to her like that. She ducked into the nearest female head and did vomit, until there was nothing left. Then she shut the door and sobbed against the bulkhead. Shock had turned to pain and then to anger. The son of a bitch! All she could think about was taking a shower. He'd made her skin crawl.

Knowing her chief wouldn't know how long she'd be with the CO, Hallie cleaned herself up, went back to her quarters, stumbled into the head there, and dry heaved. Gasping and choking and crying. There wasn't even a place where she could go and have some privacy to deal with this. Hallie stripped off her clothes and climbed into the shower.

Immersing herself in warm water, she wished for her mother. She was torn between the loneliness of missing her and the hatred she felt for her mom ever being with that man. Hallie cried with the anguish of knowing the Captain was Rick and then she doubled over with the emotional pain that he'd been so familiar with her. With those eyes. *Her* eyes. All the longings of wanting a dad in her life caused her to crumple to the deck, when she thought about Captain Amerson being that man.

But wait. Rick wasn't her dad. Her mother had been right. Rick was a bastard.

The water turned cold, letting her know two minutes were up. Reality reared its ugly head. All she wanted to do was to dry off and go crawl into her rack. Curl up into a ball and never get up. In a perfect world, she'd curl up in Philip's arms and let him rock her while she cried.

Not make love. Just cry. And rock. And he'd understand. He wouldn't ask her anything. He wouldn't ask for anything. He'd just hold her. And soothe her. Because that's the kind of man he was. A real man. A man she could count on. But she couldn't go to him. He wasn't a part of her life anymore and that was her own fault.

And she couldn't climb into her rack either. She had a show to broadcast in three hours. And she had work to do. First she had to clean herself up and then she had a few things she was planning to say on tonight's show. Trying to pretend she wasn't on the verge of a panic attack wasn't going to be easy, but as Philip had said, she was pretty good at pretending. So Hallie pulled herself together.

Dressing in a clean uniform, she dried her hair and put on make-up. The very thought of Captain Amerson "enjoying watching her" on the TV made her stomach cramp up all over again.

"Okay, Mom. He beat each of us once, but he's not going to beat us again."

* * *

It was all Philip could do to restrain himself, both from wanting to kill the CO and wanting to kiss Hallie. But he just stood there with his arms around her, whispering endearing words, swirling comforting strokes up and down her back. Holding her close and letting her cry. She clutched him like a lifeline. His heart swelled and surely it would burst with how good it felt to have her in his arms again.

Hallie raised her head to look at him through her tears and then grabbed him around the neck, pulled his mouth to hers, and kissed him hard and rough, taking away all his restraint. She whimpered and moaned at the same time. A cross between pain and desire. He hadn't kissed her in weeks, since the night she'd told him goodbye, and he had his own pain to exorcise.

This kiss was not their usual. Neither slow, nor deep. It was shallow and hungry and ruthless. Their hands were all over each other, demanding and greedy. His massaging her breasts, hers now in his back pockets, cupping his ass, bringing him closer to her. And still their kiss went on.

They tried to climb inside of each other and be one soul again.

Philip backed her against the door and writhed against her. And with her. Angry, demanding, ceaseless. All the pent-up tensions of the past month crying for release.

Frustration tore at him trying to feel her breasts through the thick pockets of her aquaflage. He slid his hands up under her shirt, ripping her T-shirt from the waist of her uniform pants.

His hands glided up her smooth stomach until they found her lace-covered breasts. He massaged them roughly, then caught himself, slowed down, and settled for stroking her nipples with the pads of this thumbs. Moans escaped from her mouth into his and he sucked them down to blend with his own sounds.

He unclasped her bra in the front and was nearly brought to his knees when her breasts spilled into his waiting hands. But it wasn't nearly good enough. He needed to have his mouth on her, to feel her heat and taste her skin.

His hips continued to grind Hallie into the bulkhead and Hallie ground right back. He slipped his hands out to unbutton her shirt, mouth plundering hers, while his nimble fingers worked. Philip pulled her shirt apart and pulled up her T-shirt, his mouth zeroing in on a nipple. Suckling, his groans mingled with her quiet moans.

Philip didn't know what they were going to do or how they were going to do it, but his primal brain told him he needed to make her his own once again.

He returned to her mouth, his hands making love to her breasts. Hallie reached for the zipper on his coveralls, her other hand stroking him through the fabric. A jolt of fire slammed into him and he practically went through the steel overhead.

Too impatient to fiddle with snaps and zippers and thankful for the elastic waist in aquaflage pants, Philip hooked his thumbs in Hallie's belt loops and yanked her pants halfway to her knees in one swift motion.

She grabbed for them. "No!" she whisper-cried. "We can't do this!"

He jerked away from her, turned, and placed his hands flat on the bulkhead, gulping in air. "You're right. I'm sorry I..."

Hallie pulled her uniform pants back up, reached under her T-shirt to hook her bra. "No, it's my fault, Philip. I'm sorry I started that." She tucked her T-shirt in, started buttoning her shirt. "I want you so much, but there's no way we can do this."

He rested his head against the cool, gray steel and tried in vain to catch his breath.

"Do you have any idea what could happen to you if..."

"Me? Not just me, Hallie. We've got your career to think about too." He sucked in a deep breath and blew it out again. "I've just missed you so damn much."

"You have?" Hallie finished buttoning her shirt, finger-combed her hair.

He turned just his head and looked at her in disbelief, his hands still leaning against the bulkhead. "Oh, God, are you kidding? You don't know how hard it's been to see you and not be able to be with you. To hold you."

"To talk to me? To write to me? To let me know if there's a chance for us?" she added pleadingly.

"I'm sorry I've been acting like such an ass."

"No. You had every right after what I did. But I've been so afraid that you'll never forgive me. I love you so much, Philip." She tried to hug him, but he took her by her forearms and kept her at a distance.

"Hallie, I was angry at you, but I never stopped loving you. I know you got in over your head and then you were trying to protect me. And you were right. I probably would have walked away if you'd told me the truth in the beginning. But I honest to God cannot imagine living my life without you. I'm sorry."

"I just need to know there's a chance we can be together again. Maybe not now, but in the future. When the cruise is over. When I get out of the Navy. When it's safe. I'll be fine as long as I know there's a chance."

Philip melted. "Look, we're pulling into Port Said in a few days. We'll get off the ship and go somewhere. We can talk about us and Rick and what we're going to do about everything. Because we can't meet like this. I'm sorry things got out of hand. And anyway, I suppose sex isn't necessarily the best antidote for being harassed or hit on. Can you hold on for a couple days and then we'll meet and talk?"

"Yes. Thank you."

"Don't do anything until then, except to stay clear of the CO. If that son of a bitch comes near you, call me on my brick. I mean it. Radio me. Don't email me. Don't send a note. Call me. I'll be there."

"I have to go back up there tomorrow to film the segment."

"No way. You stay away from him."

"I'll be okay. I'll have James Hall, my cameraman, with me, and I'll ask Lieutenant Latimer to go too. Besides," She raised an amused eyebrow. "If he tries anything, I'll just ask him to tell me if he knew an AG2 Suzanne Chandler in Atsugi in 1986." A trace of humor lit her eyes. "And I'll have his response on film. Don't worry. I can take care of myself."

"Okay. But I'd rather you didn't go anywhere alone on this ship anymore. I'd prefer you have someone you trust with you always. You don't hear the kinds of things I hear. Just sit on everything until we get to Egypt. Can you do that? Can you keep this Rick thing under your hat until then? We'll meet somewhere in town, so we can talk and I can hold you and love you. Will you be okay until we can meet?"

"I will now." She smiled a gentle, trembling smile. "All I needed to know is that you still love me." Her blue eyes took on an inner glow.

He wanted to kiss her so badly. His eyes dropped to her lips, but he forced them back to her waiting eyes. "I do love you, Hallie. By the way, in the future, don't send a guy you had unprotected sex with a month ago an urgent email saying 'Something horrible has happened. Story at 2130.' Okay?" He rolled his eyes, a wry edge to his mouth.

"What?"

"Hallie. I thought you were pregnant."

"Pregnant? We've never had unprotected sex. I would never do that. Look how I came to be."

"From my point of view, it could very well have been unprotected. Please understand where I'm coming from. That's all I'm asking."

Hallie winced. "Ouch. Weird trust issues?"

"Something like that."

"I'm so sorry," Hallie said.

"I know. It's all right now, but you scared the crap out of me. Okay, write me tomorrow and tell me how the filming went. Call me right away if you need me. I mean it. Just remember that the phones are non-secure lines. And no more emails. Oh, and promise me Trixie knows nothing about us."

"Nothing. Just that I have a boyfriend back home."

"I assumed so because she wouldn't be able to keep a secret if she knew about us, but we need to talk about a lot of things in Egypt. Okay?"

This time when he hugged her he held the embrace, but he didn't kiss her. He knew better. Philip leaned away from her and pulled down the golden tendril, playing with it.

"Don't worry. Everything's going to be okay. I promise. And Hallie? Remember. I love you." He kissed her on the forehead, cracked the door, scanned the passageway, patted her on the bottom, and sent her out.

Philip couldn't believe what they'd almost done. What had she said? "You stripped away my ability to reason?" Well, she sure as shit had stripped away his tonight. And then he thought about why she'd contacted him. The son of a bitch had hit on her. Maybe he hadn't thought he did, but if he made Hallie uncomfortable, then he had. Philip wanted to strangle him. Hallie. His Hallie. The fucking CO of the ship. And he was her father. Not that he knew it, of course, but the reason he didn't was because he was a prick.

Philip had always thought Amerson was a slick guy. Probably smart too. He knew just how much he could get away with before she filed a harassment complaint against him. He had no business meeting with her in his cabin alone. But he'd probably planned it that way.

But, oh, how good it had felt to hold her. Hallie, back in his arms again. Her body. Her breasts. Her lips. Her. He'd missed her so much and he wanted her so badly. He'd never get to sleep tonight thinking about her stroking him.

Thank God she'd had the presence of mind to stop them. If they'd gotten caught, not only would there have been severe consequences for him, but he doubted CNN would want to know she'd gone to Captain's Mast for frigging in the rigging when she was in the Navy.

And then all his anger and desire dissolved into humor. First he grinned like a fool, then he shook with laughter that echoed off the bulkheads. All tension drained from him when he realized a fan room on a Navy ship would definitely not be a good place to have illicit sex with a screamer.

Chapter 20

"Ramadan is a time of fasting—refraining from eating, drinking, smoking, or having sexual relations from sun-up to sun-down from the new moon of the ninth month in the Muslim calendar until the new moon on Eid al Fitr."

Rashid pushed his tray aside, food unfinished, to focus on McCabe's broadcast. He didn't give two hoots in hell about Ramadan, but he did feel a certain rush whenever he watched McCabe. It wasn't exactly sexual energy, but it was just as potent.

Maybe it was the fact that he held her pretty-girl life in his hands?

"Fasting is meant to teach Muslims patience, humility, appreciation, and spirituality. The devout are expected to show their devotion through self-restraint and good deeds. Not only by fasting, but also by saying extra prayers and helping those less fortunate."

He wondered if Ibrahim was observing Ramadan back in Jacksonville. Must be hard with the punks walking around with their sodas and the smells from the food court wafting into the kiosks. And he was pretty sure Ibrahim was a smoker. That would make for a long day too.

McCabe smiled at the camera. "The faithful begin observing Ramadan at puberty. Children are exempt, although many practice a scaled-down version. The elderly, pregnant and nursing mothers, and those who are chronically or mentally ill are exempt."

Would his sadiqs qualify as mentally ill? There was a fine line between fanaticism and mental illness—if there was one at all. Some might say he was mentally ill, plotting what he was about to do to the ship. But he disagreed.

His heart thudded when he found himself finally able to put it into words. Sometimes people just needed to take justice into their own hands.

Ibrahim had shared some inside stories of Ramadan. Because the date changed by eleven days every year, it occurred at different times in the solar calendar year. Winter wasn't a problem. It was easy to go without water during the daylight hours in winter. But when it occurred in summer, like it did this year, it was very difficult. And he'd said some people were so devout they not only abstained from drinking water, but refused to swallow their own spit all day too.

Crazy ragheads.

It was supposed to teach people what it felt like to do without, but Ibrahim said the well-to-do played the system and slept all day, rising at sunset for Maghrib prayer, and then spending the nights eating, drinking, and making merry. Didn't sound like much of a religious sacrifice to Rashid. The fuckers at the bottom of the food chain had to endure the heat and go without water from dawn to dusk. Just like back in the States, life sucked for the poor man.

"The word, Ramadan, came from the words, *ramida* or *ar-ramad*, meaning intense heat or scorched earth and shortness of food. The daily deprivation humbles the people and reminds them of those less fortunate, who do not have enough food or water. Water being more important even than food to those living in a desert-type environment."

Rashi smiled at the thought of the Muslims on board the *Blanchard*, some even observing Ramadan. They were quiet, pleasant, decent guys and girls. Probably what the majority of Muslims were like. But he bet security followed their asses twenty-four seven, at a distance of course. Wouldn't want to be accused of racial profiling.

His heart raced and a rush of pleasure surged through his veins. Too bad the *Blanchard's* cops were barking up the wrong tree. And expecting problems on the wrong day.

"Because Ramadan is a festival month of giving and sharing, Muslims prepare special foods and bring gifts for their family and friends. They also give to the poor and needy who cannot afford to celebrate. This holy month is also a time to slow down from worldly affairs and to focus on self-reformation, spiritual cleansing, and enlightenment. A time to establish a link between themselves and God through prayer, charity, good deeds, kindness, and helping others. Everything culminates with celebrations and fireworks on Eid, the final night of Ramadan."

A grin spread through Rashid's soul as he thought of the gifts—and the fireworks—the sadiqs would be bringing the crew of the USS *Blanchard* on Eid this year.

"Since Ramadan has already begun, I'm going to turn this broadcast over to the Command Master Chief, who will discuss limited liberty in Port Said. Master Chief."

"Thank you, Petty Officer McCabe. Let me start by stating that Ramadan is not a good time for American sailors to hit a liberty port in a Muslim country."

Hallie's heart stopped.

Was there to be no liberty? All she needed was one day or night on the beach with Philip to discuss Rick, and hopefully get a chance to—no. She shouldn't even be thinking about making love with Philip. The risk was too high. But maybe just a few hours alone so they could talk. Really talk. Just to be with him for a few hours without having to look over their shoulders.

"However," the Master Chief continued, "Port Said isn't your typical Muslim city. Being as it's the northern hub of the Suez Canal, the city caters to sailors, so it's a little more lax about Ramadan rules. Heck, they serve beer and that's more than many Muslim cities do—although you'll have to wait until sunset on this visit. Anyway, sailors are their best customers so merchants are dependent upon our business." He smiled. "And we certainly want to do our part to spread American goodwill around the world, now don't we?"

Hallie and the film crew chuckled.

"Not that Uncle Sam hasn't already contributed to Egypt's economy by paying a quarter million dollars for the Carrier Strike Group to transit the canal later in the week, but I figure we're good for a couple more bucks. So, it's been decided that a few hundred carefully selected members of the *Blanchard* will be allowed liberty in Port Said during our proposed three-day replenishing stay. It's going to be a different group each day. And, trust me, you will be carefully selected. The Navy is not about to allow anyone with a single strike in their disciplinary record to go ashore in a Muslim country during their holy month. We're only sending ambassadors."

Hallie expelled the breath she was holding. Yay, it was possible they could still meet up. Neither she nor Philip had any disciplinary action—but only because they hadn't been caught, her guilty conscience added.

The CMC took a sip from a water bottle and cleared his throat. "Those crewmembers who did not get liberty in Greece will be considered first—but remember, you will be carefully screened."

Hallie's heart raced. Had Philip gone ashore in Greece? She hadn't, but what if he had? Relax, she told herself. He would find a way for them to be together.

"Those who are chosen will take launches in starting at 1600 hours and you better be back on this ship by 0200 the next morning when the last launch returns. Don't even think about staying out all night or you will not only find your ass in a sling, but you can kiss any more liberty for the entire cruise goodbye. Since the restaurants and bars won't even open until dusk, there's no reason to start launches any earlier.

"You will not eat, drink, or smoke in public until after sunset. Let me say that again. You will respect local residents and culture and you will not eat, drink, or smoke in public until evening prayer is called. And I cannot emphasize the following enough: Not having sexual relations goes without saying. I don't care what time of day it is. So if you didn't go ashore in Greece and your record's clean, go ahead and submit chits to your chief and we'll post a schedule of who gets to go ashore and when. If you need more information on appropriate Ramadan behavior, there's plenty to research on the Internet. That is all."

Hallie crossed her fingers under the broadcast desk, hoping with all her heart that Philip had not gone ashore in Greece, and that all his possible research centered around hotels.

Chapter 21

The first time he was going to *knowingly* have sexual relations with a subordinate, Philip Johnston was going to make it worth his while. All of his training, all the rules and etiquette he'd learned since his first days at Annapolis were checked at the door. He knew full well what he was about to do and he took complete responsibility for it.

Right down to booking a room in a five-star hotel.

Hallie and Philip took separate cabs to the hotel. While he waited for her, he paced the room, deep in thought. He'd done a lot of thinking over the past three days and realized they had to come up with some kind of a plan. They would not be able to rendezvous any more after this, either on the ship or off.

At least not until they returned to the States.

Today was one thing. They needed to talk. But after this, it was too dangerous. He shuddered when he thought of how close they'd come to losing control in the fan room. It was like his brain had lost all reason, and his body had been more than happy to take charge. There was no way they could meet in another clandestine spot on board the ship. He didn't trust himself. And meeting too many times in public would definitely fuel the rumor mill. So if he wasn't going to be able to be with her, how was he going to deal with five more months of watching her being hit on by every swinging dick on board? Ad nauseum. And it wasn't just him being jealous. Hallie didn't like it either. But he couldn't exactly broadcast that she had given him her heart.

Or could he?

What if he asked her to marry him? What if he put a ring on her finger? What if the entire ship knew Petty Officer McCabe was engaged? Promised to some nameless, lucky guy back home? He hadn't wanted to rush things, but he'd been prepared to propose to her in Florida before he left, so the male population back there would know she was off the market. Little did he know she wouldn't be hanging around Jacksonville while he was gone. She'd be at sea with forty-five hundred horny guys on a Navy ship on a six-month cruise.

Proposing made perfect sense. But she hadn't exactly jumped at the idea back in Florida. Was it because of her secret or was it him she didn't want?

As he paced back and forth, Philip repeatedly ran his fingers through his hair, like he was going to find the answer there. Suddenly he stopped cold. Damn it. He was thinking with his head again, like he'd always done, except for that night in the fan room. He needed to think with his heart. Not easy for a left-brained engineer. Take the project apart and examine each part to determine...Fuck it. No way was he going to let Hallie get away again. The very idea of those aviators making her laugh in the ship's store roiled in his gut.

Philip was going to jump in with both feet and propose. And then all he had to do was figure out a way to get an engagement ring sent from the States and onto her hand for everyone to see.

Okay, so it was worth a shot. But she also had to agree to table their relationship until spring. He would not do this sneaking around stuff for five more months. The Command Master Chief had been right. Shipboard relationships played havoc on the mission.

As he paced, anticipating her arrival, he thought about how much he wanted to take her today, devour her, and mark her as his own. However, today was definitely the time to be a gentleman—especially if he was going to propose—so he would have to restrain himself. Hallie was in pain, still smarting from the shock of Rick, and she'd need tenderness and care.

So he put on his gentleman face and answered the knock at the door.

But the minute he saw Hallie in the doorway, his primal brain took charge and he forgot everything except losing himself in her. Love first. Talk later. There was no thought of manners or following rules or mission or Ramadan or happily ever after. There was just wild, primal lust. All he could think of was that night in the fan room and how much he'd wanted to back her up against the door and consume her.

And it was obvious Hallie felt the same way. The second she saw him, she flew into his arms, her mouth searching for his. They barely shut the door before he had her against it, blindly fumbling for the locks while he devoured her mouth, his hands rifling her clothes, needing to touch her, taste her. Ripping and tearing at each other's clothing, they murmured words of want. Of need. Of how much they'd missed each other.

"Do you have any idea how much—?" Philip started, before he was cut off by her tongue plundering his mouth. He only left her mouth long enough to find her breasts, now bared to him, allowing her to speak.

She managed to squeak out the words, "I've missed you so—" before his mouth again rendered her speechless. And not because he had covered it with his own. His lips and tongue on her breasts had taken her breath away.

Love now. Talk later.

He ravished her breast while fumbling for the button of her jeans. His hands shook pulling down the zipper.

Oh, hell. He was toast. She was wearing those purple skivvies. There was no way they were even going to make it to the bed now. Sliding her jeans down, he knelt and kissed her through the lace of her thong, stroking her bare ass with his thumbs, pulling her closer to his mouth.

All he could think of were the past three days of longing. Of wanting to take her in that fan room. Against the door. Even though her uniform had not been cooperative, he knew damn well he would've found a way. Thank God she'd brought them back to reality, because he sure as shit hadn't been able to think with his brain. He would have sacrificed his country to be inside her that night, had she not had some blood left in *her* brain.

But now? Even though he had her nailed against a hotel room door, his mind was back in that fan room and no way in hell was he stopping, even to move it to the bed. He doubted his legs could carry them there anyway. Especially with her encouraging him, murmuring how much she missed him and loved him and needed him and how good it felt to have his mouth on her again.

Hearing the telltale signs she was working up to a scream,

Philip stood and silenced her with his mouth. Just what he needed. Hallie coming apart at the seams and making too much noise with only a door separating them from the chambermaids in the hallway.

In a Muslim country.

During Ramadan.

Before sunset.

Hallie broke the kiss. "Oh, God, Philip, I need you now. *Please.*"

He yanked off her thong and jeans and somehow managed to unzip his own jeans. Philip couldn't fathom the idea of removing them, his need was so great. He slammed into her, filling her to the hilt, leaving her gasping. Hallie hooked a leg around his hip and reached around to bring him as close as possible, merging souls. How perfect it felt to be back where he belonged. Inside Hallie.

Her moaning intensified, alternating between mumbling his name and the Almighty's, growing to a fevered pitch. She grabbed his hips, wildly twisting them back and forth to merge him with her sweet spot, so out of control her head banged against the door, mouth open—no sound coming from it, thank God.

Philip slipped his fingers between Hallie's legs to help her over the edge and then watched through hooded eyes as she rocketed to her climax, her head thrashing from side to side, her voice keening.

He captured her mouth with his own, swallowing the scream, absorbing it into the marrow of his bones. And for one split second, he imagined them doing this in uniform. Against another door. In another room. On the ship. Her scream echoing down the steel passageways, leaving no doubt to anyone listening that he was her man. The image hit him so hard it nearly brought him to his knees and he poured a month's worth of pain, frustration, longing, jealousy, and love into her body and soul.

The knock on the door was not entirely unexpected. "I'm sorry, Philip, do you think it's the Ramadan police?"

He fought back the urge to laugh as he tried to catch his breath. "No. Probably just the Coast Guard."

After they'd reassured the maid everything was all right, Hallie told him, "It's good to be back in the saddle again, Cowboy. I'm sorry I screamed."

"It's okay. Just tell me again why you did it." He planted kisses on her neck, her hair, her shoulders.

"You were just so amazing. I couldn't control myself."

"You know how I hate that 'you were so amazing' part. And you were pretty amazing too." He looked down at his jeans around his hips and added, "You turned me on so much I couldn't even get my pants off."

"Or your glasses." She giggled and straightened them. "Look at us." Hallie stood against the door like the ravished woman she was with her bra hanging off one shoulder and her thong and jeans pooled around one knee. "I've never had door sex before."

He kicked off his jeans while his lips twitched in amusement. "Me either, but I sure have been fantasizing about it for the past three days." Then he sobered, fully realizing he had just officially stepped over the rule-breaking line. "Seriously, Hallie, we need to talk. We've got to figure out what we're going to do."

"Well, sir," she said as she kicked off the rest of her clothes, "My vote is we move this show to the bed."

Philip chuckled, took her hand, and led her there. As they lay down, he took her in his arms, kissing her temple, wanting to discuss things, but at the same time wanting to put it off indefinitely. "First of all, honey, I'm sorry about that...door sex. I didn't want it to be like that. I know I'm supposed to be comforting you, but I—"

She put her finger to his lips. "I'm beginning to think door sex might be even better than sailboat sex."

"I agree, but—"

"Shhh. Don't talk yet." They lay in each other's arms. Not talking. Not moving. Just being. Together. Again. Finally.

"Hallie, remember when you said I was your anchor? Well, you're my sails."

She turned to him, pressed her fingers to her smiling lips.

"You take me places I'd never go by myself." He waved his arm around the room. "And I don't mean places like hotel rooms in Port Said. Before you, I didn't know life could be like this. I've always played things safe. And I still need that, but you take me..."

"To paradise?"

"Yeah, that covers it."

And then she kissed him. Slow and sweet. First on the cheek and then worked her way to his lips. She pulled away, leaned on her elbow, raised an eyebrow, and smiled a smile of pure sin. She knew how much he hated it when she had her way with him. "Permission to come aboard, sir?"

His face lit up as she climbed up and straddled him. "Permission is so granted, McCabe."

"Permission-to-Come-Aboard-Sir Sex" rapidly morphed into an old favorite: "Ride-'Em-Cowgirl Sex." Once they'd expended the frustration of the past month or so, they made slow, gentle, tender love into the evening. And simply held each other in between.

They only realized it was getting dark when they heard evening prayer call being broadcast throughout the city. Their precious time was slipping away.

They would make the most of the few hours left. All thoughts of ethics and the UCMJ and Rick and Ramadan left in another world, beyond the door of this room, their boat, their paradise.

Chapter 22

Allahu Akbar. Ash-hadu an-la ilaha illa llah. Ash-hadu anna Muhammadan-Rasulullah...

The streets of Port Said came alive as evening prayer was called by the muezzin from loudspeakers throughout the city. Rashid glanced around for shipmates before opening the taxi door. All he saw were local residents rushing to prayer or to eat after a long day of fasting. The air was alive with tantalizing smells of roasting meats on spits and savory spices: garlic, curry, cinnamon, and others he couldn't put his finger on. Exotic covered it, though.

His stomach grumbled, but he knew the sadiqs would feed him. They'd emailed him an address from his "father's college roommate who would be honored to invite the son of Stanley Davis for an after-sunset feast." Right, like his dad ever went to college. As far as Rashid knew he hadn't even finished high school. Rashid hadn't seen him since he was eight years old. Good riddance, too.

He slammed the cab door behind him, but before he could hand the driver the address, the man turned to him and said, "Welcome to Egypt, Rashid."

These guys were good.

A smile lit the driver's face. "We are honored to have you visit us, sir."

Sir? Oh, yeah, Rashid could get used to this. "Thank you. I was told to go—"

"I know where you are going, sir. My name is Hakim. I will be your driver and will take you to the correct place. Forgive the traffic. It is time for Magrib—evening prayer. The faithful are rushing to perform their ablutions before prayer, but they are excited knowing the parties and feasting will begin soon after." He raised a water bottle to his lips. "I have just now had my first drink of water since dawn prayer call."

"Guess it's hard to observe Ramadan when it's so hot."

"Yes, it has been a long, hot, thirsty day for me. But that is what Ramadan is about, sir. To teach us compassion for those who do not have enough food or water. To do without things that give pleasure, each day for a month. To remind us to appreciate what we have. I'm sorry, I am a poor host. Would you like a water bottle, sadiqi?"

"No, thank you." But he sure could use a beer.

He glanced out the window at the shops and restaurants, now opening. Merchants hanging out everything from carpets to carcasses of what he figured were goats and lambs. Pretty gross if you asked him.

A few of the men were dressed traditionally in long white robes, their heads covered with white caps. Most wore western cloths, especially the women, although they did dress modestly. Some had their hair covered, at least partially. Rashid thought they looked pretty sexy with hair peeking out the fronts of their scarves. Weren't those things supposed to hide women's hair and keep them from looking tempting?

It reminded him of McCabe when that curl had fallen down a couple times on the news. And he'd watched her mindlessly play with it when she talked with her friends at chow too. He didn't even think she knew she did it. Goddamn women had no idea the power they held over men. Maybe the Arabs had the right idea. Keep the women subservient and covered up so they couldn't go turning on other men with their wily ways.

Hakim glanced at him in the rearview mirror. "Many businesses have been closed all day to observe Ramadan. Now they will remain open all night because that is when people will do their shopping—along with celebrating with their families."

"My contact back in the States told me the rich people sleep all day so they don't really benefit from the suffering part. Then they stay up all night. Is that true?"

"Yes, that is often the case. It is never fun to be a poor man, is it?"

"No, I guess not. So how far is it? Where are we going anyway?" He was starting to feel a little claustrophobic stuck in traffic in this foreign place. But what was the worst that could happen? He could die. And wasn't he already planning that? No, not like this. He had a mission to complete. He took a deep breath, sucking down his unease.

"It is only about two kilometers more. We should be there soon, once these trucks move, sir."

Rashid sure liked that *sir* stuff. Each time Hakim said it, Rashid felt a sweet stroke on his soul, like grazing his thumb across a soft blanket. It reminded him of that time Mrs. Buckley complimented him in front of the whole class in fourth grade and everyone had clapped. It had felt like sunshine flowing through his veins. It might have been the happiest moment of his life. If you'd asked him a year ago he would have said it was the day he met Rosie.

But he'd flushed all the good memories of her down the toilet with the bad. So yeah, a fucking fourth grade memory was what he was living on. Until tonight. This driver didn't even know him and yet he showed him respect.

They passed several more blocks of open-air shops, with dresses and scarves and sari-looking things. Did they have Indians in Egypt? Everything was colorful and bright and the people radiated warmth as they greeted each other on the sidewalks and in the open doorways of the shops. They passed a mosque with what looked like hundreds of pairs of shoes on the steps. He guessed the people were all inside doing that prayer to Mecca thing on carpets or something.

The taxi passed another block of stores that clearly sold jewelry, probably lots of gold. Ibrahim would have liked this. But this market probably carried real gold, not that gold-filled shit at Anchorage Mall. "This is the gold souq, sadiqi. Perhaps you wish to purchase some gold this evening? To send home to your sweetheart. Oh, sorry. Perhaps to your mother?"

"No, thanks." His heart banged as he worked overtime to erase a picture of Rosie, with bright eighteen-carat gold chains—fine as angel hair—on her soft, smooth, perfect neck. She always wore a cross and a small diamond pendant he'd given her, along with his favorite, a charm that said, "Randy's Girl." He'd gotten that on his last cruise, in a souq such as this in Bahrain.

Venom coursed through his veins as he pictured himself ripping the delicate chains from her neck, then grabbing her throat and practically tearing her limb from limb. He cranked down the taxi window enough to take in a lungful of the pungent, spice-filled air, trying not to puke, remembering how he'd almost killed her the night he'd discovered her extracurricular activities. He could feel the chains wrapped around his hands, biting into them as his hands bit into her. He breathed in more of the hot Egyptian air, shut his eyes, and exhaled deeply.

Thank God she hadn't pressed charges. She'd just walked out the door and he didn't see her again until they met with the divorce lawyers. Where had she gone? Where had she stayed? The only thing better than punishing the men she'd slept with would be if he could take Rosie out with them. He breathed deeply again, finding his equilibrium, put the window back up. Christ it was hot out there. And dusty.

The taxi turned into the carpet souq, where merchants were hanging their merchandise outside. Rashid could only imagine how much dirt the rugs absorbed from the dust blowing in from the desert.

"Here we are, sir." Hakim jumped out of the driver's seat, ran around, and opened his door. Rashid reached for his wallet. "Oh, no, sir. There is no charge. It is my honor to drive you tonight."

He led Rashid to the door of a carpet shop that had no rugs for sale outside. The shop was dark and a sign in the window sported a "Closed for Prayer" sign. The driver slipped off his sandals and indicated that Rashid should remove his shoes as well. Bells jingled over the doorway as they were greeted by a man in western clothing.

"*Assalam alaykum*," the man said with a welcoming smile.

Rashid could barely see through the blanket of cigarette smoke that engulfed him as he entered the shop. The men were probably smoking a day's worth of cigarettes now that the sun had set and they could indulge. But Ibrahim had trained him well and he knew how to respond. He blinked and sniffed once and replied, "*Waalaykum assalam*." Peace be upon you as well.

"We are honored to have you visit with us, Rashid," said the man who had welcomed him. "I am Mohammed. Please follow me."

Hakim called to him. "I will wait for you outside, sir. Let me know when you are ready to leave."

Rashid kind of wanted the driver to stick with him, as the host led him to a back room. He glanced over his shoulder and waved to the driver. "Okay." About to give him a thumbs-up, he remembered it was an obscene gesture in the Middle East. Almost as bad as showing the sole of one's shoe to someone. Crazy Arabs.

Mohammed escorted Rashid to a large room where a gigantic red Oriental rug covered the floor. Colorful piles of carpets stood stacked like barricades around the room, while geometric designs in earthy tones covered the walls.

Four men sat clustered around a table, sipping tea, eating, and smoking. They all rose to welcome him, walking over in their stocking feet. "*Assalam alaykum.*"

"*Waalaykum assalam*," he responded as Ibrahim had instructed him.

"Rashid, welcome to Egypt," one said. They each smiled warmly and shook his hand.

"Come, sit down, sadiqi," said Mohammed. "We are indulging in a light snack. It has been a long day of fasting."

"Thank you, sir," he replied as another man handed him a small glass of hot tea. The men raised their glasses and toasted him. Rashid smiled, took a sip of his tea and almost spit it across the table. One sip was enough to rot his teeth. How did they drink this sweet stuff?

They made small talk about the shop and the holiday and shared details of their fasting for that day. Ibrahim had told him the rules of etiquette. There would be at least three glasses of tea before they would discuss business. Rashid wasn't sure he could stomach three glasses of it, but he'd do his best to be polite. Even if each sip made him pucker inside.

There wasn't a lot to talk about yet. The weather? Hot. The cruise? Routine, so far. His visit to Port Said? This outing was going to be it. But rules were rules and nothing of import could be discussed until they had finished with the pleasantries.

"So what do you think of Port Said, Rashid?"

"This is my first time ashore here, sir. Although I have been through the Suez Canal on a previous deployment. It is very exciting to see so much action in the streets this late at night. I guess because of the holiday. It's kind of odd to see so many people shopping at eight, nine at night."

The man laughed. "It will go on like this into the early hours of the morning. The people will eat and drink and visit long into the night, preparing for another day of fasting tomorrow. Come join us in the meal."

He thought it was very cool how they dined the traditional way, dipping their right hands into the large tray of roast lamb, kebobs, and rice. Hummus, tabouli, and melon slices on the side. Scooping it all up with bread. Oh, well, when in Rome. Rashid picked up a piece of pita bread and joined them.

When they had finished eating, a young man cleared the table and poured each of them a third glass of tea. Everyone except Rashid lit a cigarette and worked at refilling the shop with smoke.

A man named Saied Ghassan leaned back, burped, and smiled at Rashid. He revealed yellowed teeth beneath his thick moustache. Never had Rashid seen a more chilling smile. Rashid had already figured out this was the boss man tonight. "So, sadiqi, we finally get to thank you for your help in our mission."

"I guess so, sir."

"I wish there was a better way to show our gratitude than sharing a simple meal with you, but please know that we appreciate all the information you have sent."

All the men nodded their heads, smiled at him, and mumbled "*Shukron.*" Thank you.

"*Afwan,*" he replied as Ibrahim had taught him. "You're most welcome, all of you."

"I know I am speaking for our brothers who are spread far and wide throughout the world, when I say thank you for what you are prepared to do for our cause."

"It is my pleasure, sir. It also meets my needs."

The man took out his prayer beads, flipping them in his hand, stroking the thirty-three beads. They were meant to keep track of prayers as someone recited them, but Rashid had come to understand why they were referred to as "worry beads." Wished he had some of his own to flip around in his sweaty palms while these men discussed his death as if it was business as usual. Wished he smoked too. However, with the amount of smoke in the air, he was probably inhaling as much as they were.

"So tell us. Your ship will be transiting the canal soon?"

"Yes, sir. We're going through in two days. We should be in the Gulf by September first. I don't think there will be a problem finding us on the ninth. It appears we'll be near Dubai for Eid."

Ghassan smiled, but it didn't reach his cold eyes. "Which is when you will help us celebrate with fireworks." He turned to another man at the table. "It's still several weeks, but I think we can plan to use the dhows near our southern target area. Alert the powers-that-be to make advanced preparations to transport the fishermen and the explosives to Doha." He looked back to Rashid. "But you will let us know if anything changes. Using the code, of course."

"Certainly, sir. As best I can. I believe I made it clear that we do not always have access to email."

"Yes, yes. I understand. But you will stay in contact with Hot Mama as often as possible?"

"I'll do my best."

"Everything sounds good, Rashid, although we have an important question. We understand you will be traveling with other American ships. Five, I think. Will they be a problem for our fishermen?"

"No. See, the escort ships are there to protect us." He raised his hand to counter the eyebrows that were raised at that information. "Sure they carry all sorts of advanced systems and weaponry. But they're not geared to protect us from common fishing boats. So say the Iranians decide to send a missile our way or a ship of their own or a submarine. The smaller ships of the Carrier Strike Group would intercede and protect us, but you're talking about dime a dozen fishing boats. Five out of hundreds that float around us whenever we're in confined spaces, or in port, or in the Gulf.

"I guarantee the escort ships will not pose a problem for you. And remember, I will be the one monitoring the radar on September ninth, so don't worry about a thing. Any other concerns?"

Smiles lit faces around the table.

One man who had not spoken yet this evening now spoke up. "Rashid, I have a concern for your soul."

Whoa. That sure as hell had come out of left field. "My soul?"

"Yes. Our fishermen have a cause, all part of Jihad. This is their mission for Allah. They know they will go to Paradise, but I worry about your soul, son."

"My soul is just fine, thank you." Even though his heart was pounding to beat the band.

"I just wanted to make certain to remind you that it is not too late to embrace Islam. You could still have a chance to go to your reward for your help in our Jihad."

"I appreciate your concern, sir, and I will take that into consideration."

The man seemed satisfied. "Good. I would feel remiss if I had not brought that to your attention."

Rashid noticed at least two of the men sneaking peeks at their watches. He knew it would be impolite for them to leave before the honored guest, and he really wanted to look into finding a beer. He pushed his chair back and stood, "Well, I mustn't keep you, sadiqis. I know this is a holiday night and I'm sure you have celebrations to attend. Thank you, Mr. Mohammed for your hospitality. I wish everyone the best for the remainder of Ramadan and may all of you have a satisfying Eid."

They stood to shake his hand and give him bear hugs, slapping him lightly on the back. "May Allah bless you, Rashid."

Ghassan hugged him, then cupped Rashid's face in his hands. "Peace be with you, sadiqi. And may everything go according to plan. *Inshallah.*"

As God wills it.

Stepping out of the air-conditioned store, Rashid felt as if someone had opened the oven door. He'd traded the thick, smoky air in the carpet shop for a blast of hot, dry heat that smacked him in the face. He found himself looking forward to getting back to the ship so he could breathe again. A man could suffocate in this heat.

He'd been through the canal before. Beyond its banks was barren desert in all directions, where the air baked all day long and now even at nine o'clock at night it was easily ninety degrees. Yeah, yeah. He'd heard the old, "but it's dry heat."

It was still fucking hot.

The streets bustled with shoppers as Hakim drove him back to the docks. They made small talk about the crowds and the traffic and the good smells permeating the air. He felt bad for Hakim, that maybe he hadn't yet eaten after fasting all day. He should have asked for a doggie bag or something.

"Sir, is there anything else I can do for you before I return you to the piers?"

"Yeah, can you find me a beer?" There were still a few hours before the final liberty launch sailed back to the ship. This would be his last night ever to enjoy a brew. He'd even spring for an expensive one. Forget it. His last chance to imbibe in this lifetime? He deserved whiskey. But he'd have to take it easy. It was vitally important he remain in control at all times. He'd nurse one whiskey. Two tops, then take the next launch back to the ship.

The taxi driver pulled up near the docks where bars catered to sailors who traversed the canal. He opened Rashid's door, shook his hand, then held onto it. It was clear he had something important to say. "Just remember, sadiqi, it is not too late to embrace the one true faith. If you do, you will go directly to Paradise with the fishermen, and your death will not be in vain."

"Thanks, but no thanks, Hakim. And thanks for driving me tonight. Your service made me feel good. Thank you." They hugged, then he said goodbye to the kind man who had called him sir all evening. As he walked into the closest bar, most likely filled with American sailors, he mulled over what Hakim had just said. And that other man too. He was touched that they cared about his eternal soul. Offering him Paradise along with the fishermen. But Rashid wasn't crazy like the fanatics. He didn't need seventy-two virgins in Paradise.

All he wanted was that one bitch to roast in hell with him for all eternity.

Chapter 23

Philip had room service delivered to their little corner of paradise. No way could he and Hallie chance being seen in a restaurant together by a shipmate. They were well aware that several couples had recently gone to Captain's Mast and punished for "having relationships." All of them had been enlisted. They couldn't even imagine what would happen to a commissioned officer.

Proposing to her in a fancy restaurant wasn't worth the scuttlebutt that would fly, let alone a chewing-out if they were seen together in public. So if that meant he was going to propose to her in bed, so be it. The least he could do was pull out the five-star terry cloth robes. Proposing in bed was one thing. Naked was another. He wondered how many men on the ship would give their left nut to be in his shoes.

Or his bathrobe.

He hated to spoil the ambience, but over a late dinner in bed, while curled up in the fluffy white robes, it was time to talk about serious matters. Like Rick for starters.

"Hallie, I called my dad and had him do a little checking on Captain Amerson. The aviator community is pretty tight and he contacted a couple of buddies. I didn't tell him much, just asked him to find out if Andrew Amerson ever went by Rick. He emailed me this morning. That's what the Captain's close friends still call him."

"Good work, Johnston. You want to be my assistant at CNN?"

"So we've determined the Captain is your father. What are you planning to do with the information?"

"Nothing—at least for now. Don't worry, Philip. I'm not going to humiliate him, although he deserves it. I don't want anything to do with him, because I don't trust him. Perhaps we could simply keep the secret as our ace in the hole, should there ever be a problem about you and me together."

"My sentiments exactly, but what about him being familiar with you? I've had some time to think it over and you were very clear you wouldn't tolerate it, but what if you hadn't been? We don't know what he might have said or done. What if he tries it with some other woman on the ship who can't handle it like you did? Do you think you should go talk to somebody?"

"Not yet, but I have everything documented if I need it. He can't have gotten in trouble for it before. The Navy's firing COs right and left for that kind of thing. He's not stupid, although he didn't act very smart around me. I found out a little about his wife and that he has three sons. That kind of blew me away. Philip, I have three half-brothers somewhere. Anyway, nothing else was new and we didn't find any complaints about him. I'll be vigilant and just play it by ear for the time being. Let me get over him being Rick first and who knows? I may decide to go have a little chat with him at a later date. But there's no reason to confront him yet."

"But you have every right to be angry about everything. How are you going to deal with that?"

"I'm going to do what I've always done with shit in my life. I'm going to turn it into something good. Somehow. I'll find a way to find the bright side. There has to be a reason this happened."

His mouth curled up in a wry manner. "You mean like calling it fertilizer and making things grow from it?"

"Good one. I like that idea." She reached out and took his hand. "You know, girls with good fathers grow up and marry someone just like Daddy, and girls with bad fathers often do the same *or* they're smart enough to figure out what they don't want."

"Like?"

"Like you, Philip. Maybe this is not about me finding out how bad he is, but appreciating how good you are. Do you have any idea how many flashy aviators have tried to hit on me since the first broadcast?" He didn't want to know. "If I hadn't had this experience with him and my mom, I might have fallen for that."

"Hallie, you don't know how hard it is to hear the guys talking about you and I can't do anything about it. I know you love me, but I worry about you being treated like that. We've got to figure a lot of stuff out here tonight. Like what we're going to do about the rest of the cruise. I mean, today was magical—the best day of my life—well, maybe except for a certain day on a sailboat." His voice trailed off and he kissed her mouth, her nose, her forehead, her ear.

"But we have to go back to the ship tonight and I don't know how I'm going to handle it—after this." He gestured to the room, the bed, and her. "After loving you again. It's so difficult knowing you're on board when I can't see you or touch you or even talk to you. And it's really hard to listen to men talking about you when I want them to know you're spoken for. But you know we can't meet on the ship. And we can't sneak around either. We need to figure this out and set some ground rules. We need a plan and I think..."

Hallie grinned, propped herself up on her elbows, and jumped in with both feet. "Okay, here's our plan of attack. We walk out of this hotel and go back to the ship. We steer clear of each other and we don't communicate for the rest of the cruise."

Did she want to break up?

Then why was she smiling?

"Except maybe for letters—pleeease, let there be letters. We act like every other person on board who's separated from the ones they love for the duration. We focus on our work and the mission. We remember the code: Ship, shipmate, self. The ship comes first. We do our jobs graciously and we smile inside, because we know we're loved. I have to have that, Philip. Come on. Every girl in a foxhole needs to have a guy to think about. A good man to come back to."

Philip's mouth tipped up at the corners. He liked where this was going.

"But we don't forget about each other and we don't forget promises we make today. We remember every detail to keep us warm until the ship pulls back into Mayport, or if I have to wait, until I get out of the Navy next March. And I mean it. I don't think we should even see each other in liberty ports any more. It's too dangerous."

He couldn't believe she was taking the words right out of his mouth.

"But there's nothing in the UCMJ that says you can't love a subordinate or a superior, just that you can't fraternize with them. Nobody can take away our thoughts and our feelings, not even the Navy. My mom told me that before I left for boot camp, 'Just remember, Hallie, when you get there, think whatever you want— say what you have to say in your head—just don't say it out loud. If you're standing at inspection and some chief is in your face and she's reading you the riot act, you can think 'Screw you, Chief!' But just look straight ahead and say, 'Ma'am, yes, Ma'am!'"

Philip fell back on the pillows, shaking with laughter.

Hallie was on a roll now. "So we go through this charade—by the way, somebody told me I'm pretty good at pretending—so we do this for the next hundred and fifty-nine days, or two hundred and seventeen if you're going to make me wait until I'm a civilian. Trust me I've counted them." His laughter fed her fire. "And then we'll be free to do whatever we want. So when we're ready, we *get married* and, as Trixie would say, we live happily ever after fucking our brains out!"

Philip could hardly catch his breath, laughing so hard at what could only have come from a sailor's mouth. But his heart was sending rapid-fire messages to his brain that she was putting into words everything he'd wanted to say. Was *she* proposing to *him*?

"That's when we're not on the nightly news or fixing engines or changing diapers once we settle down in some Navy town and start popping out the babies. You know after Suzanna and little

Philip and Billy Gates Junior come along, which is going to be hard because I'll have finished school by then and I'll be thinking about New York and how they probably won't want some pregnant mama on the national news anchor desk, but I'll find a way to get to New York. I just haven't quite worked the bugs out of that part yet, but I will."

God, he loved her spirit. And now she was talking about *babies*. His babies.

"And the children know nothing about Grandpa Blue Eyes, but they do know Mommy is never sad because she doesn't give a crap about Grandpa Blue Eyes. She just loves Daddy and they do too because he's such a good daddy, who coaches their swim team and teaches them how to throw a baseball and how to sail and he shows them what a gentleman is. And so the whole Johnston clan lives happily ever after. How do you feel about *that* for a plan!"

Still smiling broadly, he took her hands in his and pulled her close.

"Excuse me, Petty Officer McCabe, but did you just propose marriage to me?"

She saluted. "Affirmative, sir. And your answer?"

"Positively affirmative, McCabe. I don't suppose you had any idea I was planning to say the exact same things. Well, maybe not the 'fucking our brains out' part, but I like the idea of it." He kissed her, then squeezed her hands, and looked into her dancing blue eyes. Then he picked up her dog tags off the bedside table and leaned back against the pillows. He unhooked the chain, took off his Naval Academy ring, and slipped it onto the chain next to them.

"Does this mean we're going steady, sir?" Hallie asked with a good-humored grin.

"No, it doesn't mean we're going steady, McCabe." After clicking the chain closed, he walked around the bed, knelt by her side, hung the chain around her neck, and took her hands in his. "It means we're engaged. If you'll marry me, McCabe, Hallie L. 023-71-7048?"

"Oh, that's an affirmative back atcha, sir."

Philip loosened her robe, took the two most beautiful breasts in the entire world and squeezed them together around the ring and the dog tags. "Keep it warm for me," he said, "for the next hundred and fifty-nine days."

"Aye, aye, sir." She pressed her lips together tightly to keep from smiling and saluted again. "It's not fair though. You at least get to see me on the news every night. But I'm going to die if I don't get to see your cute little ass once in a while. So I'm letting you know I'll be going to the gym each evening after the newscast." And then she winked to get her point across. "And if you care to join me, just wear your BCGs because then nobody would suspect us of being a couple, because nobody in BCGs fools around and nobody fools around with guys who wear them."

He agreed to work out after the news when he could, but told her again how difficult it was to watch her on TV. "It's hard to listen to the guys talking about you, but I guess knowing you're promised to me will help. And I have to watch the news after chow, since I don't get a chance to check CNN during the day. I really want to know what's going on, especially as we get deeper into the Middle East. You're really good, by the way. Have I told you that lately?"

"So you're just watching me for the news?" A little smile played on her lips. "You mean you care more about al-Qaeda than you do about me?"

"Yes. Because I trust you, Hallie. I don't trust them."

Hallie melted. A tiny whimper escaped. "You trust me? Philip, that's more important to me than knowing you love me." Unshed tears shined in her eyes.

"I do." He felt tears at the backs of his own eyes. He cleared his throat and said, "I trust you. And I forgive you. A wise woman once told me that sometimes you have to forgive the people you love so you can move on with your life."

Hallie pulled off her dog tags and laid them on the table, then turned and slid into his arms. This last lovemaking would need to hold them for at least five months. More importantly, it would be the first time Hallie felt she truly belonged in his arms.

As they were dressing to leave, she turned to him and said, "You know, when you picked up my dog tags? I thought you were going to give me one of yours and you were going to take one of mine. Like going steady."

"That's not funny, Hallie. We're going into a hot zone. I hope you never need your dog tags, but promise me you'll always have them on you at all times. Just in case."

"Yes, sir." She popped tall and saluted him, while wearing nothing but his favorite lavender lace thong and bra—and a chain with two silver dog tags and a ring on it. And for the first time she thought about her dog tags as more than just a cool thing people in the military got to wear. She thought about their purpose and she felt a shiver go up her spine.

Leave one to identify the body and turn the other in when reporting the casualty.

It was the first time she really thought about why her blood type and religion were stamped into it too. In case she needed a transfusion, or last rites. Then the fact that they'd be transiting the Suez Canal in a few days on their way to the Persian Gulf wracked her with another shiver.

Hallie wished she had something to give Philip, to hold her promise until the end of the cruise, and beyond. And then she got an idea. A couple of ideas. "Philip, thank you for entrusting me with your ring. And now I'd like to entrust you with something. Some very valuable information. This is Wednesday, right? See my underwear? I know they're your favorites, so now you'll be the only man on the ship who knows I'm wearing my lavender lace skivvies on the broadcast every Wednesday night until the end of the cruise. And *then*, I'm wearing them at our wedding."

"Don't most brides wear a dress?"

She smacked him with a pillow.

"No, seriously. I'm honored. It's enough to keep a guy in a foxhole going for at least five months. Particularly on Wednesdays.

Knowing his girl back home is going to marry him wearing nothing but lavender lace skivvies."

Philip sent her out first to catch a cab back to the ship. "I love you, Hallie. Never forget that and always wear those dog tags."

"Don't worry. I'll wear them at all times. I love you too, Philip." She blew him a kiss and walked down the empty hallway.

When Philip checked out of the hotel, the concierge handed him an envelope with his name on it. He opened it in the cab on the way back to the ship and had to swallow the lump in his throat.

> *Dear Philip,*
>
> *That thing about Wednesdays will be fun, but I wanted to leave you with something you could see and touch every day—just like I can do with your ring. I want you to know I belong to you and you alone. I promise.*
>
> *I love you, Hallie*

Only Hallie could manage to put a promise in an envelope. Now Philip, and only Philip, would know that Hallie McCabe's heart belonged to him.

He knew it when he looked in the envelope and found the golden tendril.

Chapter 24

With the camera rolling, the USS *Blanchard* made its way through the Suez Canal. MC2 McCabe stood on the flight deck and shared the history of "the Ditch." Many of the crew would not be able to get topside during the one-hundred-twenty-mile transit and she wanted them to see what they were missing. She also wanted the tape for her portfolio. What an historic moment for her. Talk about "Join the Navy and see the world." How she wished she could share the footage with her mom and felt herself tearing up at the thought.

Hallie regained her composure and continued with the piece. "Although the land appears sandy and barren, life definitely abounds near the water. Besides high rise apartment buildings, there are oil refineries, power plants, and factories, many of which process Egyptian cotton, one of their biggest exports, along with oil and fish. The domed buildings you see are mosques and the tall towers flanking them are the minarets, from which prayer is called five times a day."

She paused in her report as the ship approached a cable-stayed bridge that spanned the canal, spreading its fingers skyward. There were no words to describe the feeling as the *Blanchard* slid smoothly underneath on her journey toward the Red Sea.

"You can tell there's plenty of traffic in the canal."

The camera panned to tankers and merchant vessels piled high with boxcars gliding by in the opposite direction. And it made Hallie more than a little nervous to see ordinary fishing boats, barges, and pleasure boats floating freely around and in between the destroyers, the frigates, and the cruiser that accompanied the *Blanchard*.

What had Philip told her the day they'd met? "What we worry about are ordinary fishing boats that just happen to be floating bombs." Her eyes glanced around at the lookouts posted around the roof, each manning a weapon, trigger fingers at the ready. What good would they do if one of those dhows just happened to get too close?

No, she had to trust that the Carrier Strike Group would keep them safe, even though she felt claustrophobic in the canal. All she knew was, she would breathe a sigh of relief once they exited the southern hub and got through to the Arabian Sea. Right. Then all they had to worry about were Somali pirates. And further along the trail? Iranians. But this was what Hallie McCabe had signed on for. And today it was her job to bring the Suez Canal to those below decks who could not get topside to see it.

The longer she stood there, the more she appreciated what the flight deck crews endured on a daily basis. Here it was mid-August at only 1000 hours, and the temperature was already one hundred degrees. Once they entered the Arabian Sea, when they would again launch aircraft, the afternoon heat combined with jet afterburner heat, would often rise to one hundred thirty degrees.

She closed her report with that thought. "So shipmates, remember we are now officially and literally in a hot zone. I have a new perspective about working conditions above decks. Control your own temperature by drinking lots of water to avoid dehydration. And to those of you who haven't endured these conditions? Those who remain below in the air conditioning? Don't forget to thank our Engineering Department for keeping the A/C up to speed. This is MC2 Hallie McCabe saying, stay safe and be cool."

It warmed Philip's heart to hear the shout-out to the engineers who brought them air conditioning. He wasn't able to witness the Suez Canal, and he appreciated the information she brought to the crew.

Hallie was exceptional at what she did. For some of these young men, hearing the news from Hallie was like having their own moms as their link to the outside world, all wrapped up in a super model's persona. He understood why every guy on the ship was in love with her. He began to notice the men paying her more respect as her show became successful. They were finally realizing Hallie McCabe wasn't just a pretty face. Although that didn't hurt. She truly had become what Captain Amerson had called her, the *Blanchard's* head cheerleader.

And she was his. No way could he have let her go.

If the guys on the ship only knew that "Bill Gates" was the proud owner of the now defunct golden tendril. It had fallen loose one other time since the first broadcast and now there were bets going on in every department about when it would fall again on camera. Only Philip knew the answer was never.

He sat at dinner and thought about the golden tendril in a ziplock bag in his wallet, in his back pocket. Right next to the pictures she'd finally given him. The tendril was the very essence of her. Beautiful and cohesive, but just a little misbehaved. He took it out every night when he returned to his stateroom. Smelled it, touched it, and curled it around his finger, while he read her daily letter, before scribbling out a response, and tucking in for a few hours of sleep.

Philip Johnston was the luckiest guy in the world.

He dozed off every night thinking of her. How she'd agreed to table their actions until she was discharged from the Navy, or at least until the cruise was over, knowing how dangerous things might become now that they were officially in the Middle East. Hallie understood how important it was for them to focus on their jobs. There was no room for passion now. Except for the mission. When he thought about his class ring—United States Naval Academy, class of 2006—nestled warmly in the crevice between those luscious breasts, he became aroused every time. Thinking about the gold absorbing her warmth and her scent. Protected from the world, like their secret.

Oh, they still had a secret, but it was a good secret. They'd declared their love and were promised to each other. They respected each other, each other's professional dreams, and the Navy as a whole. Respected them enough to wait. And they knew they'd each be fine doing their jobs every day, as long as when they crawled into their racks each night, they could pull their memories and their secret out of their seabags and dream about their future. Together.

Only a hundred fifty-eight more days to go.

Rashid liked the idea of the two-minute bits McCabe was doing with members of the crew. He'd thought he had his portion of the attack all figured out, but he hadn't planned on McCabe becoming so popular. He really wanted to use her somehow. Wanted to take her out with him, and now she'd presented him with a perfect opening. He thought about contacting her to see if she'd come to Combat and interview him on September ninth.

Wouldn't the McBabe make a perfect hostage if he should need one? He'd have to figure out how to get in touch with her though. He couldn't email her. Guess she was getting too much email or something. Her fucking boss had to go on the air and ask that all emails concerning the broadcast go directly to him. He said that any messages sent directly to the staff, meaning McCabe, would be deleted unread.

Because if he couldn't take Rosie out with him while he punished the men she'd slept with, McCabe might just have to do.

Yeah, this was definitely worth thinking about.

Despite all that she'd been through in the last week, Hallie fondled the ring around her neck and knew everything was going to be okay. She felt safe. And loved. And trusted.

Philip repeatedly told her in his letters how much he respected her for using her "fertilizer mentality" and moving on, continuing to view the positive side of life. Taking shit and letting things grow from it. He'd also told her he was glad she wasn't planning to pursue anything embarrassing for the Captain. What good would it do anyway? Except to ruin him. And his family. And the spirit of the ship. And possibly the mission. Hallie was not a vindictive person. And Captain Amerson was doing a good job as Commanding Officer. Did he really need to deal with the baggage of her existence while trying to run the ship, just as they headed into the Middle East?

Maybe she'd sit on it and approach him after they arrived home, although the idea of ever looking into those eyes again gave her the creeps. But the thought of him treating another woman the way he'd treated her still bothered her. She had a lot to think about. This was not a time to act impulsively. So she sat back and enjoyed knowing Philip loved and trusted her—and wanted to marry her. Was going to marry her. Life was good.

Sitting there thinking about feeling safe, she jerked back to reality when Captain Amerson walked out of Commander Scott's office and headed straight for her desk. Hallie's heart snapped to attention as he approached her with those blue eyes twinkling.

"Well, if it isn't the captain of the *Blanchard*'s cheerleading squad. How are you today, McCabe?"

She stood up respectfully, heart hammering, a mouth-only smile on her face. "Fine, sir."

"Well, it looks like we might be working together. Just talked to Commander Scott. Now that we're in the Red Sea, I want to chat with the crew every day. Going to see if I can get down here and do a short taping for you to air before the broadcast each night. We can be cheerleaders together all the way through the Gulf."

"Yes, sir." Not a good idea, but she said nothing but, "Yes, sir."

Hallie felt as if her safety net had just been ripped out from under her. Her heart thudded at the prospect of seeing Rick on a regular basis.

Maybe she'd have to move up that little chat with him.

Chapter 25

"Hallie, hurry up. There's a pilot waiting for you in the office." Gina had raced all the way back to berthing to get Hallie the next morning, because she apparently had a visitor. "He says he'll only talk to you."

Hallie scrambled up the ladders behind Gina to their office, her heart thumping. What pilot wanted to see her and why?

"Good morning, sir. What can I do for you?" Hallie asked the man in the desert tan flight suit sitting by her desk.

The cute pilot shot her a warm, friendly, country-boy grin and stuck out his hand to shake hers. "Lieutenant Crawford, McCabe. Nice to meet you." She used the word *cute* to describe him because that's what he was. Not handsome. Not hot. Not threatening. Cute. Like a big, overgrown, mischievous boy. Stocky and muscle-bound in his flight suit, with a blond crew cut and a gap between his two front teeth when he flashed his infectious smile. "My squadron would like to shoot a video to send back to the families. Any chance you could give me a tour of the studio?"

"I think you might want to chat with Petty Officer Hall, our cameraman. Let me—"

"Look." He glanced around then leaned in close to her. "If I'm going to be the best man at your wedding, I thought I should get to meet the bride first."

Hallie's face lit up. "Sky!" She'd heard so much about him, but this guy seemed more like a puppy dog than a player. "Let me show you the studio, sir." She led the way.

Hallie shut the soundproof door and anyone looking through the glass would see her giving him a tour, but they were definitely talking about other things. Sky exuded enthusiasm. She liked him right away.

"Bill put a care package together for you and—"

"Bill?"

"Sweetheart, I've called Philip Johnston 'Bill Gates' since the day I met his worthless ass. Look, I got a special delivery package for you here. There's a letter explaining everything. Read it first and follow the directions." He pointed his index finger at her. "Do not open the box until you read it."

"So what's in the box?" Hallie's curiosity was piqued.

"How should I know? I'm just the messenger." Mirth glittered in his blue eyes. "I only have a few minutes with you so let me say my piece and then I'm outta here. First of all I want to say thank you for being so awesome. And if we weren't in the public eye right this minute I'd give you a big hug because you've made my best buddy the happiest man on earth." Then he turned serious. "Do you have any idea what a good man you've got there? They don't make them like that anymore."

Hallie's eyes misted up. She knew a compliment like that coming from a guy like Sky was big.

"I do know, Sky. Trust me. I know how special he is. And I also know how special you are to him. And just meeting you I can tell why you're good for him. Thank you for being such a terrific friend. I promise to take care of him and never let you down. And thanks for standing up for us when the time comes."

"Oh, yeah, that. I've got to get busy. I'm trying to think of all the stories I know about Bill to embarrass him at his wedding. Okay, gotta run. I'm still looking for the Brasso. Buttons to polish."

Hallie laughed as she shook his hand and walked him to the door. She already felt comfortable with Sky.

Just before he left the space, Sky leaned in and flashed her one more of his wry grins. "Oh, and one more thing. You don't by any chance have a sister, do you?"

* * *

Philip sat across the desk from his Commanding Officer in the Captain's at-sea cabin. The same man who'd told him at a party, "If you ever need anything, you know where to find me." The exact same words he'd told Hallie. Philip and the CO had chatted at the party about Andy, and the CO had told him "any friend of Andy's is a friend of mine."

Never has been. Never will be. Knowing the Captain's son had been his ticket in the door today, however.

"What's on your mind today, Lieutenant?" Captain Amerson asked him.

Philip pegged him right in the cornflower blue eye. He did not want to miss the reaction. "I'm in love with a female sailor aboard this ship, sir."

The CO blew out a breath and leaned back in his chair. "I certainly hope you're not planning to do anything about it on my watch. Besides the fact that there are to be no relationships between crewmembers, you're talking about an enlisted woman, I take it. That's fraternization and it's totally illegal in this man's Navy. That's just damn foolish, son. It has the potential to be a career ender. Surely you know that."

"I'm well aware of it, sir."

"Then why in the hell are you telling me this?" He leaned forward and began to shuffle papers on his desk, noticeably pissed off that Philip was wasting his time.

"What if I came up here to ask for her hand in marriage? Since you're her father."

The CO's hands paused in their shuffling. His eyes flickered to Philip's. "Then you'd be mistaken because I don't have a daughter. And if I did, she certainly wouldn't be on board this ship." He returned to his paperwork.

"Hallie McCabe is your daughter."

The Captain's hands froze. His eyes narrowed in confusion and darted back to Philip. The fact that he hadn't responded with defensive words told Philip he was on the right track. He just hoped to hell he was on the right train. He'd obviously hit a nerve. Amerson hadn't moved a muscle, except for those eyeballs. He'd probably gone right to Hallie's blue eyes, now that somebody had mentioned it to him. Philip paused two more heartbeats, challenging him with his cool brown eyes, letting his CO know that he—Philip Johnston—was now in command of the situation.

"Tell me honestly you don't know anything about fraternization, *sir*. AG2 Suzanne Chandler? Or maybe you remember her better as Suzie Q. Atsugi Air Facility? July '86?"

The color drained from the CO's face.

"She took the five hundred dollars and invested it in Hallie's future, not her demise."

"Rick" looked like he'd been sucker punched. Something in his eyes, Hallie's eyes, showed Philip he'd hit pay dirt.

"You think I'm making this up? Take a look at her eyes. And take that fucking gleam out of yours when you look at her. No, belay my last. Don't ever fucking look at her again."

Captain Amerson remained speechless, although if eyes could kill, Philip would be a dead man.

"You know Hallie said something interesting on the news the other night. Okay if I call her Hallie, since you apparently feel comfortable enough with her to use her first name?" He didn't wait for a response. "She was talking about sunscreen, but it kind of applies to a lot of things in life. It's amazing how using protection in your twenties can definitely keep problems from coming back and biting you in the ass when you're fifty."

"What do want from me?" the CO asked, barely above a whisper.

"I want you to leave Hallie McCabe the hell alone. Your daily chats with the crew over the 1MC are going just fine. I personally don't think you need to be hanging around Public Affairs. Ever." Then he leaned across the desk, confidentially. "And just so you know, she isn't planning to do a single thing about knowing you're her father." He indicated the Captain's family photos. "*She* doesn't like disrupting families. She got some closure and she wants to put it all behind her. So don't worry about your precious admiral's selection board. I'm just here to let you know if you ever so much as breathe the same air as her again, I will fucking kill you."

The CO slit his eyes. "Are you threatening me, Lieutenant?"

"You're goddamn right I am, sir. I want you to leave not only McCabe alone, but also every other woman on this ship. If I ever hear of you being unduly familiar with a female service member anywhere, I will spill the beans so fast you won't know what hit you. I don't think this crew would need DNA proof. With the way scuttlebutt spreads around here, I'm sure the fact that McCabe's the spitting image of you would get the ball rolling. And I'm certain it wouldn't take long for it to get back to Washington."

The Captain swallowed thickly, but did not say a word. The son of a bitch was a master at control. A pulsing vein near his temple was the only indication of his rising anxiety. That, and the pallor of his face.

"Thank you for seeing me today, sir. I don't think we'll have any more problems here." Philip stood to leave. He didn't ask if that would be all. He didn't ask for permission to depart. He didn't even say goodbye. Nothing. Just arose and walked to the door. But just as he reached for the door handle, he turned back and added, "Oh, and don't even think about going the chivalrous route after twenty-five years. Petty Officer McCabe knows nothing about this little pow-wow and she never will. Got it?"

The CO scowled at him and looked away. He breathed in and exhaled deeply. The poor prick probably hadn't taken a decent breath in the last five minutes.

Good.

Philip laughed, like he was hanging with a buddy. "And anyway, sir, I gotta warn you. I wouldn't mess with her if I were you. She's got a pair of highly-polished, solid brass ones on her that you definitely do not want to tangle with." Then he paused two beats before smiling and delivering the coup de grace: "Must have gotten them from her mother."

Philip departed, lowering his imaginary sword and sliding it into its imaginary scabbard. He knew damn well he'd left the CO scrambling to cover his imaginary sword, so he wouldn't fall on it.

When Trixie arrived at work the next day, she practically burst at the seams. "Okay, you guys. Listen up. I've got some good shit here. It's all over for you losers. McBabe showed up last night with the biggest fucking diamond ring on her hand you ever seen. And I'm guessing it didn't come from one of you."

One of the guys smiled in his office. His plan had worked. Once Sky discovered they were engaged, he'd told Bill he'd ride his ass every day until he got a ring on McCabe's finger, so the men would leave her alone. With no liberty expected until mid-September and the possibility of it taking weeks to get one sent from the States, they'd slipped back off the ship in Port Said and found something that would let the rest of the crew know McCabe was spoken for. All Hallie had to do was to open the box in front of Trixie, and let nature take its course. He hoped that nobody would notice that everything else in the box was available in the ship's store.

Amidst the feigned heart attacks and groans of disappointment from the men, Trixie continued. "She got a care package from lover boy yesterday. You know. Snickers Bars, Slim Jims, magazines, and a big, honking engagement ring! There's just one thing I can't figure out. Who would've ever guessed her boyfriend was a *cowboy*?"

Oh, it had been a banner day when the care package arrived. Just before Hallie opened it in front of Trixie, Commander Scott had informed her the CO had changed his mind about the tapings.

All was well in Hallie McCabe's corner of the world, which allowed her to concentrate on the ship's passage through the Bab-el-Mandeb Strait into the Gulf of Aden. Dangerous territory. This was where the USS *Cole* had been attacked. Where she knew seventeen people had died and thirty-nine had been wounded. From here on out, they'd all need to keep their dog tags around their necks and their heads on swivels.

Taping a segment from the flight deck with Yemen in the background, Hallie relayed safety messages that had been handed down from the CO via her boss. That was as close to Rick as she ever wanted to get. As long as there weren't flight ops going on, Hallie tried to do the taping topside. After gliding through the Arabian Sea, they rounded Oman. Several days later they headed for the Strait of Hormuz, a frightening bottleneck, that would take them into the Persian Gulf, or the Arabian Gulf as the Arab side called it. If all went as planned, they'd be able to have some down time overlooking Dubai over Labor Day weekend.

Hallie couldn't wait.

Chapter 26

The steel beach party on the flight deck started early on September sixth. The sailors and airmen had worked hard for the past forty-five straight days, although some had a few short breaks in liberty ports, and they deserved a day off to honor the American worker. Labor Day took on a whole new meaning for them. Considering the temperature was expected to hit one hundred fifteen degrees by mid-afternoon, the festivities began at 0800 hours. Some of the participants wore uniforms, but most dug out civilian clothes or bathing suits. Inflatable swimming pools were filled and charcoal grills were fired up.

The crew didn't care what time it was. It didn't matter to them if they ate a full meal of ribs, chicken, burgers, and brats with all the fixings and all the sides in the middle of the morning. This was a vacation day.

And the best part of eating what came off the grill? Knowing their superiors had done the cooking.

Even Captain Amerson flipped burgers and wiped sweat from his brow with his forearm. The XO manned another grill, as did the Command Master Chief. All the chiefs cooked. Or served. Or cleaned up. That was the part the crew liked the best. Watching the chiefs and officers doing clean up. And it was finally somebody else's turn to do the dirty work: separating the trash into plastics, cans, paper, and garbage. This was a real vacation day.

The volleyball tournament was going strong in the hangar bay, beside the basketball game. Too many volleyballs had gone overboard in previous years when they'd tried to play on the flight deck. The pass, punt, and kick tournament was canceled after losing two footballs in the drink. Double Dutch jump rope was popular, but the event everyone agreed was—by far—the best, was the dress-up relay race. Especially when they got the officers and chiefs involved. Somebody had come up with a bizarre collection of clothing—many donated by the women—for each participant to have to dress and undress in during the race.

While all these activities were in full swing, live bands took turns performing. Many of the crew played instruments and jammed together in the practice rooms during their down time, so here was their chance to shine. The crew loved being able to enjoy live music as it blared out over the briny blue. Sunshine, good food, good tunes, games, camaraderie, and a day off from work helped make it a truly memorable Labor Day. The CO had even cut watches to two-hour increments, so everyone would get a chance to enjoy the day—because it sucked to pull duty during a rare steel beach party.

Hallie glanced around the flight deck and reveled in everyone's excitement. She enjoyed watching them wallow in the fun time. Deprivation will do that to you. And she looked at the people. The joy on their faces and, no matter how pathetic some of it was, their dancing. This was a celebration and this was her family.

A holiday family picnic.

And she wasn't referring to that guy over there turning ribs on the grill. Her father. He wasn't her family. This crew was her family. Rick must have put something together about her not caring for his enthusiasm toward her, because first he canceled the tapings, and now he didn't even acknowledge her when she found herself passing him in the passageways. He treated her like *persona non grata*—which was just fine with her.

Hallie, Gina, and their friends piled their plates high with brats, potato salad, baked beans, and fresh baked chocolate chip cookies from the galley, grabbed some sodas and sat down to watch the dress-up relay races. At 1200 all activities moved to the hangar bay, where the crew would continue to party until evening. It was simply too hot to stay topside, if they didn't have to be there. The flight deck crews were especially happy to have a day below decks.

"Swim Call" was opened up in the Gulf for the next hour and those who dared to brave the possibility of jellyfish and sea snakes leapt three stories down from the hangar bay. James filmed the CO jumping first, followed by many other brave souls, who called back, "Come on in! The water's fine!"

Hallie's gaze followed one swimmer. The one with the dark brown curly hair, who did a masterful butterfly stroke all the way out to the perimeter of rescue boats.

Philip's long arms and broad shoulders cut the water rhythmically. She thought about the first time she'd seen him swim like that, in the St. Johns River, a world and, it seemed, a lifetime away.

She couldn't believe they were now halfway around the world from their sailboat, yet on a boat together again. Even though they couldn't actually be together, they were more together than they'd ever been. Because he knew the truth now. And he hadn't walked away. Well, he had walked away, but he'd come back again. She flexed her left hand, glanced down at the ring on her finger, and felt a rush of warmth.

They were actually going to sail off into the sunset together.

The ring was working its magic. The word had circulated because the number of guys who hit on her had dropped dramatically. Hallie couldn't imagine being able to stand here alone two weeks ago. Life was good.

Everything was going to be okay.

Rashid watched McCabe focus on one swimmer. She didn't seem to notice another thing going on around her, either the activity in the hangar bay or in the water. Her focus was on one man as he swam out to the boats and back again.

Rashid couldn't believe how many people had gone swimming in the Gulf. It gave him the willies to even *think* of getting in that water.

If he wasn't mistaken, the guy she was watching was the same one she'd been talking to in the store at the card racks a couple weeks ago. Rashid watched her smile as she admired her new engagement ring. Maybe this was the cowboy everyone was talking about. Nah. Scuttlebutt had it that guy was back in the States waiting for her. And this was how she behaved. Cheating with this geek. Shit, McCabe could do way better than him. Probably was. Probably had a whole string of men on the ship while she was whoring behind her fiancé's back.

She turned and saw him watching her. Oh, shit. She was walking his way.

"Hi. Having fun today?" McCabe asked.

"It's okay. Better than usual around here."

"I'm Hallie McCabe. I recognize you from the aft mess deck." She paused.

Waiting for him to say something? He couldn't imagine why she was over here talking to him. The McBabe? After much thought, he'd gone back to his original plan, to leave the bitch out of it and stage the attack during the news. But here she was giving him an invitation to involve her, on a silver platter.

She tried again. "Where do you work?"

"Combat. I'm an OS. You know. Checking radar. Friend or foe stuff."

"Sounds interesting. I've never been down to the Combat Direction Center before. Would you be interested in maybe letting me come by and do a piece for the news?"

Rashid's heart raced. He had to think on his feet here. How much he'd like to take her to Paradise with him—like he was going there. And she was making this way too easy. "Maybe. Got any openings this week?"

"I'd have to check the schedule, but I can get back to you. It can't wait until next week?"

"Well, Thursday, the ninth is my birthday. That would be kind of cool to be on the news on my birthday." His heart palpitated at the very idea of having her there with him, while he took control of CDC.

"Oh, I like that idea. I'll move some people around and we'll plan on Thursday. We like to do it in the morning, so we can edit."

"No." It had to be after dark. "I work the night shift. Can you come by after the news? Around 1930?"

"It wouldn't air until the next night then. And it wouldn't be your birthday."

"Well, they're having a little celebration for me on the ninth, so that's when I'd like you to come by." Yeah, like those assholes would care if it was his birthday, which it wasn't.

"Okay. 1930. I'll see you in Combat. And...I'm sorry, I didn't get your name."

"OS2 Davis. Randy Davis."

A name that is majorly going to be in the news, honey. Real soon.

"Okay. See you then. Thanks. Have fun today."

She turned and walked back to the edge of the hangar bay, probably so she could look out and see if lover boy was still out there playing hide and seek with the sea snakes.

Rashid's pulse throbbed as he climbed the ladders to the Combat Direction Center. Holy shit, the McBabe was coming to interview him. He could already imagine the shocked look on her face when he told her the suicide boats were headed their way. How that soft, creamy face would go white. And she'd beg him to stop the boats. Maybe she'd get on her knees for him. Then she'd beg him not to kill her. She'd probably do anything if he'd surrender. He realized he was growing hard at the rush of power he would have over her. He needed to get to his computer to alert the sadiqs there had been a time change for K-Day. A smile warmed him as he felt everything clicking into place. If he couldn't take Rosie out with him, this other whore, McCabe, would just have to do.

* * *

After swim call was secured, Hallie saw Philip standing in the entrance to the hangar bay talking to some other officers in bathing suits. She couldn't believe it when he called out to her as she walked by. "Hey, McCabe, how come you weren't in there swimming?"

Philip?

This was very brazen of him to call attention to himself, especially since he was standing with his friends. And he was smiling broadly. This was like something *she* would have done.

Hallie recognized Sky, but not the others. She had to keep track of whom she should recognize.

She walked over to join them. "The kiddy pools are about my speed, sir. I saw you swimming out there. Feel any sea snakes slithering around?" She waggled her fingers and laughed.

"Nope. It was absolutely perfect. Very salty, but bathtub warm. I want to be able to go home and say I swam in the Persian Gulf." Since she'd never seen him amongst his friends before, she was surprised at how outgoing and chatty he was.

"Better you than me." she smiled warmly, but not so focused on him that anyone would guess they were lovers. "Everybody having fun?"

They all responded enthusiastically and then Sky piped up after leaning around to look down at her left hand, "Hey, McCabe, tell me it ain't so. Tell me you didn't just get engaged."

"Afraid so, Lieutenant."

Sky threw his hand on his chest and feigned a faint. "Aw, you just broke my heart, McCabe." Everybody laughed.

"Sorry, but I've got a great guy who will be waiting for me when we get back home. That's the breaks."

"Well, if you ever wise up, you know where you can find the Skylark." He patted his chest to identify himself by his call sign. Sky was having so much fun with this, as was Philip, who continued to grin.

"Oh-kay. I'll keep that in mind, Lieutenant. See you guys. Have fun."

She continued on her way toward the music to find Gina and the gang. What an enjoyable day this had been. Friendship, music, good food, a day off from work for most of the crew, and a chance to watch Philip swim.

Plus she'd befriended that lonely guy, Davis. Hopefully making his day a little nicer, knowing she'd be filming him on his birthday. He was exactly the kind of person she liked to ask for interviews. People who didn't get a chance to be in the limelight. The shy, quiet ones who deserved to shine once in a while.

And now only three more days until Ramadan would be over and hopefully everyone would be able to get off the ship in Dubai. Sometime after the most dangerous date for a U.S. Navy ship in the Middle East. A date when they would be on high alert.

September 11.

Chapter 27

"This is MC2 Hallie McCabe saying goodnight and stay safe." Once the camera clicked off, Hallie stood and stretched. "James, remember we're going to Combat after this. Are you sure you don't mind?" She knew he wasn't crazy about working late, but Hallie had pleaded with him. It was Davis's birthday and she had a soft spot for underdogs. He was the kind of person who looked like he could use a friend and some attention.

MC3 James Hall gathered up his camera equipment and followed Hallie through the passageways to their next assignment. Expecting to find some kind of celebration, they were surprised to see everyone quietly performing their jobs in the semi-darkness of the Combat Direction Center. She knew CDC was dimly lit with red lights so the Operations Specialists could better monitor their search radars. But she'd never been this up close and personal with the eerie collection of electronic gear that glowed on monitors and plexiglas screens. Hallie realized they would need to use the spotlight on the camera when they filmed.

OS2 Davis turned from his monitor, smiled, and called to her. "Over here, McCabe."

James set up the camera about six feet from where Davis sat as Hallie prepared her clipboard and microphone to begin the interview. "Hall, remember to turn the spot—"

The rest of her words died in her throat when she felt something cold against her temple. Instinct told her not to move. Not to breathe. Her blood turned to ice. Slowly she lifted her gaze.

The eerie red glow of the room reflected off the ashen pallor of James's face where he stood frozen to the spot, mouth agape.

Fear gripped her heart like a fist and squeezed hard as Davis spoke quiet, menacing words in her ear. "I suggest you do exactly as you're told since I have a gun to your head and a bomb strapped to my body. One false move and it will be your fault if the bomb detonates." Hallie bit back the urge to scream.

The thought of nodding her head, with a gun pressed against it, was not an option either. So she reached down deep and pulled two syllables out of some hidden reservoir. "Okay."

"That's a good girl, McCabe."

"Hey," called out one of the OSs from across the room. "Look at my screen. I've got—"

In one split second, the gun left her head, plexiglas shattered, and all personnel dove for the deck. The pit of Hallie's stomach dropped with them and her knees threatened to follow. She countered by trying to pull in as much air as she could through her nose, willing her body not to move. She fought to keep from trembling, willing herself not to collapse.

Hallie flinched at the heat of the gun when it returned to her head. She hadn't heard the loud crack of a shot, but she could tell by the warmth of the barrel that he had fired. Oh, my God, was there a silencer? With the thick steel bulkheads in CDC, no one outside would know what was going on. Nausea threatened at the back of her throat and she swallowed thickly.

"Every one of you assholes over here on the deck!" Davis screamed. Then he turned back to James. "And turn that fucking camera off. On the deck! Hands on your heads. You, too cameraman," he yelled. "If any one of you moves, then McCabe dies."

Panic spread from Hallie's center, but she worked to keep it in check. She gathered her defenses with several deep breaths. A sour taste burned in her mouth. She tried to swallow, but her mouth had gone desert dry. She feared so much as licking her lips.

What in the hell was going on?

"Anybody with a brick slide it over here," Davis ordered. "I find out later you didn't give me your radio *right now*, and you're a dead man. Or woman." Radios slid across the deck to his feet. Davis kicked them behind him.

Hallie considered keeping hers for only a second, but realized it was not worth dying for. She asked if she could remove it from her waistband before lifting her jacket with shaking fingers. She estimated ten to fifteen people lying prostrate in front of them. She couldn't make an accurate count, or tell how many were females, without moving her head, especially in the semi-darkness. Her leg muscles flexed in anticipation of escaping. But there was nowhere to go. She pressed her elbows tightly against her body, trying to hold herself together.

Why was Davis doing this?

"Dixon, get over here!" Davis called. One poor soul rose hesitantly and approached them. Davis handed the man the phone. "Get Haggman down here. I'm listening, so don't say one fucking word about what's going on, or McCabe gets it. Just get his ass down here. The boss needs to be here for the party."

Hallie's pulse pounded at the thought of some of the crazies she'd seen on the news. But it was always somewhere else. Happening to some*one* else. Surely this was a dream. No, scratch that. A nightmare.

But she wasn't asleep.

Dixon made the call, then returned to his spot on the deck near the computer consoles.

While they waited for the CDC Department Head to appear, Davis took target practice at the other screens in the room, shattering the equipment and further darkening the room. Hallie's hands begged to protect her face from the flying plexiglas, but she didn't move a muscle, except to shut her eyes. Everyone on the floor cringed reflexively as each screen exploded, but no one moved voluntarily. Hallie considered doing *something* each time he removed the gun from her head to shoot out a screen.

But he had a bomb strapped to his body.

Think, Hallie, think.

Surely Davis could see her heart pounding right through her uniform and would shoot her for moving. Or her knees would buckle and that would be his excuse.

Breathe, Hallie, breathe.

Damn it all, she was Hallie McCabe. She was not going down without a fight.

Act, Hallie, act.

"And don't any of you worry about me running out of bullets. All I have to do is push this plunger here." He opened the flaps of his uniform shirt to display duct tape around something yellow. "And we all go to Paradise together."

Paradise?

Was Davis a terrorist?

Hallie sucked in several short breaths to try to gain some control. Every muscle ached with tension. Her mind raced to what an explosion could set off on this ship.

Millions of gallons of jet fuel stored below decks, along with thousands and thousands of munitions, like bullets, bombs, and missiles. And the planes, each of them a bomb in itself.

And then—oh, shit—the reactors. An explosion could lead to a nuclear disaster that could affect the Middle East for generations.

Right now Hallie McCabe was the only person in any position to stop him. The only one who could possibly talk him down.

The only one left standing.

Literally.

The inner-CDC door flew open and Commander Haggman joined them in the darkened space. He glanced at the destroyed monitors and the bodies on the floor. "What the hell is going on?"

"Over here, asshole!"

Hallie could barely see the commander's face as he picked his way through the bodies lining the deck. If he'd been smart, he would have ducked right back out the door before Davis could get a bead on him in the dimly lit room. Smart maybe, but not courageous.

The CDC Officer had seen enough to know there was trouble, even if he didn't know the extent of it. As he approached them, Hallie saw horror dawn on his face, ghostly in the red light. He froze. It was too late to turn back.

"I have a chair all picked out for you, fucking *sir*! Sit down!"

Commander Haggman sat. As if he'd wiped away all emotion, his face appeared blank, but Hallie could see the fury and frustration in his eyes, and something else.

Revulsion?

Davis handed Hallie a roll of duct tape. "Tape him to the chair. You know. Around and around she goes." He sneered. "Save his mouth for last. I expect an apology."

The CDC Officer tried to speak. "Davis, we can—"

"Shut up! Just shut the fuck up! I'll do the talking."

Hallie cautiously took the tape from Davis's hand and turned to the Combat Officer, not sure if her trembling fingers would even work. She nodded slightly to him, apologizing for what she was about to do. His eyes narrowed, his jaw stiffened, but he nodded back to her. At least the gun was gone from her head, though that was small consolation.

"Sorry, sir," Hallie whispered as she pulled the tape loose from the roll and began to wind it around the officer's body and the chair.

"His hands first. Tape his fucking hands together. And his feet. Then wrap the rest around the whole chair."

She pulled off a long strip for his hands, but how was she supposed to cut the tape? Maybe if she asked for scissors she could somehow use them to—

"Tear it with your teeth, McCabe. I'm not a fool."

A chill ran up her spine. It was as if he'd read her mind. She wrapped the tape around the officer's hands and then his feet, although she purposely left it as loose as she could without being detected. Then she wound the rest around him, securing him to the chair.

"And McCabe, when you're done, turn on the lights."

The phone rang. Davis answered, keeping the gun aimed at Hallie while she taped. "Combat. OS2 Davis...Yes, sir. No, sir. We haven't picked up anything, sir. Probably just some boats watching the fireworks, sir. You'll be the first to know. Yes, sir. Thank you, sir." After hanging up, he added, "Asshole."

While she taped the CDC Officer, Davis addressed the men on the floor, ranting and raving about what they'd done to him. How they'd humiliated him by sleeping with his wife while he'd been here on duty. Hallie's heart broke for those who weren't guilty. What had James Hall ever done to this crazy man? What had *she* ever done?

"And *you*, asshole!" He aimed the gun at Commander Haggman. "You were the worst of all of them. Did you do one fucking thing about any of it when I came to you for help? You're a poor fucking excuse for a leader. You're the real loser here." He turned back to the sailors on the deck. "If you want to blame somebody for the position you're in right now, blame this flaming asshole, Haggman."

Hallie's eyes darted around, assessing the room. It was still dark but she caught a motion in her peripheral vision. She forced herself not to look, to possibly give away someone who might be able to help. Her stomach churned, her hands shook as she finished taping Commander Haggman.

"Now is your chance to apologize for telling me that I wasn't man enough to satisfy my wife."

"Davis, I never—"

"It's Rashid! My name is *Rashid*."

A locomotive roared through Hallie's head. It *was* terrorist related. Some copycat 9/11 thing? Were they doing it early because the ship's guard might be down until Saturday? And how many more tangos were on board? Or outside the ship? Was that why he destroyed the radar screens? The day she'd met Philip, he'd told her his biggest worry was fishing boats that just happened to be floating bombs. Like what happened to the *Cole*.

Philip.

Oh, God. Was he down in the hole right now? Or had he gone to his stateroom after the news? And then with a shudder, she realized it didn't matter where he was. This was a nuclear carrier and it was armed to the teeth for sustained combat operations. A few well-placed explosives would trigger catastrophic results and they would all die.

Ship, shipmate, self.

She couldn't think about Philip. She had to figure out what she could do right now to help save the ship. And all of her shipmates too—except for this asshole. Rashid.

Commander Haggman tried again. "Rashid, I'm sorry if I didn't listen to you and offer support. Maybe we can go talk about it in my office."

Davis slapped him across the face. "Shut up, you son of a bitch!" He turned to Hallie. "Tape up his mouth before I shoot him right now." Davis put the gun to the man's head. "But no. I want to see your face when the company arrives and my little surprise goes off. The company that nobody else is going to see or know about until it's too late." He laughed and removed the gun from his boss's head.

Sweat poured from Hallie's palms. The roll of tape felt slick in her hands as she covered the commander's mouth. Pieces of broken glass seemed to slide through her veins. Her brain whirled, trying to latch on to some kind of plan.

Do. Something. Hallie.

But another voice urged her to give up. She ordered that voice to take a hike, along with the white stars that floated through her vision in the darkened room. She willed herself not to faint.

And then she remembered her weapon. But this was not the time to be ballsy. She wasn't afraid to take a risk, but there were thousands of other lives involved here. Was this the time to gamble with everyone's lives? She took a deep breath against the panic, straightened her shoulders, and stood at the ready.

Hallie had no idea what she was going to do, but she was going to do something.

As the only person allowed to move about the space, she would either talk this guy down or take this guy down.

"Hallie" was Teutonic for "strong in war." Well, damn it, she was going to be strong in this war. The war right there in the Combat Direction Center. The war for survival. Flashes of her mom and John Paul Jones helping her in the Captain's cabin came to her.

But this man had weapons.

Well, so did she.

Remembering how her mother had given her the strength to deal with the CO, Hallie opened her heart and her mind and reached for her mother's presence.

And heard words spoken directly into her soul.

Camera, Hallie. Use the camera.

The camera?

The *Blanchard* was one of the first ships to be designed from the keel up to support wireless systems. She knew the camera was networked into the master computer in the Media section of Public Affairs, but she couldn't turn it on. Davis would know it was running by the red light in the front.

But what about the red light in the back?

The *audio only* connection?

Her heartbeat sped up. She prayed James had left the audio on when he'd switched off the video portion, but help would have arrived by now. Public Affairs would have heard what was happening.

Gulping in a breath and attempting to keep her voice light, she waited for a break in Davis's rant. "I'm finished taping him, Petty Officer Davis. I'll just—"

"It's Rashid, bitch! You will call me Rashid!"

A wave of dizziness hit her. Her knees felt weak. She had to pay attention with every fiber of her being and think of him by that name.

"Rashid, I'm going to walk over to the light switch now. Is that okay?" Her voice shook and she made herself slow down.

"Do it."

Her legs had turned to Jell-O, making Hallie's stumble near the tripod not a total act. She grabbed onto the camera to right herself. Thank God it was too dark for Davis to notice what she was doing.

As she steadied herself, she reached around and clicked the *audio only* button.

A tiny red light came on, not bright enough for Rashid to see, especially with the rest of the room bathed in red. She hoped.

Her eyes flickered down to James on the deck. His look reflected both fear and approval for what she'd just done. He nodded his head slightly once.

Hallie crossed the room, stepping around the bodies on the deck, turned on the lights, then walked back toward Davis. Out of the corner of her eye, she saw a man on the floor, separated from the rest. He'd worked his way behind the center consoles. She thought it was Dixon, but she couldn't be sure. Obviously his plan had been to come up behind Davis and overtake him, but now that the lights were on, surely Davis would spot him. She must keep his gaze away from that part of CDC or he would know. When she returned to Rashid she stood on the other side of him. In order to talk to her, or put a gun to her head, he would have his back to the man under the consoles.

The man who was crawling on his belly, inch by painful inch, behind him.

"Just so you know. No matter what we do or say in here, you're all going to die. And so is everyone else on this ship. There are five dhows headed this way. Each loaded with thousands of pounds of explosives."

Chapter 28

Hallie's heart thudded as she absorbed the news. *There are five dhows headed this way. Each loaded with thousands of pounds of explosives?*

Think, Hallie, think.

The pen is more powerful than the sword.

Not the pen. Words. The only weapon at her disposal.

She'd once interviewed a police negotiator. The most important thing to do in a hostage situation was to keep the perpetrator talking.

She wasn't certain how much time they had, but she knew she had to keep Davis talking. She hoped and prayed the master computer in Public Affairs was up and running, and that somebody was listening to the information she was relaying. *If* they were listening.

"It's really not necessary to keep that gun to my head, Rashid. I'm not going anywhere. I know you'd detonate the bomb strapped to your body if I tried anything. Because you're a very smart man." He actually lowered the weapon, which allowed her to breathe, and now Public Affairs would know of the danger within the ship in addition to what was floating their way.

"I'm impressed with your plans, Rashid. But tell me how you're going to get five fishing boats loaded with explosives close enough to attack the *Blanchard*."

"After you assholes had your fun with my wife, I contacted al-Qaeda." He turned to the sailors on the deck. "That's right, al-

Qaeda's on their way for a little visit. They chose this date because it's the last day of Ramadan. A celebration day." Davis smiled. "They'll celebrate their strike on a U.S. warship and I'll celebrate taking out every one of you mother-fuckers. There's a new moon tonight too, so it's the perfect night for the attack. And since I'm the duty OS, it was very easy for me to interfere with the internal and external reporting of the approaching dhows."

"The five dhows that are heading to attack the *Blanchard* right now?"

Hallie prayed he didn't notice her repeating information for the benefit of the Public Affairs office. And whoever could hear them—please, God, let them be listening—she prayed they understood this was a life and death situation.

"The lookouts won't be able to get a visual on the fishing boats for a little while yet. Even their night vision capabilities won't pick up anything until it's too late. And by the time they run though all the fucking Rules of Engagement—especially the part about whether or not there's hostile intent, without any clues from Combat..." He paused to smile broadly. "Well, by then it'll be too late. But still plenty of time for the dhows to get into position to blow this ship all the way to hell and back."

Every nerve in Hallie's body was on edge waiting for the Klaxon to blare and the call to General Quarters, but it didn't come. She refused to give up her last sliver of hope that somebody was listening, and worked overtime to slow down her speech, her breathing, her heart rate. To focus.

"And you planned to blow yourself up along with CDC, so the distraction would keep the rest of the ship from knowing that the five suicide dhows are approaching? You're brilliant."

"You're a quick study, McCabe," he said facetiously.

"Rashid, I'm sorry you were hurt, but many of these people are not responsible for what happened to you. What have I done to hurt you? I've always been kind to you."

"You're a whore. Just like she was."

"How can you say that? You don't even know me."

"I see you with the men on the ship. I saw you at the steel beach party watching some guy the whole time. That same geek you cozied up to, reading greeting cards in the store. Probably plotting your next fuck-fest in some fan room. You, who are supposed to be engaged. You're a whore. Just like the rest of them."

Hallie's skin crawled. This creep had been watching her? More like stalking her. "It's not true, Rashid. I'm not engaged. This..." She held up her hand with the ring. "This is fake. I got tired of men coming on to me. I don't go to them. They bother me, so I had my sister send this zirconium, so the men would stay away. She got it at the mall or something. It's not even—"

"Anchorage Mall?"

"Yes." If you want it to be.

He laughed. "So somebody actually buys that shit. I wondered about that."

Stall him, Hallie. Stall him any way you can.

"I'm not a whore, Rashid. I don't like the attention I get here. I'm waiting for a real man, like you."

His head jerked back in disbelief. Eyes wide.

"A man who believes in a cause. Who has a mission. Who is powerful enough to pull off something like this. Don't kill yourself, Rashid. I can get you away from here. And I'll go with you. Before the five fishing boats with bombs on them get here. I have a friend who is a helo pilot. He'll take us off. We can stay here in the Middle East. With your friends."

No way would he fall for this crap, but it was worth a try. You never know with a crazy guy. And if he did believe her, if she could get him off the ship, even if she had to go with him, she might save the ship and her shipmates. But first things first, she had to keep him talking.

If only the rest of the ship knew what was going on. If they would take care of the fishing boats, she and the man on the floor would take care of Davis. Wasn't there a SEAL team embarked with them? Maybe they were crawling through the ductwork right now. Her eyes automatically scanned the overhead, looking for vents.

Suddenly Hallie knew they were underway. Felt it in her bones. Not always easy to tell when moving over calm water, and the Persian Gulf was smooth as glass today. So she knew the motion she was feeling was because they had accelerated, meaning the turbines had kicked into high gear and they were traveling at max speed.

Davis's eyes darted around. "What the fuck? Are we moving?"

Hallie felt the ship turn and instinctively knew they were preparing to launch planes. Once the planes were in the air, they'd be able to see the big picture. Please, God, don't let them need to get permission to take out the dhows. Please let Davis's words be enough, and please let somebody be listening to every word he was saying.

What had the Safety Officer said? The ship had to be steaming at thirty knots in order to launch aircraft? But wait. He'd told them something else. Something about the helicopters.

"We always keep a couple of helos on the flight deck, so they're ready at a moment's notice." So maybe Sky was already airborne.

Surely the *Blanchard* had turned to alternate sources for radar, and Air Ops had taken over surveillance and reconnaissance by now. The helicopters and gunners on the roof could get a visual with night vision capability and search lights. And while the lookouts would be outfitted with fifty caliber machine guns, the helos could also carry laser targeted Hellfire missiles capable of shredding the dhows and every living thing on board.

Oh, please, Sky. Please get to the dhows before they get to us.

Hallie's feet, shins, and knees registered vibrations in the deck just before she heard the roar of jet engine exhaust against a blast deflector. The rumble was followed by the distinct thunder of a catapult launching an aircraft.

Davis's eyes flew to the overhead. "Goddamn it, are those planes taking off?"

Hallie lied. "Maybe one of your boats got through and it's an explosion. Come on, Rashid. You're a good man. I don't want to see you die. I can get a helo for us, but we have to leave now!" Hallie felt another slight lurch. Please let that be aircraft launching and not an explosion. Surely the ship had gone to General Quarters by now and the rest of the crew had been alerted.

He shoved her away with his free hand. "Shut up, bitch! No way am I falling for your whore bullshit. A good man. Right."

Philip had died a thousand deaths when the Chief Engineer passed the word they were at General Quarters because "Petty Officer McCabe was being held hostage in CDC by a shipmate with a bomb strapped to his chest."

While Philip was secretly proud she was broadcasting live, he also knew she'd likely be the first to die if the hostage-taker found out. Once the Combat Systems Officer had shut off all 1MC announcements in the vicinity of CDC, the Commanding Officer on the Bridge was able to inform the crew of the situation, using bricks, phones, and email to pass more detailed information to key personnel.

Thank God for technology. This battle was being fought with handheld radios, sound powered phones, and computers—along with a few F/A -18 Super Hornets and Seahawk helicopters with Hellfire missiles thrown in for good measure. While executing the emergency launch induced a bit of panic on the roof, getting the ship up to speed down in Engineering was fairly routine.

But not for Philip Johnston. The announcement that Petty Officer McCabe was being held hostage in CDC kept echoing through his soul. Every nerve in his body screamed at him to get to her, as he did his part in assisting the Chief Engineer.

He forced himself to focus on his priorities: Ship, shipmate, self.

Only the officers and chiefs had been given the specific details: McCabe was being held at gunpoint by a disgruntled OS2

Davis, who was wired to explode. He'd conveniently allowed five suicide dhows to literally slip under the radar and gain access to the inner zone. There were roughly fifteen OS watchstanders in the space that would die if the bastard blew up. Despite the guilt Philip felt about it, his overriding concern was that OS2 Davis had a gun to Hallie's head.

Philip removed all thoughts of her from his brain. If they didn't get moving faster and those dhows got into range, the entire ship could be in mortal danger. One spark in the wrong place would set off the jet fuel and/or the weapons magazines. They had to be underway in order to launch the planes. The helos would be airborne already, but the fixed-wing planes needed thirty plus knots of wind in order to take off. And with next to no wind tonight, it meant they'd have to travel that much faster to generate the required wind to launch a fully loaded F-18.

It gave him hope knowing Sky was probably already up there, searching out the dhows. And once Sky was airborne, his crew would be locked and loaded and ready to fire.

This is what you've trained for, Sky. Go get those sons of bitches!

He couldn't let thoughts of Hallie distract him. And he couldn't think about his men—and woman—down here in the hole, within spitting distance of the reactor spaces. Close to where the dhows would hit if they didn't get the fucking ship moving faster. The ship came first. Then he could worry about his division and the woman he loved who currently had a gun held to her head—and then, and only then, would he consider thinking about himself.

The hell with himself.

He had to focus on doing his part in getting the ship underway. He hoped and prayed Hallie and the duty OSs could hold on until Security—or more likely the embarked SEAL team—could neutralize the asshole who was set to blow in Combat. He knew the men would have the brawn to do it and Hallie certainly had the brains. Who better to manipulate that sorry fucker than Hallie McCabe?

What had her mom called her? A daughter with balls?

"Well, this would be the time to pull 'em out and use 'em, honey," Philip mumbled under his breath. It was the last thing he did before an explosion rocked his world and everything went black.

A thud shuddered through CDC, strong enough for Hallie to lose her balance. She reacted quickly, afraid Davis would think she was moving of her own accord.

"What the hell was that?" Davis said, glancing around.

Hallie grabbed his attention before he could turn to see Dixon making his way toward them on the deck. "Maybe it's one of the fishing boats that got through." She got right up into Rashid's face and turned the charm on full blast, praying he wouldn't see how badly her hands were shaking. "Look, you *are* a good man. You've just had a bad experience. Please, come with me. Let's get away while we can."

Her peripheral vision reported that Dixon had worked his way out from under the console and into plain sight. She willed her eyes not to look over Davis's shoulder.

Every cell in her body screamed at Rashid: *Do not look behind you!*

Dixon would need another minute to get close enough and then what? She knew if he jumped Davis now and knocked him forward, the bomb could go off. But what other choice did they have? Maybe if she stood in front of Davis, he'd fall against her and—

But Davis was done pussy footing around. "There's no more time for this crap. All kinds of shit's going on out there. It's time to do my part. Kiss your asses goodbye. We're going to Paradise, folks!"

He laughed. He actually *laughed.*

Rashid opened his camouflage shirt, exposing the explosives. His fingers fondled the top of the plunger as he smiled at her with eyes that were now cold and dead. She picked her heart up off the deck and prayed for long life.

In one swift move, Dixon lunged for Rashid's back, yanking his arms behind him. "You son of a bitch!" Dixon cried out. The gun fell free to the deck and Hallie grabbed for it out of blind instinct. She pointed it at Davis. Her minimal weapons training kicked in from somewhere. But what about the bomb?

"You think I'm afraid of a gun, McCabe? You shoot me and the bomb goes off. We're all going to die one way or the other." He struggled against Dixon, trying to free his arms to push in the plunger.

Dixon yelled, "Shoot him, McCabe! Shoot him!"

"The bomb! I'll hit the bomb!"

Davis wrapped a foot around Dixon's leg, tripping him, and as the two fell backward, one of Davis's arms came free. He reached for the plunger, grinning madly. "This is for you, Rosie!"

Hallie cried, "Duck, Dixon!" and blew the grin right off Rashid's face.

Chapter 29

"Freeze!" Dixon yelled. "Nobody move!"

Hallie had slammed her eyes shut and prayed she didn't hit both of them, or the bomb, when she'd pulled the trigger. Her heart started beating again, because Dixon sounded strong, and apparently she was still alive. They all were.

Except Davis.

She felt herself slipping into shock, but willed her body not to move, except to lower the gun and open her eyes. She glanced around madly, avoiding the carnage on the deck, refusing to poison her mind with the vision. Turning just her head, she met Commander Haggman's eyes. How she wished she could remove the tape from his mouth so he could take charge, but she didn't dare move.

He nodded to her as if he could read her mind.

"Talk to me, Dixon!" called out the senior chief OS.

"Except for dripping in who-the-fuck-knows-what, I think I'm okay."

Hallie gagged, swallowed, refused to look.

Dixon spit. "I don't think you hit me, McCabe, but I'm sure as hell not moving 'til this bomb is defused to find out."

The senior chief took over, addressing the CDC Officer and then the men. "Sir, I'm going to take the con until we can get you free. The person closest to the door, walk out very carefully."

"No! Don't move." Hallie reported to the air. "This is MC2 McCabe. We have a bomb in CDC. Send EOD ASAP. The suicide bomber is dead, but he's wired with explosives and we don't know what to do. Maybe...maybe twenty personnel in here. Send help now!"

Every head turned as the inner-door to CDC opened and a suited-up explosive ordnance disposal team slowly filed in. "Make a hole! Make a hole!" the leader said and the line of OS watchstanders parted like the Red Sea.

The senior chief was stunned. "How'd you do that, McCabe?"

"The audio portion of the camera was broadcasting through the wireless system the entire time. The digital signal feeds a monitor in Public Affairs. Thank God somebody up there was listening. EOD must have been waiting in the passageway."

"Damn, I'll never trash the press again in my life. Good job, cameraman."

"Don't thank me," James replied from the deck, still lying stock-still. "McCabe turned it on when she went for the lights."

"Whoa, McCabe! You're a McHero!" cried the senior chief without moving. "You too, Dixon. You both deserve a medal for this."

"Keep your medal, Senior. Just get me out of this clusterfuck," Dixon mumbled, as if afraid to move his lips.

"Don't anybody move," one of the EOD techs from the bomb squad said in a surprisingly calm voice. "Except those of you behind me. You're cleared to exit this space and report directly to Medical for evaluation. The rest of you stay where you are for now."

For the first time since this bizarre ordeal started, the reality of what just happened—that she'd killed a man—soaked in. Hallie's body began to shake uncontrollably. She willed herself to remain calm but panic was rapidly winning the battle. Her stomach threatened to slide from her body, the way the blood was draining from her face. Her hands grew cold. The gun still held tightly in her right. She wanted it out of her hand now. But no way she was going to move. Hallie had the rest of her life to move freely. And she hoped that would be a long, long time.

But not now.

She refused to pass out, or look at the two bodies entwined on the deck in front of her. She brushed aside every horrible thought and picture that tried to invade her brain, filing them away into a little compartment she would deal with later.

Besides they weren't out of the woods yet. There was still a bomb to defuse.

Turning her head a fraction of an inch, she saw the Combat Officer still taped and gagged, his eyes focused on the EOD squad. He caught her glance and his eyes softened as he nodded to her. She felt her mouth tremble, but he nodded again repeatedly, trying to tell her that everything was okay.

Just hold on.

She couldn't turn far enough to see any of the other OSs, some standing, some probably still lying on the deck. And James was back there too. Thank you, sweet Jesus, there was someone she knew. Someone she could hold on to once they could move. And she wanted to hug Dixon and make sure she hadn't hurt him, once he was cleaned up. She quickly filed away what he must look like right now. And Davis. Holy Mother of God, she had just shot him in the...the hell with the rules of no touching. Hallie knew somebody needed to hold her pretty soon or she was going to come apart at the seams.

Philip.

She'd locked Philip away in another corner of her brain and now she almost lost it. What was that last unexplainable thud that reverberated through the ship. It certainly wasn't a plane launching. What if the ship had been hit? What if he was down in the hole? What if—?

No, she couldn't go there.

Two members of the EOD team were now moving past her. Slowly. "Everybody just stay calm and don't move until we tell you to."

"Holy shit," one of them muttered under his breath as he approached what must have been Davis' faceless body draped over Dixon. "Okay," he said to the other one. "Looks like a standard 'do-it-yourself Saturday Night Special' from the Internet." He turned back to face all of them. "Listen up. We're going to get the rest of you out of here before we dismantle this bomb. One by one, starting with the person closest to the door, I want you to slowly walk out. And do not even think of slamming it." Turning to Commander Haggman, he smiled and said, "We'll cut you loose as soon as they're all out of here, sir."

While the OS watchstanders slowly filed out, he noticed the gun in Hallie's hand. "Don't tell me you did this, McCabe."

All she could do was nod her head yes; her chest tight, her jaw clenched, her eyes still averted from the bodies.

"Bravo Zulu! Damn good job. You managed to kill this fucker without setting off the bomb or taking his cuddle buddy with him? We're going to have to cross deck you to Gunner's Mate."

How could they joke about this?

Hallie sucked in a breath, exhaled deeply, and ordered her face not to crumple into tears. She was not going to lose it in front of these men. She was Hallie, "Strong in War." But the horror of what had just happened hit with a nauseating wave and kept trying to seep out of the tightly closed compartment in her mind.

When the last of the OSs had departed, one of the EOD techs said, "Okay, McCabe. You're up. Hand me the gun, butt first. Now turn around very slowly and walk out the door."

Hallie was surprised her feet worked as she made her slow approach to the door. Surely this was the longest walk she would ever take in her life.

Just before she exited, she heard an EOD tech talking to Commander Haggman. "Hold on while I cut you loose, sir. Haven't cut anyone with this para-knife yet today, but wigglers are always at risk."

Although she felt herself beginning to hyperventilate, Hallie held it together as she walked the passageway lined with Security personnel in full battle gear—including a couple of Navy SEALs if she wasn't mistaken. All silently cheered her with thumbs-up as they ushered her toward Medical with the rest of the former hostages. Once she arrived, Hallie's eyes searched through the blue camouflage to find a familiar face, so she could let down her guard.

Finally she saw James and curled into his arms. Relief rushed to every cell in her body. He put his arms around her and patted her back. Closing her eyes, she drew in a slow calming breath and tried unsuccessfully to keep the tears at bay. The hell with the regs. She didn't care who saw them comforting each other.

"I'm sorry, Hallie, I can't believe I didn't think of the audio," he said.

"It's okay, James. I'm just glad you're all right. I was so scared." Hallie wiped away her tears, sniffled, and tried to maintain her military bearing. But she couldn't stop shivering.

James wrapped a blanket around her. She was glad he kept his arm around her and discretely stroked her back as they assessed the scene around them.

She realized she was not alone in processing the horror of the past hour. It was reminiscent of a refugee scene. These were not battle-hardened infantrymen. They were Operations Specialists whose job it was to gather and process tactical information. They were analytical types. None had been trained for close combat. They looked as stricken as she felt, but she had just killed a man. She had every right to cry openly.

But she didn't. She would suck it up and carry on.

Hallie turned as Commander Haggman joined them. The color was back in his face, but he still appeared quite shaken. She wanted to throw herself into his arms. They had, after all, almost died together.

Instead she reached out her hands to him. "Is Dixon okay? I was so afraid I hit him."

The CDC Officer squeezed her hands before dropping them. "He's okay, but, trust me, you don't want to see him yet." He exhaled a sigh of relief. "McCabe, that was masterful. I can't even begin to thank you." He raised his brick and made a call. "Gun Boss, CDC. Have you got a spare body to shadow McCabe for the time being? Prefer someone big and intimidating, if possible."

"No problem, Hag," squawked from the brick. "I have just the guy. I assume she's in Medical with the rest of the CDC folks."

"She is. Thank you."

Hallie's heart lurched. "Am I in trouble, sir? I didn't need *permission* to do that, did I?" She would have laughed if she could.

"Permission? Hell, no. The guy was going to kill us. And everyone else on the ship. We all heard it and a very savvy member of the press even recorded it all. You're not in trouble, McCabe, but you might need some protection against well-wishers mobbing you. You heard the senior chief. You're a freaking McHero!"

Finally the Klaxon blared. "General Quarters! General Quarters! With the exception of personnel receiving medical attention, all hands man your Battle Stations. I say again, General Quarters! General Quarters! With the exception . . ." It was punctuated with the roar of a jet blast from overhead. Or something else. They didn't know.

Commander Haggman gave a sharp whistle to get the attention of everyone gathered in Sick Bay. "Okay, listen up. I don't know much more than you do right now. See a corpsman if you need aid and make sure you get your name on the sign-up sheet that's being passed around so we know who to talk to later. If you're not injured and have been cleared by a corpsman, then make your way up to Air Ops. That will be our Battle Station until the EOD guys clear us in CDC. As soon as General Quarters is over, expect to be told to report back to me. Plenty of people are going to want to interview you and get your perspective on what happened. Do not discuss details with anyone until we've been debriefed. Petty Officers McCabe, Hall, and Dixon are to remain here in Medical. By the way, great job up there, men—*and woman!*"

This caused an eruption of cheers for Hallie and more than a few shout-outs.

Gesturing with his hands for them to keep it down, Commander Haggman added, "Okay, calm down. Taking out a tango is just another day at the office for a *Blanchard*-trained MC." He smiled broadly. "Surely you didn't think she was just a pretty face that read cue cards. Now lay off McCabe, get in the proper Battle Dress, and follow me to Air Ops."

Again the 1MC boomed. "Attention all hands. This is the XO. We are still at General Quarters. Remain at your Battle Stations until further notice. We have four confirmed kills on suicide dhows. We took one indirect hit, when it exploded in close proximity. We suffered some damage and have a few casualties—mostly from the concussion just below the waterline and from flying debris in the hangar bay. Reactor spaces were not compromised and we are under our own power. We will continue to transit to safer waters. We have aircraft airborne to provide early warning, including a handful of fixed-wing and most of our helicopters. Everyone involved did an outstanding job getting them to the roof and launched. We have the rest of our pilots and aircrews on Alert Five, Alert Fifteen, or Alert Thirty until we know for sure that the threat is over. Damage Control is still assessing damage and casualties in Engineering..."

All of Hallie's resolve disappeared as she slipped from James's arms.

Chapter 30

She didn't know if it was the smelling salts or the 1MC that brought her around, but Hallie was mortified to find herself on the deck, faces hovering over her. The hospital corpsman wielding the smelling salts was a female, flanked by two male corpsmen with genuine looks of concern on their faces, as they gently lifted her to a sitting position. Hallie relaxed knowing she was in their care.

"Attention all hands. This is the Captain. We believe all external threats have been eliminated. However, one of our own was involved in the attack, and that greatly increases the possibility of sabotage. We're going to relax Battle Dress, but we want everyone to remain at their GQ stations while we do a search. I want every square inch of this ship scoured for possible bombs. Unless you are directly involved in the search, limit your internal phone use and stay off the bricks. That is all."

Hallie scrambled to stand up and signaled Commander Haggman, telling him she needed to talk with him privately. "Before you go, I need a favor, sir. Please."

"I owe you my life, McCabe. Shoot." The word hit both of them at the same time. "Sorry."

"Sir, this has to be confidential."

He nodded.

"My fiancé is in Engineering. Can you find out his status?"

"Ah, so you *are* engaged. That was a good story in there, by the way. But we can talk later. I'm headed topside. I'll check it out and call down here. What's his name?"

Hallie hesitated. "Um...he's an officer, sir."

A flicker of something passed across Haggman's face and a smile tugged at the corner of his mouth. "Okay, McCabe, like I said, I owe you my life. I promise to be discreet. Who is the lucky son of a bitch?"

"It's the AUXO, sir. Lieutenant Johnston."

That threat of a smile gave way to a full-fledged grin. "You and Bill Gates? No way."

"Please, sir," she implored him.

"I'm on it, McCabe. I'll call you here at the Sick Bay desk as soon as I know anything." He chuckled as he departed. She figured he was probably thrilled to find something humorous in an otherwise traumatic evening.

"Captain wants to see you on the Bridge, McCabe," said the corpsman holding the phone.

The Captain? Hallie hadn't seen him since that day in Public Affairs. She was still pretty shaken about the whole Combat experience and didn't know if she had it in her to face Rick right now. She was glad the female corpsman was going with her and realized the burly petty officer the Gun Boss had sent wasn't letting her out of his sight either.

When Hallie stepped onto the Bridge, the senior officers present broke into applause. And she knew it wasn't the same kind of cheering and clapping that had accompanied her first broadcast. After handshakes from the officers and a few words from the CO, Captain Amerson announced he needed to talk with McCabe in his cabin for a few minutes. In private.

The corpsman offered to go with her, but Hallie said she'd be fine. She was unafraid and followed Captain Amerson off the Bridge. She needed to find out about Philip and was prepared to bargain.

"Sit down, McCabe." He indicated the chair. He sat and looked at her seriously from across his desk. The first thing she noticed was the twinkle was gone from his eyes. Something had taken its place, but she couldn't quite put her finger on it.

"I have a few things to say here, so bear with me. First of all, thank you for saving the lives of so many of our shipmates tonight and possibly the entire ship. I am indebted to you. And I want you to know if you ever need anything from this man's Navy—or this woman's Navy—for the rest of my life, I'm there for you. And I mean that."

Hallie's spine relaxed a few notches. This was about thanking her. She decided to take him up on his offer by discreetly asking about Philip. She'd subdued the terrorist and alerted the ship. He owed her big. She might even push the limits and ask him to allow Philip to come up and be with her for a few minutes. Certainly she deserved that after what she'd been through. And after what she'd done.

Unless Philip was dead. She shivered.

"And secondly, I want to say I'm sorry. About everything."

"Sorry, sir?" Hallie's voice quavered.

"I'm sorry if I ever made you feel uncomfortable. And I'm sorry about hurting your mother."

A fist slammed into her chest. "My mother!"

He knew Suzanne was her mother?

"I didn't know about you. I'm sorry. I had no idea. How is your mother?"

Surely her heart was going to burst right through her jacket. "She...she..." He was being way too matter of fact about this. "She died several years ago from breast cancer, sir."

"I'm sorry to hear that. But I can tell she did a bang-up job of raising you. She'd be very proud of you tonight. As I am." He paused and looked at her intensely. "I never knew I had a daughter. Suzanne told me that she..." He cleared his throat and looked away before continuing. "And then she stopped answering my letters and was discharged from the Navy and disappeared. I would have helped, if I had known...about you. Look, I hope we can discuss this another time. We only have a few minutes here."

"How long have you known about this, sir? About me? That I'm your daughter?" The words sounded foreign coming from her mouth.

"Your knight in shining armor came to see me a couple of weeks ago. To defend your honor. He told me everything." Captain Amerson looked down at her left hand. "Johnston's a good man."

This time the fist slammed Hallie in the gut, forcing her mouth to pop open. Philip had put his career in jeopardy to defend her?

"I promised him I wouldn't say anything about that meeting, but I think under the circumstances, he would approve."

Circumstances? Was he...? Oh, God! Tendrils of fear crept into her body and wrapped around her soul, choking it. She hadn't even processed that she'd narrowly escaped death and killed a man tonight. But the thought of something happening to Philip on top of all of that was too much.

"Circumstances, sir?"

"Your quick thinking helped us avert everything except for the repercussions from one of the dhows exploding. There's damage to some of the engineering spaces. I'm afraid we have casualties down there."

She forgot how to breathe. Terror enveloped her. Squeezed. Hard. "Is he okay?"

"Lieutenant Johnston was wounded, McCabe."

Hallie took a shot to the ribs.

"He's unconscious. He has a head injury."

"Noooo!" A traumatic brain injury could mean anything. And none of it good.

"We're not equipped to deal with a TBI here. I've arranged for a Med-Evac to take him off the ship immediately. We'll fly him off via one of our own helicopters to Bahrain, and from there he'll be transported by military airlift to Germany."

"Oh, God!" Hallie's hands flew over her open mouth to keep herself from keening. She rocked, trying to counter what he'd said with one word: No! No! No! No. No!

* * *

"McCabe!"

Rick had to get her back. As much as he wanted to reach out and touch her in some form of comfort, he didn't dare. If this was all he'd had to tell her, he would have brought the corpsman in with her, but he'd needed to be alone with her to discuss Philip, and Suzanne.

"He's going to be okay. I promise you." Rick had no idea where those words had come from, but he knew he needed to say them to get her back. "A corpsman will accompany him in the helicopter to Bahrain and the Air Force Cargo plane there has a fully staffed Med-Evac team to monitor him all the way to Germany. The Army hospital in Landstuhl will have the right specialists to ensure nothing's overlooked."

Hallie continued to rock, her hands covering her mouth.

"The good news is I'm sending you with him, if that's what you want. I think you should be on that helicopter, holding his hand, and talking to him all the way."

This could be a win/win situation if she'd accept his offer. Maybe she'd forgive him for the paternity snafu if he allowed her to go with lover boy. And he'd get her off his ship before any photographers got "father/daughter" pictures out to the media.

"I have every confidence that you're the one to bring him back to us, McCabe."

"Yes! I want to go." Hallie stood and headed for the door.

"You've got a few minutes. Make sure you have your ID and some money," he said as he pulled bills from his wallet and handed them to her.

"Sir?

"You'll need cash in Germany. Just in case. Don't worry about anything else. I'll see you're taken care of there and we'll send all your things once you arrive."

"My things?"

"McCabe, who knows how long this will take. He'll probably be sent home to the States after everything's okay. I want you to stay by his side as long as he needs you. It's the least I can do."

"I'm not coming back to the ship?"

"Let's not go there yet. Let's get Lieutenant Johnston the right medical care and we can talk later. Just take care of him. And, McCabe, I would very much like to talk with you at another time about...you know." This was his daughter. "I'm afraid this is not the time or place to discuss it, but I hope it will be okay to contact you after this is all over. I'll make sure your things are sent. I'll see to it personally."

"Yes, sir. I'm sure that would be all right. To meet with you sometime later. I'd like that. About my things, there are some personal letters." She dug out her locker key. "I'll just give this to my cameraman and he'll make sure my bunkmate sends my things. And, sir? I'd like to ask that Lieutenant Sky Crawford be allowed to process Lieutenant Johnston's things if you're sending those too."

"No problem." He jotted down the name.

"Actually, sir. Can I ask a favor?"

"I told you 'anything you need.'"

"If he's not out on patrol or something, could Lieutenant Crawford accompany us to Bahrain? He's a pilot with HSM-23. I really could use his support right now, if he's available."

"Consider it done." He continued taking notes.

"And, sir? Just so you know. There isn't anybody else on this ship that knows about you, that you're my...you know. Not even Lieutenant Crawford. Lieutenant Johnston and I are the only ones who know. We didn't feel it would serve any purpose to say anything. We thought it best that it stayed between us."

Rick looked up at her with visible relief. He couldn't have said it better himself. "I appreciate that. Let's get through this crisis first."

They were interrupted by the 1MC. "Attention all hands. This is the XO. All personnel who witnessed the crisis in CDC are to report to the Officer's Wardroom for debrief. That is all."

Hallie looked at the Captain for answers. "I'll take care of it," he said. "It's all on tape and there were plenty of witnesses. Since you're 'suffering from severe shock and PTSD,' we'd really better get you on that Med-Evac plane to Germany for further evaluation." He winked at her.

As Hallie rose, he stood and walked around the desk. "I look forward to talking with you about other things another time. When all of these crises have resolved themselves. Go now and God bless. Get on that helo and do whatever you need to do for Lieutenant Johnston for as long as it takes. I'll keep tabs on both of you. Email me directly if you need anything."

Captain Amerson was filled with mixed emotions. On the one hand he truly was indebted to them. On the other, he wanted them gone. Far away from his ship. He walked her to the door, sincerely wanting to reach out and touch her. Not only was she his *daughter*, but she had saved his ship. No way was he going to touch her though. Except maybe to extend his hand for her to shake it. Hallie looked down at it and then reached out with her own. He took her hand in both of his and held it for a heartbeat longer than necessary, looking into her cornflower blue eyes with his own. Eyes that he hoped reflected admiration, respect, and regret.

"Good luck, McCabe." He paused. "Hallie." Letting go of her hand, he added, "I wish you both the best. Godspeed."

She focused on his identical blue eyes. "Thank you, sir." Then she turned and departed.

Rick knew he needed to get back to the Bridge, but he gave himself ten more seconds to regain his composure.

His daughter.

Whoever would have guessed that the seed he'd literally planted twenty-five years earlier would grow to come back and save his ship, his crew, and his ass?

Chapter 31

"I've never been on the roof during flight ops, sir, and I'm already a nervous wreck," Hallie said to the Air Transportation Officer, when he finished outfitting her with disposable ear plugs, a cranial with integrated goggles, and an emergency flotation device.

"Just pay attention, McCabe, and do whatever I tell you. We're going to walk topside to the back of the island and I'll point you in the direction of the helicopter. It's going to be loud out there, with a lot of things happening all at once. Keep your head on a swivel to make sure you don't walk into the exhaust area of a jet or trip over anything, like arresting gear cables or catapult launch shuttlecocks. And watch out for the tractors and aircraft being towed. Once you get on board the helo, do whatever the aircrewman tells you. From the pilots' seats back, he's in charge and he'll keep you safe.

"Do not enter the rotor arc until the plane captain signals you in by pointing at you and motioning you to come aboard. Walk straight in at the nine o'clock position, directly toward the cabin door. You don't need to duck as the rotor arc is far overhead but you can if it makes you feel more comfortable. Whatever you do, keep your goggles over your eyes, since the jet exhaust and rotorwash out there can cause permanent eye damage. Now follow me."

As Hallie and the ATO rounded the island, the noise of jets taxiing and helicopters turning on deck was deafening, even with ear protection. Her heart went out for everyone who worked on the roof on a daily basis. The ATO turned to her and pointed across the flight deck at a helicopter, although it was nearly midnight and her eyes had not adjusted completely to the darkness.

A shiver ran through her when she remembered there was a new moon tonight, which was why Rashid had planned the attack for this evening.

Had that just happened tonight?

She was jerked back from her reverie when the ATO grabbed her by the back of her flotation device and walked her toward the aircraft.

Focus, Hallie, focus.

The helo's cargo door slid open and an aircrewman jumped out. He flashed a red light signaling her aboard. Hallie ducked instinctively as she walked under the spinning blades. Approaching the starboard side of the helo, she spotted the boots of another flight suit-clad crewman, who grabbed her and whisked her the last few steps. Rising up to her full height, she turned to thank him, and froze, mouth open in mid-speech.

Sky.

Hallie flew into his arms for a brief hug. Then he yelled over the noise of the flight deck, "Hey, Wonder Woman! I just heard what you did!" He kissed her full on the mouth, then grinned. "Sorry, I wasn't thinking. But cool! Now everyone will think I'm your cowboy. Don't worry about Bill, sweetheart. Everything's going to be fine. The Skylark is going to take care of both of you. All the Sierras took the rest of the casualties, so the Skipper radioed me personally to get you where you need to go. Welcome aboard! She's all yours, Quinn."

The aircrewman, Petty Officer Quinn, grabbed her by her floatation device and screamed above the noise, "Get in now, McCabe!"

He planted her in the main Sensor Operator's seat and began adjusting the five-point harness to lock her in. Then he attached a long cord to a "pigtail" on her cranial and spun around to close the cabin door. The noise deadened considerably and Hallie realized she was connected to the helo's Inter Communications System. She could hear Quinn talk with Sky now as if he was speaking right into her ear.

"Hey, sir, I thought we were doing a Med-Evac. Petty Officer McCabe looks like she's in pretty good shape to me."

Hallie heard Sky reply, "Hold your horses, Quinn. We've got one more coming. Thankfully Maintenance removed the sonar system from this aircraft for repairs, or we wouldn't have room for our other passenger. Heads up, Quinn. Here comes our guest now."

Hallie watched as Quinn slid open the cargo door and jumped out to assist a group of red-shirted "Ordies"— ordnancemen—bearing a patient strapped into a Med-Evac litter. They somehow managed to shimmy the litter into the helo's tunnel between the enclosed racks of electronics. Hallie leaned forward in her straps to get a better look.

Philip.

A wave of nausea swept over her and she struggled to stay conscious. Although his neck was braced in a cervical collar, his head was swathed in gauze, and an oxygen mask covered his nose and mouth, she could tell from his jawline that it was Philip. Her heart sank further as she took in the bruises and abrasions on his face and the IV bag on his chest, with a line snaking down under the blanket that covered him. It was odd that her first thought was: where are his glasses?

Every breath of life in her cried to get to his side, touch him, kiss him, reassure him that everything would be okay. And she prayed to God it would. But just as she was actually considering unstrapping to go to him, Quinn pulled the corpsman in, slammed the sliding cabin door shut and strapped both of them into the remaining seats.

He flipped a switch on the console. "McCabe, reach down on the left side of your seat and grab the round handle. Now move it forward to lock your harness. Okay, sit back, relax, and enjoy the ride." Then he called out, "After-Station secured. All locked aft, ready for takeoff, sir."

Sky's co-pilot replied, "Pre-Takeoff Checklist complete, locked aft, locked left, clear left."

Sky's voice now. "Locked right, clear right, coming up."

Hallie felt them rise into a hover over the flight deck, her heart thrumming with the rotors, wishing she could get to Philip. Maybe if she could hold his hand, he would know she was there and it could make the difference between him living and...

Stop. Stop that right this minute.

Believe, Hallie, believe.

Sky's voice soothed her through her cranial. "Gauges green. Power coming on. One...two...three rates of climb. Safe single engine airspeed. Stabilator programming. Passing through three hundred feet heading to five."

He said something under his breath to his co-pilot, but Hallie didn't care what it was. Just hearing Sky's voice anchored her, let her know that somehow he was helping to make everything all right. Sky was in command here and no way would he let Philip die on his watch.

"Five hundred feet, one hundred knots, altitude hold engaged. Give Tower a call and let them know we've got Bahrain TACAN singing sweet and ask them to relay to Bahrain Control that we'll enter their airspace in fifteen mikes. Speeding up to one-thirty."

"Copy, Sky. After-Takeoff Checklist complete. Calling *Blanchard* Tower now."

"Hey, Quinn," Sky called aft. "Can McCabe hear me?"

"Yes, sir. She's all miked up."

"Hallie, you okay?"

She didn't know how to respond, until Quinn showed her how to engage the *Push To Talk* button. "Just fine, sir. Though I'd really like to talk to Phil—uh, Lieutenant Johnston."

"I understand he's still unconscious, but it sure couldn't hurt. And, hell, he might be able to hear for all we know. Quinn, put a Gunner's Belt on her."

"Yes, sir."

"Hallie, you've got five to ten minutes before Quinn will need to get you strapped back in for landing. So keep it short and sweet."

Quinn moved her to a Gunner's Belt so she had free movement in the cabin, but remained tethered to the aircraft. "And McCabe, I'm gonna switch seats with you, so you can talk to the patient. Don't worry about strapping into my seat. All you need is that belt for now.

As soon as she switched places with Quinn, Hallie dropped to her knees beside Philip.

She kissed his cheek gently, otherwise afraid to touch him, fearful it might hurt him. Her hand found its way carefully under the blanket to find his, and she squeezed just a little. Then laying her head down gently on their clasped hands, she prayed. Next Hallie put her mouth next to his ear and talked soothingly to him, even though she felt the stirrings of panic rising back up in her gut. She had taken Philip back out of that closed compartment in her mind, but now she had to keep shutting the door on Rashid's evil grin.

"Philip, I'm here. I love you so much. You've got to come back to me. Remember the lavender lace skivvies I'm going to wear at our wedding? Just like I do every Wednesday night on the news? Just for you? I'll wear them every day if you'll just come back. Remember how much you love it when I scream when we're making love? I promise to scream every time if you'll just come back so we can get married and make those babies together. Remember Suzanna and little Philip and Billy Gates Jr.? I need you to come back so we—"

"McCabe!"

Sensing the panic in Quinn's voice, she feared something was wrong with the helicopter, but the faint light of the cabin revealed a red-faced grin, hard to do with his mouth hanging open.

She heard him clear his throat through her earphones. He tried to speak, but started laughing. Finally he said, "Um, McCabe, you're on Hot Mic."

Hallie screwed her face up in confusion.

"You must have bumped the ICS switch when we traded places. And...um...Everyone on board just heard what you said."

Now she heard muffled laughter coming from various crewmembers. Sky's voice chimed in, "So will the bridesmaids be wearing lavender lace skivvies too, McCabe? I'm up for wearing purple boxer-briefs myself, but only if I'm color-coordinated with the ladies. Hey, maybe you and Bill can do, like, a Victoria's Secret theme. That would be a wedding to remember."

Didn't matter. Nothing mattered except getting Philip the care he needed.

Sky continued. "Don't worry, sweetheart. I probably won't be at the wedding anyway. Once Bill finds out we didn't cut you off sooner he's gonna come back and strangle me anyway. Which would be a good thing, the him coming back part, not so much the strangling part."

She tuned them all out. The details of her and Philip's sex life, let alone the admission of blatant fraternization, didn't matter. Keeping Philip alive was all that was important at this point. She stroked what little of his hair she could find around the gauze and kissed each bump, bruise and laceration on his face.

Careful to click the right button this time, she soothed him as best she could. "It's all going to be okay, Philip. We'll be landing in Bahrain soon and then we'll board an Air Force plane to take us to Landstuhl. I'll be at your side every minute. Just hang on." She looked up to see the corpsman watching her, wide-eyed. She smiled at him for good measure. This was a trip he'd not soon forget.

Sky's voice broke through. "Attention all hands. Attention all hands. This is the Skylark, your beautiful and sexy flight attendant. Thank you for flying with Operation Enduring Freedom Airlines. I have a few parting words before we land. In case you didn't know, Petty Officer McCabe most likely saved all of your asses tonight with her quick thinking and bravery in CDC. So I am asking you to have the decency to forget everything you saw or heard on this flight that might compromise my best buddy and the love of his life, Hallie McCabe. Actually, it was all just a figment of your imagination. And just to let you know that if you feel it necessary to spread rumors about what you *think* you saw and heard, I will make it my mission in life to go the ends of the earth to seek you out so I can kick your sorry ass all the way to kingdom come. It's been a pleasure flying with you tonight. We hope you have a pleasant stay in Bahrain or wherever your travels take you. That is all."

Hallie laughed out loud along with everyone else. What an awesome brother-in-arms Sky was. She couldn't wait to share the story with Philip. Laughter felt good amidst the tension of the night, and the nasty images that kept clawing at her mind. She knew Sky's little chat might not keep scuttlebutt from reaching the ship, but at least he'd tried. They were both powerless to do much more for Philip right now, but at least they hadn't lost their ability to laugh.

Looking directly at Hallie, Quinn clicked through. "I'm good with keeping McCabe's secret, sir. Only I might need confirmation on the underwear color first."

An astonished Hallie looked at him, only to discover him winking and laughing out loud at her expense.

Sky responded, "Agreed, Quinn. Too bad she's leaving the ship. I bet you were looking forward to next Wednesday's broadcast. But for now, you need to get her strapped back into her seat, as we're about to check in with Bahrain Control for landing."

The aircrewman motioned for her to begin the Chinese Fire Drill seat swap with him.

Sky chimed back in. "Hallie, when we land, there will be an ambulance waiting. Sometimes those crews are afraid to enter the rotor arc, so Quinn may need you and the corpsman to help hoist Philip and transport him to the ambulance. Then you and the corpsman go with the ambulance to wherever they've staged the *Blanchard* crewmen headed for Germany. We're shutting down here for the night, so I'll come find you and Bill at the hospital as soon as possible. Word is, the plane to Germany won't depart for a couple more hours."

"Yes, sir. Thank you for getting us here safely. This has been the most insane day of my life. I keep thinking I need to pinch myself and wake up from this crazy dream."

"Whether you pinch yourself or pinch Bill or whatever other kinky stuff you two do, I'd keep that on the down low for the rest of your trip and your time in Germany." Sky was interrupted by Bahrain Tower's call, clearing him to land in the far corner of a parking ramp where an ambulance awaited.

Sure enough, the ambulance crew stood and waited outside the rotor arc. With Quinn on one side and the corpsman on the other, Hallie grabbed the narrowest end of the litter, near Philip's feet and loaded him aboard. She climbed in after him, then heard Quinn shouting.

Realizing she was still wearing the cranial and flotation device, she promptly removed them and handed them over. "Thanks for everything, Quinn."

"Good luck, McCabe. I hope your guy's okay." Then he grinned. "Let me know when Billy Gates Junior is born. I'll send a card. And hey, no screaming on the plane tonight, you hear?" He winked before walking back to the helicopter.

Hallie wheeled Philip's IV pole as she followed him into the holding room for the other *Blanchard* casualties. She thought the sight of the injured might be more than she could handle, but knowing Philip was in the right place, calmed her.

A senior chief corpsman approached her. "Are you Petty Office McCabe?"

"Yes, Senior Chief."

"My duty staff is stretched a little thin with all these *Blanchard* arrivals. Would you mind chatting with a few of the patients to keep their spirits up until we can get them loaded onto the plane?"

"No problem, Senior. I think it would help me to stay busy, because when I have time to sit and think, I feel like I'm going to lose it." Her heart rate ratcheted up at the thought of what had happened tonight.

"That's a pretty normal response after what I heard you've been through, McCabe. But don't worry. My staff knows what happened and they'll keep an eye on you too."

"Thanks, Senior Chief." Hallie adjusted the blanket on Philip, bent over and kissed him first on the lips and then on the forehead.

She turned on her heel to check on the other patients and was greeted by the dancing eyes of none other than Trixie Williams. Her arms and hands were swathed in bandages and her face looked like she'd been badly sunburned. She stared in open-mouthed disbelief. Obviously she'd just witnessed Hallie kissing "Mr. Gates." Trixie closed her eyes and made a half-hearted attempt to smile as Hallie made her way over and knelt down at her side.

"Shit, Hallie, this is better than the morphine they just gave me," Trixie said in a hoarse voice. "Bill Gates and the McBabe. Whoever would've thunk it? Not in a million years. What I can't figure out is the cowboy part. I mean Mr. Gates is about as far from a cowboy as you can get."

Hallie nodded her head. There was no use in denying it. "It's kind of a private joke. But yeah, I won't lie to you. He's the guy who's going to be waiting for me 'back home.' And he will be because he's going to be fine and so are you, Sarah." Hallie wanted to take her hand, but didn't dare touch her so she used her eyes to nurture her as best as she could.

Trixie raised one of her bandaged hands a few inches in the air and said, "Call me Sarah again and I'll have to figure out how to punch you out."

"Well, I see they weren't able to take your spirit. Honestly sweetie, you're going to be fine. I'm going all the way to Germany with you guys and I'll watch out for you there. I promise. And I won't let them call you Sarah either."

Trixie smiled stiffly and started to speak, although her speech was rough and beginning to slur. Hallie had to lean in close to hear her whispers. "God, Hallie, I was so scared." Tears pooled in her eyes. "We knew there was something going on and we went to General Quarters and the ship was hauling ass but we didn't know what was out there and then there was this big explosion." She tried to blink back her tears. "I've never been so fucking scared in my life."

"It's okay, sweetie. It's all going to be okay. We got them all and they're never going to hurt you again."

Hallie thought she'd fallen asleep, but then she spoke again. "You know what I always envied about you, McCabe?" She didn't wait for a response. "How smart you are."

"Smart?"

"Yeah, Mr. Johnston is probably the nicest man in the whole world. I mean, he's not my type or anything, but he's a really good man. I never would've put you two together. But now it makes perfect sense." She opened her eyes and continued. "You're a really lucky girl. Whoa. Wait a second. You're the one who broke his heart. Okay, I'm getting it now. All those stories I brought back to berthing? You were hanging on every word, weren't you?" She smiled as best as she could. "Damn. Did Gina know? Is that why she was feeding me all that shit so I'd take it down in the hole? You guys crack me up. Bill Gates and The McBabe. Too funny. Don't worry. I won't say anything to anyone. I'd never do that to Mr. Johnston. But Bulldog would shit if he knew this." She tried to look around. "Bulldog isn't here, is he? God, who else is here?"

"I'm not sure. Mr. Johnston was the only patient on the helicopter I came in on, but I'll find out all the names. You rest now. Go ahead and sleep. I'll keep checking on you. And remember, you're going to be fine. I promise."

"Yeah, well, if those terrorists messed up any of my tats, I'm going to cross deck to Aviation Ordnanceman, so I can put bombs together for special delivery on tangos' ignorant asses," she said as she drifted off.

It was true. They might have burned her and they might have even messed up some of her tattoos, but no way had they put a dent in her soul.

Hallie found another coma victim and she felt compelled to take his hand and talk soothingly in his ear. She didn't know if he was married or even had a girl back home, but she talked about how someone was waiting for him and he needed to come back for her. She didn't know whether or not he had kids. She just told him there would be kids in his life that needed him some day so he needed to come back and teach them how to throw a baseball. "I know. I didn't have a dad and it was very lonely, so you've got to hold on and come back for them."

She knelt and talked to the others about their girls back home too. And the guy who said he didn't have anyone? She told him he just hadn't met The One yet, but she was out there somewhere and he would know it when he met her. She asked the married men about their families and the young guys about their parents and their brothers and sisters. She asked everyone where he was from and what their hometown was like.

She got close and looked each man in the eye, then talked sincerely and tenderly. Her soothing voice reassured them and her concern made each person feel special. All of this allowed the corpsmen to do their jobs: to treat wounds, to relieve pain, to change IVs, until they, too, found themselves falling under her calming spell, along with one particular helicopter pilot who had stopped in his tracks to listen to her words of comfort.

Hallie was afraid to touch any of the burn cases, even to hold their hands. So she bent close to their ears and comforted them with her voice. Between patients, Hallie made her way back to Philip to check on him and whisper in his ear. She juggled checking on him with getting water bottles for the thirsty and wiping tears for the fearful. But despite the positive energy she was exuding for the patients, her brain continued to churn.

She finally, truly understood that all the wounded were snipes. It was just what Philip had feared on the beach the day they'd met. What if one of the dhows had hit directly? What if the others had hit too? What if they'd compromised the reactors? Flashbacks of the nightmare kept trying to invade her brain. As much as she tried to focus on the wounded, images flashed through her head. The kick of the gun after she'd pulled the trigger. The split-second horror that she might have killed Dixon too. The not knowing if the noise and vibrations were the catapults and aircraft launching or the dhows hitting the ship.

Do not go there.

Focus, Hallie, focus.

Right here. Right now.

While they transferred the wounded to the Med-Evac plane, the senior chief corpsman appeared out of nowhere. "Hey, Florence Nightingale, thanks for what you just did. You were like the perfect mom or girlfriend for these guys. You were like, I don't know, an angel or something. Be safe and take some time to heal in Germany."

Just as quickly as the senior chief vanished, Sky sidled up and put his arm around her.

"I have no idea how I'm going to handle being in your wedding now that I know what you'll be wearing under your dress, but just keep telling Bill about it, okay? Whisper 'lavender lace skivvies' in his ear. That ought to bring him back."

"Thank you for coming with us, Sky. Thank you for caring and making us all laugh. I'm touched. It means a lot to me and I know it will mean a lot to *Bill* when I tell him."

"Hey, thank you. What you just did here at the Trauma Center? You were like hypnotic. You ought to bottle that bedside manner stuff and go into business. And the fact that you could talk to them like that after what you went through yourself tonight? Man, you're something else.   Hey, when Bill comes to, just tell him the Skylark says you're definitely The One and I'm freakin' jealous. And tell him I'll never call him a dumb ass again. No way can he be a dumb ass, if he's got you." Then Sky hugged her and kissed her temple. "Don't worry, sweetheart. We'll all laugh about this someday. And you better believe I'm telling the Hot Mic story at your wedding."

"Oh, I hope you do."

"Even the skivvies part?"

"Even the skivvies part. It means we'll all be there. All of us."

He got it. "Okay, but I'm skipping the screaming part. Bill's mom is not cleared for that kind of information."

Sky walked over to his alpha male wingman, squatted down and spoke quietly in his ear. "You got a real winner there, buddy. You're not going to believe what that woman did on the ship tonight. I just want you to know that if, whatever happens, just know I'll take care of her if you need me to."

He paused, blinked, pinched the bridge of his nose, cleared his throat several times before trying to continue. Then realized he couldn't, too overwhelmed with the events leading to this moment. Hallie alerting them. Guns firing. The dhows exploding. His missiles taking out one of them—he'd never forget that explosion as long as he lived. Learning of Hallie shooting the traitor and Bill in a coma. The laughter that had obliterated all of it when Hallie spilled her guts on Hot Mic, then becoming a different person, impersonating an angel with the wounded.

He was the Skylark, king of the skies and the bedroom. He wasn't going to cry. So he turned to his tried and true therapy.

Humor.

"Hey, I finally got the perfect nickname for Hallie. You gotta come back so I can tell you. And you have to come back, you sly dog, so I can kick your ass for not telling me she's a screamer. Never mind. I wouldn't tell you either if she was my One. But I guess I owe you a beer—hell, sounds like I owe you a whole keg—so you better bring your sad ass back to the world so I can buy it for you."

Then he choked up all over again. "It's really important to me that you come back for that beer, Bill." But, once again, humor won out. "Cuz we need Billy Gates Jr. to get born. You know, Cowboy. Billy the Kid?" He smiled through tears that refused to go away, then made a fist and gently touched Philip's shoulder with it. "All right, gotta run. Hang in there, buddy."

Sky turned to Hallie and hugged her, stealing a moment to regain his composure. "Hey, fair winds and all that. For both of you. Just take care of him and remember 'lavender lace skivvies' right in his ear." Then his mouth curved up into his gap-toothed grin before adding, "Okay, *Lacey*?"

Fair winds and following seas.

The sailors' blessing for good luck. May all the conditions be right for good things to happen on their journey.

They were going to need it.

Chapter 32

Philip was swimming under water and he could not break the surface. He needed air, but no matter how hard he stroked, he couldn't get any. Everything was murky and brown, or was it green? Like swimming in a bay or was he in the St. Johns River? It was salty like the St. Johns, but very, very salty. He could taste it. And warm. Bathtub warm. Was this the Persian Gulf? He hoped there weren't any sea snakes if it was.

The sunlight filtered down, but he couldn't reach it. And then he saw a distorted face above the water. The person was all wavy and fluid, but then he knew it was Hallie, because he could hear her. Faint and watery. She was calling to him and he tried to respond, but nothing came out. "Come back, Philip, I love you," she was saying, but he couldn't. "You can do it. I know you can. You always do everything you put your mind to. I know you can hear me and I know you're going to come back."

He kept trying to tell her he was doing his best.

And then she was gone again and he just floated, until he heard Sky. Why was Sky talking about beer? There wasn't any beer at the steel beach picnic. Suddenly his arms and legs stopped working and he started to sink. It gave him the creeps to go deep in this water, if it was the Gulf. All kinds of strange creatures lived here.

Philip willed himself to kick and stroke, but his body wouldn't work. He kept sinking, but there didn't seem to be any bottom. He kept sinking down, down, down. It grew darker and colder. He couldn't see the streaks of sunlight near the surface anymore. He just kept slipping down in the deep, dark, icy water.

Suddenly it became light again. Very light. Everywhere. Like being lost in the fog. And someone was talking to him again. It was a woman. Not Hallie—but she was *like* Hallie, only she had dark eyes. Soulful eyes. "Go back to Hallie," she said. "She needs you."

And then the fog was gone and he was back in the dark, chilly water. This time his arms and legs worked so he breaststroked his way up. He knew it was up by the bubbles. Bubbles always float up. Way off in the distance, he could see it getting lighter.

He kicked and stroked harder, but he was getting tired. He wasn't certain he could make it all the way to the light. The water grew cooler again and he didn't think he had the strength to swim back to the sunlight. Suddenly he felt something lift him. It was the woman with the soulful eyes, pushing him up, lifting him. She swam behind him, helping him, and guiding him. Up. Back to the light.

It became clearer. No, not clearer. Brighter. It was still fuzzy, like under the St. Johns, but warm like the Gulf. Something blocked the light above him. Something was in the way. Not his ship, but a small boat, with waves slapping against it. The boat rocked ferociously and he sensed a storm around it. There were raindrops pelting the surface above him.

A hand reached down into the water. He knew it was Hallie by the ring. Wait. This was his sailboat. She was on his sailboat trying to save him. What was his sailboat doing in the Persian Gulf? Philip reached for her hand, but he was too tired. He started to sink again. The woman pushed harder from underneath, until he felt Hallie's fingertips. But he kept slipping away, sliding back. Down. And the water became so rough, the boat kept rocking and the hand disappeared. The woman pushed him up again until he could finally grasp Hallie's hand. Maybe she could pull him out of the water now.

Philip held on for dear life and when he looked up through the water, he could see Hallie's face now, leaning over, all rippley in the waves. And he could see the sails moving wildly above them in the storm. It was raining hard and the water looked red.

He heard Hallie say, "Hold on, Philip. I know you can hold on." So he did. But then she started talking about her skivvies. Was it Wednesday? Did he miss the news?

"It's going to be okay. Just hold on. Squeeze my hand, Philip. I know it's hard to hold on, but squeeze my hand if you can hear me." So he squeezed it as hard as he could, and Hallie screamed. He was happy he could make her scream, but this wasn't that kind of scream. It was too loud and it hurt his ears.

"He squeezed my hand! Oh, hold on, Philip. I love you!"

He started to sink again, and then he heard a man's voice, but it wasn't Sky. Why was Hallie on his sailboat with another man, screaming? Hallie belonged to him. She promised. She gave him her hair. It was in his wallet.

Hallie was finally allowed to be with Philip again after surgery. The hours had been interminable. The Army medics had balked at first when she answered, "not yet," to the question of whether or not she was his next of kin. She dug deep and figuring she had nothing to lose, told them the story about the flight and that she'd been ordered to whisper "lavender lace skivvies" into his ear until he came to. Then she added for good measure, "Tell me honestly you have a better plan." When they stopped laughing, they allowed her into ICU, as long as she promised to invite them to the wedding.

As next of kin, Philip's parents had been notified and were on their way to Germany. Oh, they were in for a few surprises, but Hallie didn't care. All that mattered was bringing Philip back. Once they arrived, they'd all gang up on him. He would have to wake up. There was no way he would be able to resist the three of them.

She could tell exactly when Captain Amerson's message had gotten through to the CO of the hospital. Philip was moved to a VIP room, for a general or an admiral, and food and civilian clothing were brought to her. Which was a good thing, because there was no way she was leaving Philip's side, except for a few quick, discreet visits to check on Trixie and the others.

It was clear the medics now knew who she was, offering her copies of the overseas American military newspaper, *Stars and Stripes*, or to turn on CNN for her, but she didn't want to know about the *Blanchard* attack. She didn't need reminders of what had taken place in CDC. Or in the engineer spaces. She didn't want to be reminded that there had been several deaths. Hallie was in the news business. She knew how the press worked and she only wanted positive vibes in that room. She saw just enough to know her boot camp picture was plastered all over them and that Hallie McCabe was "recovering from shock at an undisclosed location."

She couldn't believe she was saying it, but she was: "Protect me from the fucking press."

Hallie picked up Philip's wallet and again wondered about his glasses. He would need new ones when he woke up. Had to think positively. She made a mental note to email Gina and have her look into it. Surely Philip's prescription was in his medical record.

Looking through the wallet, Hallie found pictures of herself and a lock of hair. The golden tendril was sealed in a small plastic bag. In his wallet. Which he always carried close to his body.

She reached down and fondled the warm ring still around her neck. With her dog tags. She shuddered when she thought that Philip had been right about wearing them. He had needed them. And then she sent up a thank you prayer that she hadn't needed hers. But that brought back memories, so she put all thoughts of that night and dog tags away.

In the meantime, Hallie would sit there keeping her demons at bay, holding his hand, and reminding him of everything: A lock of hair, a warm class ring, a fan room, terry cloth bathrobes, and yes, lavender skivvies. And a kiss in the rain, a sailboat, a cowboy hat, a red sky at night and how Sky was going to embarrass them at their wedding and the babies they would make together some day. And how much she loved him.

Hallie would whisper it all to him. Over and over again. Until he came back to her.

Retired Navy Captain Doug "Spurs" Johnston was exhausted. He'd been traveling with his wife for close to twenty-four hours with only fits and snatches of sleep and dry sandwiches washed down with way too many cups of coffee for sustenance.

He'd been delighted to discover a car and driver from the hospital waiting for them when they arrived in Landstuhl, Germany. He was not pleased however, when the Military Policeman posted outside Philip's door patiently explained that the Johnstons were not on the list of persons cleared to enter Philip's room.

Just another instance where he did not miss being in the military.

"Corporal, we've just traveled from the States to see our wounded son who is behind that door." He pulled out his military ID card and added, "We're his parents for God's sake. What could possibly be the problem with us entering that room? Why does he need a bodyguard anyway? And why is he in a VIP room? I'm sure there were other wounded brought here from the *Blanchard*. Are they all getting this treatment? What in hell is going on here, Corporal?"

The M.P.'s eyes flickered up and down the hall with uncertainty. "I'm not here to protect your son, sir. I've been assigned to Miss McCabe."

"Who?" both parents said in unison.

"I'm Miss McCabe's bodyguard. And I'm sorry, but I can't allow you to enter."

Mrs. Johnston stepped up to the plate. "Corporal, my son is in that room and as far as I know he's in a coma. Now I'm going to walk through that door to be at his side. I will give you thirty seconds to get permission for me to do just that or you're going to have to shoot me because I am going to enter."

"Who's Miss McCabe?" a confused Doug Johnston asked as the baby-faced M.P.'s walkie-talkie squawked with permission for them to enter. His relief was evident as he stepped aside to allow them in.

Philip's mom strode directly to Philip's side. His dad strode directly to Hallie. "Who are you? What are you doing here?" Hallie looked him right in the eye, but walked past him to Philip's mother and introduced herself.

"Mrs. Johnston, I'm pleased to meet you. I'm Hallie McCabe and I've been watching over Philip for the past two days."

"Hallie." She opened her arms to her. "Philip talked of nothing but Hallie this summer. It's so good to meet you. Thank you for being here with him."

Doug Johnston was still confused and he couldn't let it drop. "But how did you get here? And why do you need a bodyguard?"

Hallie glanced at him but continued to avoid his questions. Instead she updated them both on Philip's condition. "I assume you know Philip suffered a traumatic brain injury in the explosion on Thursday. He'd not regained consciousness by the time we arrived here and they've kept him in an induced coma to keep the swelling down. Fortunately he's been able to breathe on his own, although they've got him on oxygen as a precaution. He had surgery right after we arrived to determine the extent of the damage." She put up her hands in surrender. "I'm sure the doctor can explain that part a lot better than I can. All I know is they repaired and cleaned out some hematomas and contusions or something."

Philip's mother's hand flew to her chest. Her other hand stroked Philip's arm.

Her husband walked to her side and put his arm around her. "It's alright, Margaret. He's going to be fine." Not that he had any idea of how fine his son was going to be, but as far as Spurs Johnston was concerned it's what a man tells his wife.

Hallie continued. "They don't know how the TBI will affect him yet. We won't know much until he wakes up and they can do tests. But so far all his reactions are good. Anyway, they took him off the sedative this morning so it's possible he could wake up any time, and he will. I know he will. Talking to him is the best thing we can do. I've been talking non-stop." Her eyes pooled with tears. "I'm so glad you're here. It's going to be so much better now that he can hear your voices."

"Miss McCabe, I still don't understand why you—"

"Doug, you will either conduct yourself appropriately or you will leave the room."

Damn it, his wife was always doing that. And she was usually right.

"But Margaret, I don't get..."

Hallie glanced over her shoulder toward Philip, then turned back to Doug and answered a little too defensively, "I flew on the Med-Evac flight with him. From the ship."

His brow furrowed. "What were you doing on the ship?"

"Because I'm in the Navy, sir. I'm stationed on the *Blanchard*. I was on board when the terrorists attacked."

"Philip never mentioned you were on his ship. He never even told us you were in the Navy."

Hallie looked down and bit her cheek, then turned to him and replied, "He didn't know—before we left. Look, I'd rather we didn't get into this now."

"He didn't know? What are you saying?"

Hallie hesitated, looked at each of Philip's parents, inhaled deeply, and blew out her breath. Then answered proudly. "I'm a Mass Communications Specialist in the United States Navy. An MC2, sir."

His eyebrows shot up.

"Yup, I'm an everyday, garden variety sailor."

"You're enlisted?" Incredulous. "Why would Philip...? And the Navy sanctions this? What the hell's going on here?"

Hallie took two steps forward, breaking into his personal space. She lifted her chin and challenged him with her eyes. "I am in no position to give you parenting advice, Captain Johnston, but I would think that the health of your son and the idea of us working together to bring Philip back to us is a hell of a lot more important right now than who I am, why I'm here, or how I earn my living."

Doug took it like a slap to the face. What really pissed him off was that she was right. "Well, of course Philip is the issue here, but—"

"I have worked my damndest for the past forty-eight hours to ensure that your son is surrounded with positive energy. So if you insist on focusing on negative issues, I must ask you to leave. Sir."

How dare she speak to him that way? But his wife's quiet clapping from Philip's bedside confirmed that it was two against one. "Touché, Hallie. Go find us some coffee, Doug."

He replied, "I'm going to find the CO of the hospital and get to the bottom of this is what I'm going to do." He walked over to Philip, laid his hand on his forehead, then about-faced and headed toward the door before adding, "And yes, I'll get coffee too, Margaret."

Women.

Hallie turned to Philip's mother. She was seated at his bedside, stroking his bald head, while squeezing his hand with the other. "I'm sorry about that Mrs. Johnston. I just didn't feel his accusations were going to benefit Philip right now."

Margaret Johnston continued to stroke her son's hair. "Don't give it another thought, Hallie. Of course Philip's more important. Doug's been very upset since we got that call and we've barely slept since Friday. But forgive him, please. He's known for speaking his mind, although he's usually not quite so rude. I promise you his bark is worse than his bite. I think it's just his way of dealing with not having any control over this. And it was a little confusing finding you here, but I'm glad you are here with Philip. We just didn't know you were back in the picture."

"Thank you, ma'am. It's a long story and I'd prefer not to discuss it here. I believe he can hear everything we say and I want to keep the atmosphere as positive as possible." Hallie paused, no idea why tears were forming in her eyes again. They kept doing that. "Philip always spoke so highly of you and now I can see why. I know he feels your presence." She paused. "I'll step outside if you'd like to have some time alone with him."

"It's okay, sweetie. I don't have anything to say to my son I can't say in front of you."

She turned to him. "Honey, Dad and I are here. We've been worried about you, but now I know you've been in good hands the entire time. Everything is going to be all right. Just come back to us. And come back to Hallie. I know she needs you."

Hallie sat down across from her. Each of them stroked one of Philip's hands. Hallie held Philip's left hand with hers. Mrs. Johnston reached across and turned it so she could better see Hallie's ring. Her face, although etched with concern, blossomed into a tired smile. She continued her one-way conversation with her son.

"Looks like you found The One. I'm so happy for you. Even Dad's glad. He just doesn't know it yet. Didn't I tell you to be patient and the right woman would come along? Well, it looks like she has. Didn't I tell you the smart ones would be looking for someone like you?" She chuckled to herself before continuing. "And there's no question Hallie's smart. She had your father figured out in a New York minute."

Chapter 33

The woman was back. The one with the beautiful brown eyes. Philip couldn't see her but she was definitely back because he could hear her whispering in his ear again. "Come back to Hallie. She needs you." At least he thought that was what she was saying. It was kind of hard to focus on her words because his head hurt like a son of a bitch.

Maybe she had an aspirin.

He tried to get his bearings, but he couldn't get a fix on things. He was out of the water for sure. He felt like he'd been swimming for days on end. Maybe that's why he was so tired. But he was definitely out of it because the water had been bathtub warm and it was sort of chilly here. He could only see fog, but not wispy fog like when he first met the woman

No, this was different. This was like coming to in the morning with a bad hangover. Afraid to even open his eyes. Wondering just what in hell he'd done the night before.

"Come back to us. Come back to Hallie," the woman whispered again in his ear.

Wait a second. *Come* back to Hallie? Not *go* back to Hallie? Come back to us? Who was us? What was going on here?

And suddenly Philip recognized this woman's voice as his mother's, not the woman with the soulful brown eyes – not that his mother didn't have soulful brown eyes. No, this wasn't the woman who'd been in the water with him. This was his mom talking now. What was his mom doing on the ship?

Did she have an aspirin?

And then he realized his eyes were closed. No wonder he hadn't been able to figure anything out. It suddenly dawned on him that his eyes had been closed through this whole weird journey. If he could just open them, he'd be able to figure out what was going on.

And where the hell he was.

He peeked out from under his eyelids just enough to know that it definitely was his mom talking to him, because she was sitting beside his bed. His bed? Why was he in bed and why was his mom there? He sensed, more than saw, that there was someone else there, but he couldn't make it out. He tried to turn his head to get a better look, what with his eyes only opening to slits and his glasses gone—where were his glasses?—but his head hurt too much to turn it.

And then the woman was leaving. Yup, as she passed the end of the bed he knew for sure it was his mom. What was his mom doing here? He wanted to call out, "Hey, Mom, you got any aspirin?" but his mouth wasn't working quite yet. Well, beyond knowing he was mighty thirsty.

And can I get some water with it?

Moving only his eyeballs under the heavy lids—damn, what was holding his eyelids down?—Philip was able to take in a footboard of some kind, some machines, and a lot of wires and tubes. One appeared to be snaking out of his nose. No wonder it itched so much. Now he understood what all the mechanical beeping had been about. This was some kind of hospital room. Sick Bay on the *Blanchard*? But it was definitely a hospital-type place and he was in some kind of bed so he must be sick or hurt or something.

And then he remembered some kind of explosion.

Whatever had happened, he realized he was gazing at a beautiful sight.

His feet. Both of them seemed to be there. He wiggled his toes under the sheet just to be sure. And then flexed his fingers. Yup. Two hands reporting as ordered, sir. All extremities present and accounted for. That was always a good sign. So maybe he'd just hit his head or something, because it hurt like...Wait a minute. Good. If he was in a hospital, it meant he hadn't gotten drunk last night and done something stupid. Whew.

And then he heard another familiar voice in the room—or wherever he was. It was definitely his dad. Uh oh. If his dad was on the ship, he'd probably tell them how to run it.

And then his dad said something that connected all the dots.

"...nut job in CDC..."

Oh, shit. OS2 Davis in CDC had a gun to Petty Officer McCabe's head.

Philip's heart kicked into high gear. His body screamed for him to get to Combat and save Hallie, but he couldn't seem to move a muscle. He had to tell his dad to go save her. But his mouth wouldn't work.

"He told me everything," his dad continued. "Margaret, you can't believe what this young lady did."

"Sir, I only..."

Hallie?

What was Hallie doing in Sick Bay? Everyone on the ship would know about them if Hallie was here with him. But wait. If she was here, then she was okay.

Relief flooded his body. He summoned all his strength and managed to turn his head ever so slightly and...there she was.

Hallie.

His Hallie.

Hallie was alive.

Relief pumped from his bloodstream into his soul.

He could only see her back as his dad hugged her. Wait, *his dad was hugging Hallie?* And thanking her. Thanking her for saving his son. This show was way too good to miss and Philip willed his eyes to open wider. Yup, there was his mom, watching them and smiling. And now hugging both of them.

"I apologize for being rude to you, Hallie. Please forgive me. I was tired and frustrated and I didn't understand why you were here, but that's no excuse. Why didn't you tell me what you'd done to save the ship? You could have shut me up but fast."

"Because Philip is more important, sir."

Captain Johnston sighed and turned to his wife. "Isn't she something, Margaret? Honey, we missed it all while we were traveling." His dad stood back and whipped out a newspaper to show his mom. "The CO of the hospital gave me the *Stars and Stripes*. Look at this story that just broke this morning..."

So he was in some kind of hospital. Probably in Bahrain or Kuwait. But he was off the ship. That's why his dad and mom were here. But how did Hallie get here? And what happened to the ship? Were his men—and Trixie—okay?

"See right here. 'Sailor Saves Ship.' She practically did it single-handedly. Okay, the aircraft did their thing too, but Hallie's the one who alerted them. She was taken hostage, but managed to alert Public Affairs through her camera. Everyone on the ship knew what was going on, but OS2 Davis in Combat didn't know they knew. So they went to General Quarters via the phones and TVs and computers."

Philip's brain was on fire now. Come on, Dad, did they get the dhows? And how did Hallie get away from Davis?

"And the aircraft took out the fishing boats and Hallie took out the nut job."

Thank God!

"Sir, I really don't want to talk about it now. Especially in here."

"But you shot him, right? You killed Davis. And then they defused the bomb, right?"

Hesitantly, Hallie answered, "I did."

Hallie shot him?

Hallie killed Davis?

Hallie?

"Oh, honey," Philip's mother said as she embraced her.

"I had to. He was going to blow up the ship."

She's apologizing?

"Of course you had to, sweetie," his mom said as she rocked Hallie from side to side. "But this can't be easy for you. My goodness, you've lived through a nightmare."

Doug Johnston was back in the game. "But I still don't understand how you got to leave the ship and come here with our son to Germany."

Aha. They were in Germany.

"I'd really rather not go into that right now, so let's just say the CO thought it best if I accompanied Philip here."

"You mean he knew about you two? When I was in the Navy, fraternization was considered—"

"Doug, not now."

Yup, that was his mom, all right.

But Philip knew how Hallie had gotten here. She'd probably played her paternity card and threatened to expose the Captain if he didn't let her go with him.

He would have laughed if he could. That was his Hallie. He wondered if the CO had reneged on his promise not to tell her he knew he was her father. It didn't really matter anymore. Guess it worked out for her if she was here. All Philip knew was he was damn glad she was here.

Philip wished that he could get his hands on Hallie to make sure she was all in one piece, but all that seemed to be working were his eyelids, and they had sandbags or something on them.

"They're calling her a McHero. I mean she saved the entire ship, Margaret. Our little Hallie saved that ship and everyone on it. And she saved our son's life." Captain Johnston joined the hug and murmured, "Thank you, Hallie. God bless you, darling."

Again, Philip wished he could laugh. His dad in a group hug?

Whoa. Wait a minute. Was his dad crying? Spurs Johnston? Crying?

No way.

It was definitely time to intervene and join the party.

Philip reached down into the marrow of his bones for the strength to nudge the words off his tongue and push them out into the room. He was certain they'd be slurred. He just hoped they'd be loud enough.

"...mom was right...daughter with balls...s'my girl."

The three turned as one. Although Philip's eyelids were still at half-mast, his cracked lips had curved into a gentle smile.

His mom spoke first. "Philip?"

"Yeah, Mom...hey...you got any asp'rn?"

His dad took care of alerting the staff while his mother moved to the end of the bed, allowing Hallie first dibs on face time and kisses.

"Mmmm," Philip murmured, "...feel better already. Give me some more of that med'cine, wud'ja honey?" She kissed him again. Oh, good. It seemed all his bodily functions were in working order.

"Hey, Cowboy. I missed you. Where you been?"

"Pretty sure I have been to hell and back, but sounds like you did, too. Way to go. You kicked some major ass. Not surprised. Nothing you do s'prises me." His mouth curved up. "I think I'll stick around and see what you pull out of your seabag next. First give me another one of those kisses."

He saw his dad return to his mom's side at the foot of the bed. And just as Philip closed his eyes for Hallie's kiss, he watched his dad put an arm around his mother and heard him say, "You see, Margaret, like I always told you: 'Every man in a foxhole needs a good woman to come back to.'"

Photo by: Straley Photography

Heather Ashby

Heather Ashby is a Navy veteran, whose mother was one of the original Navy WAVES in World War II. After leaving the service, Heather taught school and raised a family while accompanying her Navy husband around the United States, Japan, and the Middle East.

In gratitude for her son's safe return from Afghanistan and Iraq, she now writes military romance novels, donating half her royalties to benefit wounded warriors and their families. She lives in Atlantic Beach, Florida with her retired Naval Engineer husband. Reach Heather at www.heatherashby.com.

**Don't miss the next book
in the Love in the Fleet Series**

Forget Me Not
by Heather Ashby

Suffering from survivor guilt, Navy pilot and renowned playboy, Brian "Skylark" Crawford, swears he'll never marry, uncertain he deserves happiness. Besides there are too many hot chicks out there to choose from.

War widow and veterinarian, Daisy Schneider, swears to love only animals after her Marine pilot husband is killed in Afghanistan—but work fails to ease her loneliness, or the guilt that she might have saved him.

Between one stray matchmaking cat and a fiery battle with drug runners at sea, the fur flies as Sky and Daisy learn valuable lessons about life, love, and second chances.

Available December 2013
For more details, visit www.henerypress.com

IF YOU LIKE MYSTERY,
TRY THESE HENERY PRESS MYSTERIES...

Lowcountry BOIL
by Susan M. Boyer

Private Investigator Liz Talbot is a modern Southern belle: she blesses hearts and takes names. She carries her Sig 9 in her Kate Spade handbag, and her golden retriever, Rhett, rides shotgun in her hybrid Escape. When her grandmother is murdered, Liz high-tails it back to her South Carolina island home to find the killer.

She's fit to be tied when her police-chief brother shuts her out of the investigation, so she opens her own. Then her long-dead best friend pops in and things really get complicated. When more folks start turning up dead in this small seaside town, Liz must use more than just her wits and charm to keep her family safe, chase down clues from the hereafter, and catch a psychopath before he catches her.

Available Now
For more details, visit www.henerypress.com

FRONT PAGE FATALITY
by LynDee Walker

Crime reporter Nichelle Clarke's days can flip from macabre to comical with a beep of her police scanner. Then an ordinary accident story turns extraordinary when evidence goes missing, a prosecutor vanishes, and a sexy Mafia boss shows up with the headline tip of a lifetime.

As Nichelle gets closer to the truth, her story gets more dangerous. Armed with a notebook, a hunch, and her favorite stilettos, Nichelle races to splash these shady dealings across the front page before this deadline becomes her last.

Available Now
For more details, visit www.henerypress.com

DINERS, dives & DEAD ENDS
by Terri L. Austin

As a struggling waitress and part-time college student, Rose Strickland's life is stalled in the slow lane. But when her close friend, Axton, disappears, Rose suddenly finds herself serving up more than hot coffee and flapjacks. Now she's hashing it out with sexy bad guys and scrambling to find clues in a race to save Axton before his time runs out.

With her anime-loving bestie, her septuagenarian boss, and a pair of IT wise men along for the ride, Rose discovers political corruption, illegal gambling, and shady corporations. She's gone from zero to sixty and quickly learns when you're speeding down the fast lane, it's easy to crash and burn.

Available Now
For more details, visit www.henerypress.com

PORTRAIT of a DEAD GUY

by LARISSA REINHART

In Halo, Georgia, folks know Cherry Tucker as big in mouth, small in stature, and able to sketch a portrait faster than buck-shot rips from a ten gauge–but commissions are scarce. So when the well-heeled Branson family wants to memorialize their murdered son in a coffin portrait, Cherry scrambles to win their patronage from her small town rival.

As the clock ticks toward the deadline, Cherry faces more trouble than just a controversial subject. Between ex-boyfriends, her flaky family, an illegal gambling ring, and outwitting a killer on a spree, Cherry finds herself painted into a corner she'll be lucky to survive.

Available Now
For more details, visit www.henerypress.com

BOARD STIFF

By Kendel Lynn

As director of the Ballantyne Foundation on Sea Pine Island, SC, Elliott Lisbon scratches her detective itch by performing discreet inquiries for Foundation donors. Usually nothing more serious than retrieving a pilfered Pomeranian. Until Jane Hatting, Ballantyne board chair, is accused of murder. The Ballantyne's reputation tanks, Jane's headed to a jail cell, and Elliott's sexy ex is the new lieutenant in town.

Armed with moxie and her Mini Coop, Elliott uncovers a trail of blackmail schemes, gambling debts, illicit affairs, and investment scams. But the deeper she digs to clear Jane's name, the guiltier Jane looks. The closer she gets to the truth, the more treacherous her investigation becomes. With victims piling up faster than shells at a clambake, Elliott realizes she's next on the killer's list.

Available Now
For more details, visit www.henerypress.com

malicious masquerade
by ALAN CUPP

Chicago PI Carter Mays is thrust into a perilous masquerade when local rich girl Cindy Bedford hires him. Turns out her fiancé failed to show up on their wedding day, the same day millions of dollars are stolen from her father's company. While Carter takes the case, Cindy's father tries to find him his own way. With nasty secrets, hidden finances, and a trail of revenge, it's soon apparent no one is who they say they are.

Carter searches for the truth, but the situation grows more volatile as panic collides with vulnerability. Broken relationships and blurred loyalties turn deadly, fueled by past offenses and present vendettas in a quest to reveal the truth behind the masks before no one, including Carter, gets out alive.

Available Now
For more details, visit www.henerypress.com

ARTIFACT

BY GIGI PANDIAN

Historian Jaya Jones discovers the secrets of a lost Indian treasure may be hidden in a Scottish legend from the days of the British Raj. But she's not the only one on the trail...

From San Francisco to London to the Highlands of Scotland, Jaya must evade a shadowy stalker as she follows hints from the hastily scrawled note of her dead lover to a remote archaeological dig. Helping her decipher the cryptic clues are her magician best friend, a devastatingly handsome art historian with something to hide, and a charming archaeologist running for his life.

Available August 2013
For more details, visit www.henerypress.com

CPSIA information can be obtained at www.ICGtesting.com
Printed in the USA
LVOW05s2131160314

377663LV00009B/80/P